The Black Prince
and Other Stories

The Black Prince

AND OTHER STORIES

SHIRLEY ANN GRAU

ALFRED A. KNOPF 1955 NEW YORK

Three of these stories were first published elsewhere. Acknowledgment is made to *The New Yorker*, where "Joshua" originally appeared, to *New World Writing*, for "White Girl, Fine Girl," and to *The New Mexico Quarterly*, for "The Black Prince," first printed in somewhat different form, under the title of "The Sound of Silver."

L. C. catalog card number: 55-5037

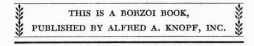

THIS IS A BORZOI BOOK,
PUBLISHED BY ALFRED A. KNOPF, INC.

PUBLISHED JANUARY 17, 1955
SECOND PRINTING, FEBRUARY 1955

For Jimmy

CONTENTS

The Black Prince
and Other Stories

White Girl, Fine Girl

THERE are these two places—Stanhope and Kilby—and there are seven miles between. These are the only two towns that state records list in Clayton County. One of them is the state capital and the liveliest little place in the South: the pine ridges around town, the back yards of outlying houses, hold dozens of stills. And from them come the best corn likker in the state: smooth and the color of good Scotch. The legislators always manage to take a few gallons home with them. (After a man's got used to the doings of the capital, there's nothing so tedious as months spent at his home way out in the counties somewhere.) And for the three months when the two houses or the state supreme court are in session, the price of the likker always rises until it is beyond the reach of the colored people. The wise ones, of course, have laid by a supply, if they have had the money to do that; and those who haven't must sweat out the time sober. The police have learned to be vigilant during this time: extra squad cars circle around the colored part of town, which on these nights hums with a restless aimless anger. The state police come in, too, and

3

their white-painted new shiny cars move up and down the streets. There are more fights this time of year than any other. More knifings. The price of burial insurance goes up. And the warden's desk at Kilby is full of yellow tissue-paper triplicate records of new prisoners.

That's what Kilby—the other place in Clayton—is, the big colored prison. It's a town: just three or four buildings for a grocery; and a railroad platform with the name KILBY painted in white letters on a green board and hung from the edge of the roof, right over the room that has a smaller sign: Post Office; and a few houses around, the biggest one with the yellow clapboard walls and the green shutters for the warden's wife, and the smaller ones painted all yellow for the guards' wives. (The men rarely come down to these houses; they spend most of their time inside the walls; it is as if they have a sentence to serve.) There are other houses for the colored washwomen and the cleaning women and their men and their children. This is the town of Kilby; this is what the county records show. But the real Kilby is half a mile north: the white brick walls and the machine-gun turrets, two on each side, and the men inside: the white guards and the colored prisoners.

You can't see Kilby from any point inside the limits of Stanhope, though if you stood on the capitol steps, on the spot where Jeff Davis took his first oath, you'd be staring in the right direction, and if your eyes were sharp enough, you'd see. But you don't.

But you can see the town from Kilby. On clear days in broad daylight the smoke from the mills comes up plain and still and fans out like a branch in the sky. And the

4

white guards prop their rifles between their knees and the parapet wall and lean on their elbows and watch. And the colored trusties dangle their billies between limp fingers and fold their arms and watch the branch bloom out in the sky.

At night you can see even plainer. During the war, when the mills worked full time on army contracts for tents and sheets and bandages, you could see the smoke come up red against the black sky. After the war, when the mills closed down at night, you could still see a glow —a different one—over where the town was. The lights from the cafés and the clubs: sometimes low under clouds before a storm, sometimes rising straight up, soft like cotton into a clear black sky, sometimes a yellow and small circle under the moonlight. Just lights, from seven miles away over blue pines and fallow patches and little streams that have water in them only during the spring rains; and whole hillsides of hackberries with thorns thick as a rooster's spur; and one river, slow, yellow, and without a bottom; and red dust that any wind—summer or winter—is going to lift and send sliding off down the air. And there is always a wind and the dust moving.

It was a flat hot sun in a powdery white sky when Jayson Paul Evans walked out of Kilby prison. He leaned against the white brick wall and hitched up his belt.

The guard behind him at the gate said: "Waiting for a car to come along and pick you up?"

Jayson moved his mouth in slow chewing circles: "Don't reckon I expect none."

5

From the top wall another guard called: "Get started there." He was directly overhead looking down.

Jayson stood clear of the wall and bent his head back to see. In the light his wide black eyes turned shiny like the sun.

"Sweet Jesus," the man at the gate said. "Ain't you ever gonna get out of here?"

Jayson stopped looking at the guard directly above him. "I reckon I will," he said to the man behind him. "I reckon I will now."

There was a strip of asphalt to the town, black asphalt with a white painted line down the center. A carefully painted line. He had done some of the work himself a couple of days earlier. That was how he'd cut down his twenty years for manslaughter, working it out in the road gangs.

He did not see a single white person in the town of Kilby; only the colored washwomen hanging out clothes on fences and bushes. The white wives would be inside. He thought of them briefly: in their slips, lying on beds, with shades drawn, fanning themselves slowly, waiting for the evening to come.

Beyond Kilby on the main highway he turned south, the sun beating hot against his left cheek and his eyes beginning to water from the dust. After he had walked nearly a mile, after the white walls were out of sight, he left the road, cutting across the fields, walking in a straight line for Stanhope. These were old fields; the plowed ground had hardened with rain and frost and sun until it was solid as boards, only a little uneven. And it was easy walking.

"I got no cause to hurry," Jayson told a dusty black crow that scratched on the bare red earth. "No cause to hurry." The crow looked at him sideways out of a light yellow eye and hopped into the protection of the barberry bushes.

Jayson laughed and pulled off his shirt. "Scared of me?" He hooked the shirt through his belt and went off at a jogging trot, his heels striking hard against the ground: a big man making long steps. The dust that came up white from the red ground settled on his skin, and sweat ran crisscross lines in it.

There were trees along the low places away to the right; he could have skirted through them. They were pines: no underbrush to make rough going, just a soft floor of needles and a clean smell when his feet crushed them.

He stood and looked at the trees, and wet his lips with his tongue and spit out the dirt taste. But he kept going, the quickest way, right across the old fields that had been plowed wrong first years ago and that nobody would bother with now and that each year got drier and darker and more washed into gullies and more full of powder, so that each time the wind blew across them, summer or winter, their dust would come swinging up on it. Jayson went on, stumbling a little on the sharpest gullies, swinging his arms wide for balance, and singing for company:

> *"The sun is real hot,*
> *Oh Lord. The sun is real hot*
> *And the wind is hot*
> *And the dust is rolling around,*
> *Oh Lord, Oh Lord, Oh Lord."*

The old plowed bare ground went down across two hills like a ribbon trailing and ended on a line of staggering fence posts and dragging wire. Jayson kicked at one post; it crumbled without sound: the center had dried away. Jayson wiped one hand across his bare chest, leaving a black streak in the red-white dust. Then he began to push his way through the bushes. They were elderberry mostly, green and yielding. When his fingers touched the soft round stalks, they bent aside smoothly. From a single laurel he pulled a broad leaf and chewed it slowly, bit by bit, until he had eaten it up the stem.

He was going downhill now. He had to work his way along sideways to keep from falling. The rocks—granite most of them, with sparks of fire in the light—rolled under his feet and he had to hold to the elder stems, pale and smooth. For just a moment he stopped and looked at one and rubbed his thumb up and down its length, from the ground up to as high as he could reach.

The thicket ended as a sharp gully, in its bottom during the summer months just a thin trickle of water, so narrow he could almost straddle its breadth. Jayson scrambled down one of the sharp deep crevices of the side and put his fingers in the water. Then he knelt down and carefully reached in his arm, feeling for bottom; he stretched out his fingers and touched nothing. He drew back his arm and wiped fingers across his lips to taste the water. It was warm from the sun and strong with leaf taste. But he was thirsty and he drank from his cupped hands.

A train whistled to his right. He lifted his head and listened, cocking just a bit to guess the distance. Then he moved off in that direction, following along the bottom of the gully. The tracks, he remembered, were on the far side of the Scantos River, and the whistle had been close, not more than a mile. He had to walk much farther in the twisted gully—two, maybe three miles; but it was easier going than across the fields or the thickets. (You never could tell when you would have to walk miles around a batch of hackberries all tangled together.)

He was beginning to be hungry by the time he reached the river—the broad yellow river moving slowly under the afternoon sun, moving so slowly that you could swear it was solid like ground; moving slowly because it had no bottom.

Jayson tossed a stone out as far as he could, almost to the other bank. "Sweet Jesus," he said, "I reckon you can just rest quiet, you old hungry man inside me. There ain't nothing I can do."

He followed the river south, looking for a way across, looking for a sandbar or a skiff. On the other bank a train went past, a diesel, shining silver in the sun, going all the way to New Orleans.

The heat of the day was beginning to make him sleepy so that he did not see the boys until he could bend over and touch them: squatting on the sands, peeling willows for fishing poles. They turned heads up to him, mouths open with surprise, eyes popping.

"Why," he told them, "if it ain't two nice little boys; two nice little boys my color."

They got to their feet very slowly and began to back away, feeling carefully behind them for each step. The bigger one, light-brown colored, had a hunting knife at his belt. His fingers unsnapped the guard and took hold of the handle.

Jayson laughed. "That a mighty big knife you got there, boy."

The boy held the leather sheath in his left hand; the right loosened the blade.

"You acting like a real man there," Jayson told him. The little one, who had been standing next to him, had disappeared. There wasn't even a sound when he slipped away. "You might could be thinking that you a man."

The knife was out now. The boy held it crosswise in front of him.

"I can see you ain't so foolish to go throwing that thing," Jayson said. He bent down and picked up a brown paper bundle with the grease markings that food leaves. He smelled it briefly. His eyes did not move from the boy, who was on tiptoe now, swaying back and forth, balancing himself for a fight: afraid, but holding his knife steady. And when his lower lip began to tremble, he took it firmly in his teeth.

"I reckon you think you a man," Jayson said. Out of the corner of his eye he had seen the skiff, pulled up on the river sand. He backed toward it, tossing the food package inside, and began pushing it out. Once he stumbled on the uneven bottom, but recovered his balance without taking his eyes from the boy.

The boy shifted his grip on the knife; he held it lightly with two fingers on the blade.

10

"Ain't no knife gonna stop me," Jayson said, "and I come back and kill you with it."

The muddy yellow water reached his knees. He climbed into the boat and picked up the long pole. He gave two hard shoves and the pole no longer touched solid ground. Then Jayson stood in the boat, the pole held crosswise in his two hands, and looked down at the river and waited until he could drift across the bottomless part and could use the pole again.

On the other side, he left the skiff on the sands and, holding the package of food in his left hand, scrambled up the bluff: the going would be easier along the bed of the railroad. At the top he turned and looked across the yellow river. On the other side the boy had not moved; he was still standing there, the knife ready. And the second boy, the little one, like a black monkey slid down the trunk of the bay tree where he had climbed to be out of the way.

Jayson Paul saw the tall twin chimneys of the cotton mill that was on the outskirts of town. "Right over that little bunch of pines." His shoes, which he had tied together by the laces, he swung in circles around his finger. "Right over yonder." He sat down on the ground and crossed his feet under him. A big yellow and black spider dangled from a honeysuckle bush, sliding up and down on its web. Carefully, with one finger, Jayson Paul shifted the thread to another branch. "That ought to mix you up some, Mr. Spider," he said. Then he stretched himself out full along the ground and sang into the heat of the late evening.

> *"I been in the pen so long,*
>   *Yes, I been in the pen so long,*
>   *I been in the pen so long, baby,*
>   *Baby, that where I been so long."*

He drew his knees up close to his chin and wrapped long arms around them.

> *"I been in the pen so long, baby,*
>   *Too long, baby,*
>   *I gonna stop lying alone, baby,*
>   *Baby, I been away so long."*

For a while after he stopped singing he lay there, his eyes closed, thinking how it would be.

Jayson Paul leaned against the tarred black wood of a lamppost and began to put on his shoes. Smoke from the trash incinerator of the mill made him shake his head and sneeze.

"Sweet Jesus," he said. "I done forgot how to breathe."

The mills had closed down for the day. There was no one on the streets; they would be inside eating now. Over the burning the smell of frying was heavy on the beginning night.

"I be mighty glad to get home," he told himself. "For sure. It be real fine.

> *I'm working my way back home,*
>   *Oh Baby,*
>   *Working my way back home,*
>   *Oh Baby,*
>   *Working my way back home."*

He recognized the neighborhood: it hadn't changed. First the scattered houses with stretches of bumpy weedy places between them and a few cart horses and a cow or two pulling the tops off the longest grasses. Then houses closer and closer together until at last there was no space or grass between them, just dirt alleys and dirt streets and dogs licking the dirt off their paws on front porches and dust lying over everything; a church, brown-painted with a crooked steeple: they had had a still in the basement once; he wondered if there was any there now—he would have to find out. (Once he could have told you exactly where every batch of brew could be found. It would take time to learn all the new spots again.)

The street lights went on. He looked up at them, strung out yellow against a sky that wasn't dark yet. Jayson remembered them looking that way. He hadn't forgotten anything.

Over to the left was the Pair-a-Dice Bar with its green-painted door and on each side the full-length posters of white girls drinking Jax beer. He pushed open the door and went in. There was only one light burning, a small one without a shade over the bar. The first table was so near the bar he stumbled into it and stood for a minute blinking. He saw that they had added more tables but that nothing much had changed. Behind the bar, the cracked mirror framed in scrolled black wood; the pin-up pictures stuck into the frame and pasted on the glass; the three peacock feathers—red and blue and black—dangling by a cord from the ceiling and turning around and around in each draft—he had seen all this before.

13

The man behind the counter leaning on his elbows reading the funny page of last Sunday's paper was coffee-colored and young—too young for Jayson to remember him. And his eyes when he looked up at Jayson were the same color as his skin.

"Man," Jayson told him, "I come looking for somebody."

The light eyes blinked twice. "Who for?"

Jayson pulled out a chair and sat down, backwards so that he could lean his folded arms on the back. "I come looking for somebody but I ain't got no idea where she living at."

"That right?" The young man bent his head toward the funny paper again.

"I ain't seen her in quite a while and now I got to find her."

The years in prison had made him careless. He hadn't noticed Joe standing across the room. Joe, with the red and green baseball cap and the light kinky brown hair that stood up straight in front, almost as high as the snapped-up visor; a short man but very heavy and with the curved baling hook of a warehouseman stuck in his belt. Jayson stood up so quickly that the chair caught against his leg and fell over.

"Hey," the light-colored young man said and lifted his funny paper straight up. "What you doing?"

"I done thought I was seeing wrong but I reckon I ain't," Joe said.

"How you?" Jayson told him quietly. He didn't have a knife or a razor, so he kept his hand on the back of the

14

nearest chair and he bent his knee against the edge of the table, ready to send it over.

"Hey," the young man said, and rubbed his light hairless chin with a quick nervous hand. "What you all doing?"

"You was looking for Aggie." Joe leaned back against the wall, his fingers rubbing the wood cross handle of the hook.

"I might could be doing that." Jayson hunched his back and waited.

"You ain't gonna do no fighting in here," the young man said, and pulled at his fingernails. "You ain't gonna do nothing like that."

Joe turned and looked at him and laughed. "No," he said. "We ain't gonna do nothing like that. Iffen he wants to find Aggie, I reckon I ain't gonna stand in his way."

"You ain't used to talk like that," Jayson said softly.

Joe kept on laughing. "Man, I ain't got no more interest in Aggie. I done had it and finished there."

Jayson stood watching him until he stopped laughing.

Joe said: "I reckon I gonna buy us a couple of beers." He sat down and Jayson took a chair about ten feet away. "Ain't got no cause to be scared of me," Joe said, and rubbed his round black face with his hands. "Ain't carrying no meanness for you for the time you like to kill me."

The young man pulled two bottles out of the rattling ice and brought them over, still dripping, and stuck out his thin yellow hand until Joe paid him.

"Why, Jay, man." Joe turned his head around and pulled off his baseball cap; the base of his skull was crossed by thick white scars. "You like to kill me right. Like you did to Mannie."

"Yes," said Jayson. "I done thought about that time." *He couldn't remember it though. Not very clearly. He had been fighting, but he couldn't swear who he was fighting with. He had killed Mannie and he didn't remember it. Nights in Kilby he had tried to call it back and couldn't. All he could remember was fighting and his mouth open and dry and the taste of dust in it.*

"I done thought about it," he said.

Joe tipped back his head and put the bottle to his lips. When he put it down again, he shook his head and rubbed his hand across his mouth. "I used to could take off a whole bottle one gulp that way."

"I remember," Jayson said. *And he did remember that. His mind was full of pictures of Joe emptying a bottle at one gulp. In some of them there'd be a girl in his lap or hanging around his shoulders. He remembered the feel of their skins, soft and moist.*

"I remember," Jayson said.

"A whole bottle," Joe said. "I used to could do."

"I remember," Jayson said. *He remembered: the stuff they'd made. The best corn likker there was: smooth and sweet on the tongue. They could make their own price for it and find buyers any time.*

It was Mannie who found buyers in the white people from the houses on Capitol Hill, the most important people, who had money and a taste for good corn. Mannie had sold to all of them. That's what he did best—sell. With his broad black face that was always shiny with perspiration even in winter, he had a way with white people; they were always glad to buy from him. He was chauffeur to Senator Winkerston's family, but his money did not come from that job. He only used their car to deliver the likker. It was a plan the police never would have caught on to.

"Never in a million years," Jayson said aloud. They had to go ruin it themselves, the three of them. And because of Aggie.

Mannie spent most of his time up at the Winkerston house. He had a room over the garage. Mrs. Winkerston had had it specially painted for him because he was such a splendid driver. He spent most of his time up there (when he was not actually driving the car or washing it) stretched out on his bed, wearing the silk pajamas he always bought with his share of the likker money.

Jayson had never seen the room, but he had seen the pajamas when they had just come and were still in the box that had the name in fancy Old English letters of the store in New Orleans. And when he saw them he wished for a moment that he had some, too, but just for a moment, because he was wishing for other things.

Mannie had a wife, whom he married in church on Easter Sunday—a tall light-brown woman whose name was Aggie. She lived in the colored section of town because at the Winkerstons' with Mannie there was no room for her and their son.

Jayson remembered: a tall woman, light-colored, a thin face, pinched almost; darkness under the cheekbones; and long eyes set wide apart. A thin woman with full nursing breasts. He saw her sitting on the steps of the house in the

17

colored section that Mannie rented and hardly ever lived in. Mannie preferred his room over the garage with the white family. He knew where his wife was; he could find her when he needed her. When he did, he would take one of the Senator's cars and drive down (the family had no objections to his keeping the car overnight), certain that he would know where to find her. And one time he found Jayson, too.

He was surprised. Even Jayson saw that. His round black face (the smiling affable face that the white people liked) was completely blank with surprise. And he staggered a little bit; he had had a few drinks coming down, the best of the stuff they made.

"I remember," Jayson said. *But he did not remember exactly what happened after he looked up and saw Mannie. He had fought and there had been the blood taste in his mouth and there had been the screaming from Aggie somewhere: he heard it far off. His head was swinging from the whisky and the excitement of the fight. And when Mannie's razor slashed along the side of his neck, he felt the blood run but no pain. There wasn't anything but breath coming short and not air enough and dust taste and smell. And from the corner of his eyes he saw the icepick on the table and grabbed for it.*

He remembered: *after he had finished with Mannie and was straightening up for breath there had been a short jab along his ribs. He had spun aside and brought down a bottle on Joe's neck (Joe, who was Mannie's friend and the third partner, who had driven over with him and*

18

*stayed out in the car to keep an eye on the stuff they had in
the back seat).*

Joe held the bottle up to the light. "Used to could take
off a whole bottle that way once. Used to once."

"I remember," Jayson said.

"Can't no more. Getting old, maybe. All us getting old."

"Maybe," Jayson said.

"Now you come back looking for Aggie."

"That right." Jayson said.

"She ain't gonna have nothing to do with you."

Jayson grinned. "Just tell me where she at."

Joe shook his head. "She ain't gonna have nothing to do
with you." He looked up quickly as Jayson shifted in his
chair. "Don't be getting riled up, man. I just telling you
what going on."

Jayson put both hands on his knees and bent forward.
"What going on?"

"Drink you beer, man."

"What going on?" Jayson said slowly. "You tell me what
going on."

"That what I trying to do." Joe sighed and reached for
Jayson's bottle. "Iffen you can let me."

"Go head," Jayson said.

"Aggie ain't having nothing to do with no men."

"Go head." Jayson said, staring at him. He ran his
tongue briefly over his lips; they tasted dry and dusty.

"She ain't had no luck with them, the three or four.
They just give her kids and no money.

"She got three—all of them girls. The boy, the one that

was Mannie's, the one that got baptized in the church, he
went and drunk some lye water that his ma was washing
in and died. The biggest girl, she yours all right. Looks like
you.

"And Aggie got plain mad. So she ain't having nothing
to do with no men. She don't let anybody come in her
house no more. And she got the kids so they don't let their
daddies walk down the street. They got to go round the
next block or the kids throw rocks at them. And they big
enough to hurt." He grinned and poked one finger down
the neck of the beer bottle. "You ought to seen what they
done to me, walking past. Just walking past. Just coming
here, not an hour ago past. Not noticing Aggie. Not even
studying on her. Just walking past."

*The street was narrow and without sidewalks. On
the north side a brick wall began at the edge of the
gravel; the late evening sun struck color off the broken
glass on the top. Behind the wall and out of sight were
the low brick buildings and the vegetable gardens of
the white poorhouse. On the south side of the street
ran another wall—of houses, mustard color; in front of
each, four wooden steps. A solid wall: wood house,
alley gate, wood house, and so on for the entire block.
Aggie lived in the second one from the corner with her
three girls, who were all half sisters.*

*Evenings it rains in Stanhope. Not hard. Not hard
enough to make it any cooler; not hard enough to settle the dust really. The drops mostly stay as they fall
and roll around the top layer of dirt in round blobs*

until they dry away. Althea, who was the second girl and was eleven, walked up and down in the street, breaking the heavy drops with her bare toe. Anna, who was five, sat cross-legged on the top step, the broadest one, the one with the pile of brick fragments. Alice Mary, who was the oldest and Jayson's child, was sitting on the bottom step. She was thirteen, big for her age, with the beginnings of a heavy woman's body. She sat with her head bent into her hands, dozing in the heat of the late evening.

Althea skipped back in from the street with her quick skip and jammed sharp little fingers into Alice Mary's side. "There he come," she said.

The sun was still so bright: Alice Mary blinked and rubbed her eyes. The piece of brick she had fell into her lap. "Who coming?"

"My Daddy Joe." Althea picked up the brick and juggled it in her hand. "I reckon I could hit him way off where he at." She was big for eleven, with the broad shoulders and back of an older boy.

"There he come," little Anna said. "There come Althea's Daddy Joe."

Alice Mary leaned back against the wood steps. "I sure see him now. Come right slam down the middle of the street."

"I can hit him now for sure." Althea did not stand up, but her right hand snapped forward and the piece of brick hit the man squarely in the stomach.

He gave a quick growl of pain and cupped his hands over the sore spot. The three girls laughed.

"*Sweet Jesus*"—*he rubbed his square chin with one hand*—"*iffen I ever get my hands on you.*"

Althea stood up, another rock in her hand, and shouted: "Go off, Daddy Joe. You can't walk down our street. You can't walk by our house."

The three girls called: "Go off, Daddy Joe. Go off. Daddy Joe. Go off, Daddy Joe." Then they stood up and, fast as they could, threw the rocks at him. He dodged around the corner at a scuttling run.

Alice Mary stuck her head in the front door and told her mother: "Daddy Joe was coming down the street."

"I reckon I know," Aggie said. She was lying on the bed in the first room, in her slip to be cooler. She worked as a cook in one of the big houses on Madison Street and when she got home she always lay down for a while before she looked for supper. "I reckon I heard all the racket."

While Joe stood around the corner watching them, Alice Mary helped Althea and Anna find other pieces of brick. They always kept a pile on the front top step.

Joe rubbed his hands over his face and stared at Jayson. "That plain what happened."

Jayson grinned and did not answer.

"That it, all right."

"Let kids chase you," Jayson said.

Joe chewed his underlip. "It ain't worth getting you face bashed none. Just to walk down a street."

"I reckon I best visit her for a spell," Jayson said.

"They ain't gonna let you near the house."

Jayson was still grinning when he stood up.

Joe pointed one finger at the Jax beer poster: a girl, a white girl with red hair and green eyes and a mouth open and waiting. "You ought to go looking for one like that."

Jayson hooked thumbs in his belt and studied the poster. "Hell, man," he said. "Where I gonna find something like that?"

Joe grinned.

"You ain't knowing where."

"Sure," said Joe. "I reckon I know where there one looks like that."

"Jesus," Jayson chewed his lower lip. "Why ain't you got her?"

Joe grinned and made crisscross lines on the wet table oilcloth. He was embarrassed. "She won't have nothing to do with me. She says she don't go for nobody little."

"She ain't white."

"Plain near almost," Joe said.

"She ain't like that." Jayson was staring at the poster.

"I done said she is. Hair and all. You plain got to go take a look."

"Where I got to look?"

Joe grinned. "Iffen you went walking through the houses back of Lansford Mill, she come walking up to you."

Sweat tickled down the side of Jayson's neck and he rubbed at it with the back of his hand. "You reckon she would?"

"Iffen she took a liking to you. You wouldn't even need no money."

"You reckon she would?"

"Hell, man," Joe said. "She there almost like she waiting for you."

Jayson swung his leg in wide circles. "I reckon I better see Aggie first."

Joe rubbed his chin and pulled at a stray hair on his cheek. "She's a lot better-looking than Aggie."

"Maybe," Jayson grinned. On the upper left-hand side of his mouth most of the teeth were missing. "But I reckon I will all the same."

"I plain don't study you."

"Man," Jayson said. "I go to Kilby account of Aggie and I sure gonna want her now I out."

"Now you out," Joe said. "What you planning for money?"

"Don't figure trouble getting none, long as people still drinking."

Joe rubbed his hands and grinned. "Like it used to be. Before the fight where Mannie got killed."

"Maybe," Jayson said. "But I got something else I want now."

Joe shook his head and rubbed his teeth with his knuckles. "Aggie ain't young no more."

"Don't reckon I am neither."

"Hell, man," Joe said. "There ain't no use fussing with a woman when she get old."

Jayson grinned. "She was a mighty lot of woman, I remember."

"Okay," Joe said, and tipped back his chair. "You go head. But I'm telling you. She got religion now. She ain't gonna have nothing to do with you."

"Ain't no woman not going to have nothing to do with me," Jayson said. "Now where she living at?"

Over in the direction of the river the chimney sweeps were swinging wide across a sky that was filling with faint summer-night haze. The night wind was beginning to stir the first top dust of the streets.

Inside the mustard-colored wood house Aggie had got up and was beginning to fix supper. The kitchen was two rooms away from the front steps but the noises carried plainly: the banging of pots and the singing, a hymn:

"King Jesus lit the candle by the waterside
To see the little children when they truly baptized.
Honor, honor
Unto the dying Lamb."

In the house where she worked on Madison Street she was very quiet; here she listened to the sounds of pots with pleasure. On Madison Street she was an elaborate cook (to the joy of her employers); here she boiled potatoes and tossed a chunk of bacon in a frying-pan. Then she wiped her face with her hands and went back into the front room to lie down again on the bed with the week-old copy of *Life* she had brought from the house on Madison Street.

Outside, Anna had gone back to sleep, her head pillowed on the step above. Althea was building a little arch of the pieces of rock; whenever it reached a certain height

Alice Mary would laugh and poke it with her finger.

The arch of rocks collapsed. "You plain got to stop that," Althea said.

"Why I got to stop?" Alice Mary said. "Why I got to stop?"

"You plain got to stop."

"You build it up," Alice Mary said, "and I knock it down." She reached out, but her hand stayed in mid-air. She had seen Jayson coming toward them, coming down the middle of the street, the wood walls of houses on one side and on the other the brick wall with the pieces of glass on top shining faintly under the street lamp. Jayson stopped in the round circle of light and stood looking at them, his fingers hooked in his belt.

"What you looking for?" Alice Mary called. She had her head turned sideways and she was frowning.

"I come looking for somebody called Aggie," Jayson said.

Anna woke up and reached for the nearest little rock.

"Nobody here called that," Alice Mary said.

Althea tossed a rock from one hand to the other.

Jayson stood still in the circle of light, without moving, and grinning.

"Why you want to find her?" Alice Mary's voice hesitated slightly.

Jayson stretched out one arm to the lamppost and leaned against it. "You got no cause to ask," he said. "You got no cause to ask."

From the lowest step Anna stood up. "Iffen you come up on our sidewalk we're gonna bash you."

Jayson laughed. "Ain't no little rock gonna stop me when I pull you head right off you neck."

Anna threw the rock. It struck Jayson's shoulder and bounced into the street, lifting a little cloud of dust.

"Ain't no little rock gonna stop me," Jayson said, and stood clear of the lamppost, hitching up his pants.

"Pitch him one." Anna pulled at the skirt of Alice Mary's dress. "You pitch him one that'll make his head spin."

"Like I did to my Daddy Joe," Althea said.

Alice Mary did not answer. She was staring at him, and her face was puzzled. A thin face, a girl's face twisted into a woman's.

"Come ahead," they said. "Pitch one. Reckon he you daddy. Pitch him one."

He took one step, grinning.

"Reckon I better," she said.

Her aim was good. He ducked as the rock passed his shoulder. But the second one, the one she threw from her left hand, caught squarely on the head. In dodging one, he had walked squarely into the force of the other.

"Sweet God Almighty." He put his hand to his head and then looked at the blood on his fingers. The ground was shifting under his feet like the trick floors at sideshows.

Another rock hit his shoulder. And another the center of his chest; the pain flashed hot through the length of his body. Objects were passing him, missing him and striking into the ground.

Inside his head was the sound of rocks falling. And all around him dust was heavy in the air, so heavy he couldn't see clearly because of it. But then he saw Aggie.

She was calling to the girls through the front window. "Pitch some more," she kept calling. "Pitch some more."

He decided then. He held his arms in front of his face and started walking toward them. Not running. Not hurrying. But walking. The rocks hurt, but as long as they did not hit his head it was not too bad.

Aggie was screaming. He did not look up but he recognized the sound. He had heard it before, the night Mannie was killed. A door slammed somewhere close. He had heard that sound, too, the same night. She had run away then like she'd be doing now. But there was a difference now. And he could not be sure of it.

He could not see where he was going, with his head covered by his arms. He walked straight into the steps, stumbled and sprawled out full-length on them, one of his hands squarely on the pile of rocks. He wondered what had happened to the kids who had been standing there.

He turned his head slowly, looking up. Alice Mary stood on the porch, her hands raised over her head, and in them a whole brick. He jerked his body aside and the brick gouged a piece out of the wood steps.

He remembered she was his kid when he caught her shoulder and pushed her off the porch. She stumbled backwards and sat down and a little cloud of dry dust rose.

He went through the house. Aggie was not there. In the kitchen a pot of potatoes was boiling on the stove. He knocked it to the floor and then rubbed the side of his hand where the pot had burned it. The potatoes were over-

28

cooked. They burst on the floor. He stepped into one; it made it hard for him to walk without slipping.

The bacon was burning. The smoke at the bottom of the pan was so thick he could not see the meat. He knocked that pot off, too, and kicked it into a corner.

He walked all the way through the house, back to the kitchen. He opened the door and stood looking out into the back yard. Behind the shed, through a crack of the boards he caught sight of white cloth. Aggie was out there, hiding and watching him as he was watching her.

And suddenly he began to laugh. The white cloth disappeared. He thought of her running away, dodging along in the alleys between the houses; and he laughed still harder. He stood in the doorway and laughed until he had to hold to the door for support.

He turned and walked back to the front of the house, kicking at whatever came in his way. In the room he yanked the mattress off the bed and the effort made him stagger. He would have liked to smash the house to bits, but suddenly he felt too tired. And he was very hot. He felt the perspiration run down his face and drop with a pulling tickle from his chin. The perspiration ran in his eyes, his vision blurred; he could have sworn that the walls swayed inward, ready to fall on him. He lunged for the door and the safety outside.

He stood on the front steps breathing hard, blinking, until he could see again. Then he remembered the hurting and began to rub the spots on his head and body where the rocks had hit him. He noticed his girl still sitting where she had stumbled on the bare ground of the front yard.

She was leaning back on her hands, staring at him. "Don't you know you daddy?" he asked her. It was too dark to see much of her face, but her mouth was open and she was staring up at him. He held on to the porch rail and laughed at her. He let his body swing back and forth as he laughed.

There was a song going through his head. And because he knew Aggie would be close enough to hear, he sang it aloud:

> *"Head is like a coffee pot,*
> *Nose is like a spout,*
> *Mouth is like an old fireplace*
> *With the ashes all raked out.*
> *Oh Aggie, po gal,*
> *Oh Aggie, po gal,*
> *Oh Aggie."*

The railing was rotten and cracked under his weight. He went down the steps with the tune of the song in his ears.

He stood in the street under the lamp and rubbed his head with both hands; there was a kind of buzzing in it. He could have sworn that the mill was working, but it was all in his head. There was blood on his hand too; he wiped it across the front of his shirt.

He turned so that his heel grated against the asphalt street and looked back at the house where Aggie lived. The two little girls were still gone: they would be hiding under the house. His kid was standing up now, on the steps, her foot raised in mid-air as if she were about to come down and was not sure where the next step was, while it was there, right in front of her. She stood watching him, with her foot out stiff and not too steady. He could hear Aggie calling her: "Alice Mary, you come in here. Alice Mary!"

Alice Mary came down one step as if she hadn't heard. Aggie opened the front door a crack and put her arm through, trying to reach her. "You come in here." Just an arm waving up and down in the air, trying to touch something that wasn't in reach.

He saw that and laughed. He said aloud: "Man, you ain't got no call to be laughing," and shook his head. But he only laughed harder and his voice slid off down the lengths of evening air.

He turned and walked down the street, chuckling and singing.

> *"Mouth is like an old fireplace*
> *With the ashes all raked out.*
> *Oh Aggie, po gal,*
> *Oh Aggie."*

He stumbled a couple of times and caught himself just before falling. Once his knee brushed the ground. "Man, you ain't got no call to be singing," he said aloud. But he only sang louder so that he could hear himself over the buzzing in his head.

Joe called to him: "You, Jayson!" But he did not stop.

Joe came running alongside. "Christ sake, man," Joe shouted at him, "what you yelling for?"

Jayson stopped singing. His mouth was so heavy that he let it hang open.

31

"Christ sake, man," Joe said, "the police pick you up sure, with you going around acting like that."

Jayson looked at him, and slowly lifted his left hand and pushed up his lower jaw and closed his mouth. His hand stayed on his chin, rubbing it slightly.

"Man," Joe said, "you sure a mess."

Jayson blinked at him, his vision clearing slowly.

"You got blood all over you face."

Jayson rubbed his sleeve across his face and winced at the soreness.

"Come on inside." Joe took his arm and pointed to the Pair-a-Dice Bar. "And get cleaned up some."

"No," Jayson said, and pulled free. "No."

Joe smiled and tugged at his arm again, persuasively. "You just come on in and have a drink, man."

"No," Jayson said, and swayed on his feet.

There was another man standing beside Joe, a younger man, not much past twenty, tall and thin. Jayson's eyes fastened first on the blue and red print of his sport shirt and then lifted to his face. There was something familiar in it and he stared, trying to remember.

"This here is Al," Joe said. "You remember Al."

Jayson crinkled up his lips with the effort.

"He wasn't nothing but a boy," Joe said. "Before. You remember. Nothing but a little boy."

"I remember," Jayson said. A little boy. Tall even then and skinny. Black legs, running, in short trousers, running up and down, fetching and carrying. And two black eyes, shiny as oil in the light, watching. "I remember," Jayson said.

Al stuck out his hand without a word. Jayson stared at it a moment, then took it.

Joe said: "I been telling him how you come back. I been telling him we going in business again. And get the stuff really flowing."

Al said: "That right?" He was wearing a hat, a brown straw with a red flower-printed band. "You gonna do that?"

Jayson did not answer. He turned away from them. He let his eyes swing in a circle around the street, looking.

"What you looking for?" Joe asked.

Jayson did not answer. He took a deep breath and began to move off. Joe and Al walked with him.

"Where you going?" Joe asked him again.

"That right," Al said. "Where?"

Jayson did not answer. He kept walking slowly.

Suddenly Joe chuckled. "Jesus," he said. "Ain't we plain stupid?" He chuckled again.

"How we stupid?" Al said quickly and, frowning, hunched his shoulders. "What call you got to say we stupid?"

"Don't get riled up, man." Joe was still grinning. He patted Jayson on the back. "We gonna fix you up, man. We sure gonna."

Jayson shook his head and looked at him.

Joe said to Al: "Go tell Nancy what we got for her. You tell her we got somebody here who used to be the biggest fellow around here and he aiming to be it again. That what you tell her."

Al opened his mouth in a quick smile and went off, al-

most at a run. Jayson stared at his legs, moving like a
boy's had, back and forth, on errands.

"Sure," said Joe, and patted him on the back again.
"That what you want."

"What?" said Jayson. "What I want?"

He swung his eyes around until they rested on the
posters on either side of the bar door, the Jax posters of
white girls drinking beer and smiling; girls with long red
hair, and mouths open just a little.

"I done told you I know where to find one like that,"
Joe said. "I done told you that. And now I got to show
you."

"Show me," Jayson said.

"That what I fixing to do, man," Joe said. "That what I
plain fixing to do."

Jayson remembered the part of town back of the Lansford Mill. It had been a low stretch, marsh almost. He
remembered catching frogs there. It was filled with houses
now, the yellow painted barracks that the government had
built for workers at the cotton mill when they were doing
three shifts a day on army orders. The barracks were
mostly empty now; a few almost white people had slipped
into one of the buildings so quietly that no one had seen
them come: three or four families with over a dozen kids
and heavy-bellied pregnant women.

Jayson stopped and rubbed his head in both hands. He
could see again, almost clearly. But it seemed like the
ground was a long way off. His feet scarcely touched it.

"Where I got to look?" Jayson asked.

"Down there," Joe said. "Second one from the end on this here side."

"Ain't no call for you to come," Jayson said. "I reckon I can find it."

Joe grinned. "She know you coming. Al done run all the way to tell her."

"No call for you to come."

"Okay," Joe said. "I'm leaving." He turned around and noticed for the first time that Alice Mary had followed them. "Jay, man," Joe said, "look what we got here."

Jayson turned and noticed his girl for the first time. "You been following me?" he called. She did not answer. Looking at him, her eyes were wide open, so wide open that they did not seem to have any lids. And they weren't brown anymore; they were two flat round pieces of silver.

He walked over and took hold of her shoulder. He shook her so that her body struck into the hardness of his thigh. She was perfectly limp; even her arms flapped.

"You ma say for you to follow me?"

She shook her head but did not answer. The pressure of his arm was steadily increasing. She kicked at his shins sharply and pulled free; he grabbed at her as she slipped back out of reach. He grabbed for her again and his hand brushed her dress, but she was too quick. She stood just beyond his hand, body bent forward slightly, waiting, ready.

"Why you coming after me now, when I ain't want nothing to do with you?"

He studied her for a while between half-closed lids and then turned away. "You quit following me or I fix you good." He walked away and, glancing over his shoulder, saw that she had not moved. He searched with the toe of his shoe in the weeds by the side of the road until he found a rock: a piece of concrete, white, with round brown pebbles in it. Even in the dark he could have hit her easy when he threw the rock, but he did not want to, suddenly. The piece of concrete hit the ground a little to one side of her. She disappeared.

He looked around for Joe, and he was gone, too. Jayson straightened up and took a deep breath: the air was full of night and damp. He rubbed his hands down his sides. His eyes, dark and shiny as oil, moved down the row of barracks on the left side of the street.

He began to walk along slowly, dragging his feet in the dirt road. It was completely dark now; over the broken stand of a street light, the evening star was tangled in the electric wires. The night wind caught the top layer of dirt from the road and spun it in slow circles.

He walked until he saw her. She was standing in the doorway of one of the barracks, the second from the end. Like Joe said, she was white or nearly white, and she had red hair, bright red hair. It hung over her shoulders in long perfect waves, like water when the wind passes over it. Red hair like a curtain that would draw down like a shade.

She came down the two steps and walked toward him— slowly, putting one foot in front of the other so that her walk was wavy as her hair. The light from the corner shone on the luminous green shadow of her eyelids. She leaned against the gatepost which was all that was left of the fence the government had built. And she waited for him.

Looking at her he began to grin. The skin on his face felt dry and hard and he could imagine it cracking when his mouth moved as wide, bright, he began to grin. "You waiting on me?"

"I might could be," she said.

The Black Prince

"How art thou fallen from heaven,
O Lucifer, son of the morning!"

Winters are short and very cold; sometimes there is even a snow like heavy frost on the ground. Summers are powdery hot; the white ball sun goes rolling around and around in a sky behind the smoke from the summer fires. There is always a burning somewhere in summer; the pines are dry and waiting; the sun itself starts the smoldering. A pine fire is quiet; there is only a kind of rustle from the flames inside the trunks until the branches and needles go up with a whistling. A whole hill often burns that way, its smoke rising straight up to the white sun, and quiet.

In the plowed patches, green things grow quickly: the ground is rich and there are underground rivers. But there are no big farms: only patches of corn, green beans, and a field or two of cotton (grown for a little cash to spend on Saturdays at Luther's General Store or Willie's Café; these are the only two places for forty miles in any direction). There is good pasture: the green places along the hillsides

38

with pines for shade and sure water in the streams that come down from the Smokies to the north; even in the burnt-out land of five seasons back, shrubs are high. But in the whole county there are only fifty cows, gone wild most of them and dry because they were never milked. They are afraid of men and feed in the farthest ridges and the swamps that are the bottoms of some littlest of the valleys. Their numbers are slowly increasing because no one bothers them. Only once in a while some man with a hankering for cow meat takes his rifle and goes after them. But that is not often; the people prefer pork. Each family keeps enough razorbacks in a run of bark palings.

It is all colored people here, and it is the poorest part of the smallest and worst county in the state. The place at the end of the dirt road leading from the state highway, the place where Luther's Store and Willie's Café stand, does not even have a name in the county records.

The only cool time of the summer day is very early, before the mists have shriveled away. There is a breeze then, a good stiff one out of the Smokies. During the day there is no sound: it is dead hot. But in the early mornings, when the breeze from the north is blowing, it is not so lonesomely quiet: crickets and locusts and the birds that flutter about hunting them, calling frantically as if they had something of importance to settle quick before the heat sets in. (By seven they are quiet again, in the invisible places they have chosen to wait out the day.)

A pine cone rattled down on Alberta's head and bounced from her shoulder. She scooped it from the ground and threw it upward through the branches. "You just keep your cone, mister birds. I got no cause to want it." With a pumping of wings the birds were gone, their cries sliding after them, back down the air. "You just yell your head off. I can hit you any time I want. Any time I want." There was a small round piece of granite at her feet and she tossed it, without particular aim, into the biggest of the bay trees: a gray squirrel with a thin rattail tumbled from the branches and peeped at her from behind the trunk with a pointed little rat face. She jammed her hands in the pockets of her dress and went on, swaggering slightly, cool and feeling good.

She was a handsome girl, taller than most people in her part of the county, and light brown—there had been a lot of white blood in her family, back somewhere, they'd forgot where exactly. She was not graceful—not as a woman is—but light on her feet and supple as a man. Her dress, which the sun had bleached to a whitish color, leaving only a trace of pink along the seams, had shrunk out of size for her: it pulled tight across her broad, slightly hunched, muscled back, even though she had left all the front buttons open down to the waist.

As she walked along, the birds were making even more of a row, knocking loose cones and dry pine needles and old broad bay leaves, and twice she stopped, threw back her head, and called up to them: "Crazy fool birds. Can't do nothing to me. Fool jackass birds." Up ahead, a couple of minutes' walk, was the field and the cotton, bursting white out of the brown cups and waiting to be picked. And she did not feel like working. She leaned against a tree, stretching so that the bark crumbled in her fingers, listening to the birds.

Something different was in their calling. She listened, her head bent forward, her eyes closed, as she sorted the sounds. One jay was wrong: its long sustained note ended with the cluck of a quail. No bird did that. Alberta opened her eyes and looked slowly around. But the pines were thick and close and full of blue night shadow and wrapped with fog that moved like bits of cloth in the wind. Leaving the other bird calls, the whistle became distinct, high, soaring, mocking, like some rare bird, proudly, insolently.

Alberta moved a few steps out from the tree and turned slowly on her heels. The whistle was going around her now, in slow circles, and she turned with it, keeping her eye on the sound, seeing nothing. The birds were still calling and fluttering in the branches, sending bits of twig and bark tumbling down.

Alberta said: "A fool thing you doing. A crazy fool jackass thing." She sat down on a tumbled pile of bricks that had been the chimney of a sugarhouse burned during the Civil War. She spoke in her best tone, while the whistling went round and round her faster. "I reckon you got nothing better to do than go around messing up folks. You got me so riled up I don't reckon I know what way I'm heading in." The sound went around her and around her, but she held her head steady, talking to the pine directly in front of her. "I don't reckon there's nothing for me but set here till you tires out and goes away." The whistle circled her twice and then abruptly stopped, the last high clear note running off down the breeze. Alberta stood up, pulling down her faded dress. "I am mighty glad you come to stopping. I reckon now I can tell what direction I got to go in."

He was right there, leaning on the same pine she had been staring at, cleaning his front teeth with a little green twig and studying her, and she told him to his face: "That was a crazy mean thing, and you ain't got nothing better to do."

"Reckon not," he said, moving the little green twig in and out of the hole between his lower front teeth.

She pushed her hands in the pockets of her dress and looked him over. "Where you come from?"

"Me?" The little green twig went in and out of his teeth with each breath. "I just come straight out the morning."

She turned and walked away. "I be glad to see you go."

He stood in front of her: he had a way of moving without a sound, of popping up in places. "I be sorry to see you go, Alberta Lacy."

She studied him before she answered: tall, not too big or heavy, and black (no other blood but his own in him, she thought). He was dressed nice—a leather jacket with fringe on the sleeves, a red plaid shirt, and new blue denim pants. "How you know what I'm called?" she asked him politely.

He grinned, and his teeth were white and perfect. "I done seen it in the fire," he said. "I done seen it in the fire and I read it clear: Alberta Lacy."

She frowned. "I don't see as how I understand."

He blew the little green twig out of his mouth. "I might

42

could be seeing you again real soon, Alberta Lacy." Then he slipped around the tree like the last trail of night shadow and disappeared.

Alberta stood listening: only the birds and the insects and the wind. Then everything got quiet, and the sun was shining white all around, and she climbed down the slope to the field.

A little field—just a strip of cotton tucked in between two ridges. Her father and her two biggest brothers had planted it with half a morning's work, and they hadn't gone back to tend it once. They didn't even seem to remember it: whatever work they did was in the older fields closer to home. So Alberta had taken it over. Sometimes she brought along the twins: Sidney and Silvia; they were seven: young enough for her to order around and big enough to be a help. But usually she couldn't find them; they were strange ones, gone out of the house for a couple of days at a time in summer, sleeping out somewhere, always sticking together. They were strange little ones and not worth trouble looking for. So most times Alberta worked with Maggie Mary Evans, who was Josh Evans's daughter and just about the only girl her age she was friendly with. From the field there'd be maybe three bales of real early stuff; and they'd split the profit. They worked all morning, pulling off the bolls and dropping them in the sacks they slung crosswise across their shoulders. They worked very slowly, so slowly that at times their hands seemed hardly to move, dozing in the heat. When it got to be noon, when they had no shadow any more, they slipped off the sacks, leaving them between the furrows, and turned to the shade to eat their lunch.

He was waiting for them there, stretched out along the ground with his head propped up on the slender trunk of a little bay tree. He winked lazily at Alberta; his eyes were big and shiny black as oil. "How you, Miss Alberta Lacy?"

Alberta looked down at him, crooking her lips. "You got nothing to do but pester me?"

"Sure I got something to do, but ain't nothing nice like this."

Alberta looked at him through half-closed lids, then sat down to the lunch.

"You hungry, mister?" Maggie Mary asked. She had stood watching, both hands jammed into the belt of her dress, and her eyes moving from one to the other with the quickness and the color of a sparrow.

The man rolled over and looked up at her. "Reckon I am."

"You can have some of our lunch," Maggie Mary said.

Crazy fool, Alberta thought, standing so close with him on the ground like that. He must can see all the way up her. And from the way he lay there, grinning, he must be enjoying it.

"That real nice," he said to Maggie Mary, and crawled over on his stomach to where the lunch bucket was.

Alberta watched his smooth, black hand reaching into the bucket and suddenly she remembered. "How you called?"

44

He put a piece of corn bread in his mouth, chewed it briefly, and swallowed it with a gulp. "I got three names."

"No fooling," Maggie Mary said, and giggled in her hand. "I got three names, too."

"Stanley Albert Thompson."

"That a good-sounding name," Alberta said. She began to eat her lunch quickly, her mouth too full to talk. Stanley Albert was staring at her, but she didn't raise her eyes. Then he began to sing, low, pounding time with the flat of his hand against the ground.

> "Alberta, let you hair hang low,
>   Alberta, let you hair hang low,
>   I'll give you more gold than you apron can hold
>   If you just let you hair hang low."

Alberta got up slowly, not looking at him. "We got work to finish."

Stanley Albert turned over so that his face was pressed in the grass and pine needles. "All you get's the muscles in you arm."

"That right." Maggie Mary nodded quickly. "That right."

"Maggie Mary," Alberta said, "iffen you don't come with me I gonna bop you so hard you land in the middle of tomorrow."

"Good-by, Mr. Stanley Albert Thompson," Maggie Mary said, but he had fallen asleep.

By the time they finished work he was gone; there wasn't even a spot in the pine needles and short grass to show where he had been.

"Ain't that the strangest thing?" Maggie Mary said.

Alberta picked up the small bucket they carried their lunch in. "I reckon not."

"Seemed like he was fixing to wait for us."

"He ain't fixing to wait for nobody, that kind." Alberta rubbed one hand across her shoulders, sighing slightly. "I got a pain fit to kill."

Maggie Mary leaned one arm against a tree and looked off across the little field where they had spent the day. "You reckon he was in here most all morning watching us?"

"Maybe." Alberta began to walk home. Maggie Mary followed slowly, her head still turned, watching the field.

"He musta spent all morning just watching."

"Nothing hard about doing that, watching us break our back out in the sun."

Maggie Mary took one long, loping step and came up with Alberta. "You reckon he coming back?"

Alberta stared full at her, head bent, chewing on her lower lip. "Maggie Mary Evans," she said, "you might could get a thought that he might be wanting you and you might could get a thought that you be wanting him—"

Maggie Mary bent down and brushed the dust off her bare feet carefully, not answering.

"You a plain crazy fool." Alberta planted both hands on her hips and bent her body forward slightly. "A plain crazy fool. You wouldn't be forgetting Jay Mastern?" Jay Mastern had gone off to Ramsey to work at the mill and never come back, but left Maggie Mary to have his baby.

46

So one day Maggie Mary took her pa's best mule and put a blanket on it for a saddle and rode over to Blue Goose Lake, where the old woman lived who could tell her what to do. The old woman gave her medicine in a beer can: whisky and calomel and other things that were a secret. Maggie Mary took the medicine in one gulp, because it tasted so bad, waded way out into Blue Goose Lake so that the water came up to her neck, then dripping wet got up on the mule and whipped him up to a good fast pace all the way home. The baby had come off all right: there wasn't one. And Maggie Mary nearly died. It was something on to three months before she was able to do more than walk around, her arms hanging straight down and stiff and her black skin overtinged with gray.

"You wouldn't be forgetting Jay Mastern?"

"Sure," Maggie Mary said, brushing the dust off her bare feet lightly. "I clean forgot about him."

"Don't you be having nothing to do with this here Stanley Albert Thompson."

Maggie Mary began to walk again, slowly, smiling just a little bit with one corner of her mouth. "Sounds like you been thinking about him for yourself."

Alberta jammed both hands down in the pockets of her dress. "I been thinking nothing of the sort."

"Willie'll kill him."

Alberta chewed on one finger. "I reckon he could care for himself."

Maggie Mary smiled to herself softly, remembering. "I reckon he could; he's real fine-appearing man."

"He was dressed good."

"Where you reckon he come from?" Maggie Mary asked.

Alberta shrugged. "He just come walking out of the morning fog."

That was how he came into this country: he appeared one day whistling a bird call in the woods in high summer. And he stayed on. The very first Saturday night he went down to Willie's and had four fights and won them all.

Willie's was an ordinary house made of pine slabs, older than most of the other houses, but more solid. There were two rooms: a little one where Willie lived (a heavy scrolled ironwork bed, a square oak dresser, a chest, a three-footed table, and on its cracked marble top a blue-painted mandolin without strings). And a big room: the café. Since anybody could remember, the café had been there with Willie's father or his grandfather, as long as there had been people in these parts. And that had been a long while: long before the Civil War even, runaways were settling here, knowing they'd be safe and hidden in the rough, uneven hills and the pines.

Willie had made some changes in the five or six years since his father died. He painted the counter that was the bar with varnish; that had not been a good idea: the whisky took the varnish off in a few weeks. And he painted the walls: bright blue. Then he went over them again, shaking his brush so that the walls were flecked like a mockingbird's eggs. But Willie used red to fleck—red against blue. And the mirror, gilt-edged, and hanging from

48

a thick gold cord: that had been Willie's idea, too. He'd found it one day, lying on the shoulder alongside the state highway; it must have fallen from a truck somehow. So he took it home. It was cracked in maybe two dozen pieces. Anyone who looked into it would see his face split up into a dozen different parts, all separate. But Willie hung it right over the shelves where he kept his whisky and set one of the kerosene lamps in front of it so that the light should reflect yellow-bright from all the pieces. One of them fell out (so that Willie had to glue it back with flour and water) the night Stanley Albert had his fourth fight, which he won like the other three. Not a man in the country would stand up like that, because fighting at Willie's on Saturday night is a rough affair with razors, or knives, or bottles.

Not a man in the country could have matched the way Stanley Albert fought that night, his shirt off, and his black body shining with sweat, the muscles along his neck and shoulders twisting like grass snakes. There wasn't a finer-looking man and there wasn't a better: he proved that.

The first three fights were real orderly affairs. Everybody could see what was coming minutes ahead, and Willie got the two of them out in the yard before they got at each other. And everybody who was sober enough to walk went out on the porch and watched Stanley Albert pound first Ran Carey's and then Henry Johnson's head up and down in the dust. Alberta sat on the porch (Willie had brought her a chair from inside) and watched Stanley Albert roll around the dust of the yard and didn't even blink an eye, not even during the third fight when Tim

49

Evans, who was Maggie Mary's brother, pull a razor. The razor got Stanley Albert all down one cheek, but Tim didn't have any teeth left and one side of his face got punched in so that it looked peculiar always afterward. Maggie Mary went running down into the yard, not bothering with her brother, to press her finger up against the little cut across Stanley Albert's cheek.

The fourth fight came up so suddenly nobody had time hardly to get out of the way: Joe Turner got one arm hooked around Stanley Albert's neck from behind. There wasn't any reason for it, except maybe that Joe was so drunk he didn't see who he had and that once there's been a couple of fights there's always more. Stanley Albert swung a bottle over his shoulder to break the hold and then nobody could see exactly what was happening: they were trying so hard to get clear. Willie pulled Alberta over the bar and pushed her down behind it and crouched alongside her, grinning. "That some fighter." And when it was all over they stood up again; first thing they saw was Joe Turner down on the floor and Stanley Albert leaning on a chair with Maggie dabbing at a cut on his hand with the edge of her petticoat.

He got a reputation from that Saturday night, and everybody was polite to him, and he could have had just about any of the girls he wanted. But he didn't seem to want them; at least he never took to coming to the houses to see them or to taking them home from Willie's. Maggie Mary Evans swore up and down that he had got her one day when she was fishing in Scanos River, but nobody paid her much attention. She liked to make up stories that way.

He had a little house in a valley to the east. Some boys who had gone out to shoot a cow for Christmas meat said they saw it. But they didn't go close even if there was three of them with a shotgun while Stanley Albert only carried a razor. Usually people only saw him on Saturday nights, and after a while they got used to him, though none of the men ever got to be friendly with him. There wasn't any mistaking the way the girls watched him. But after four or five Saturdays, by the time the summer was over, everybody expected him and waited for him, the way you'd wait for a storm to come or a freeze: not liking it, but not being able to do anything either. That's the way it went along: he'd buy his food for the coming week at Luther's Store, and then he'd come next door to Willie's.

He never stood up at the counter that was the bar. He'd take his glass and walk over to a table and sit down, and pull out a little bottle from his pocket, and add white lightning to the whisky. There wasn't anything could insult Willie more. He made the whisky and it was the best stuff in the county. He even had some customers drive clear out from Montgomery to buy some of his corn, and, being good stuff, there wasn't any call to add anything: it had enough kick of its own; raw and stinging to the throat. It was good stuff; nobody added anything to it—except Stanley Albert Thompson, while Willie looked at him and said things under his breath. But nothing ever came of it, because everybody remembered how good a job Stanley Albert had done the first night he came.

Stanley Albert always had money, enough of it to pay for the groceries and all the whisky he wanted. There was always the sound of silver jingling in his trouser pocket. Everybody could hear that. Once when Willie was standing behind the bar, shuffling a pack of cards with a wide fancy twirl—just for amusement—Stanley Albert, who had had a couple of drinks and was feeling especially good, got up and pulled a handful of coins out of his pocket. He began to shuffle them through the air, the way Willie had done with the cards. Stanley Albert's black hands flipped the coins back and forth, faster and faster, until there was a solid silver ring hanging and shining in the air. Then Stanley Albert let one of his hands drop to his side and the silver ring poured back into the other hand and disappeared with a little clinking sound. And he dropped the money into his pocket with a short quick laugh.

That was the way Stanley Albert used his money: he had fun with it. Only thing, one night when Stanley Albert had had maybe a bit too much and sat dozing at his table, Morris Henry slipped a hand into the pocket. He wouldn't have ever dared to do that if Stanley Albert hadn't been dozing, leaning back in his chair, the bottle of white lightning empty in one hand. And Morris Henry slipped his little hand in the pocket and felt all around carefully. Then he turned his head slowly in a circle, looking at everybody in the room. He was a little black monkey Negro and his eyes were shiny and flat as mirrors. He slipped his hand back and scurried out into the yard and hid in the blackberry bushes. He wouldn't move until morning came; he just sat there, chewing on his little black fingers with his wide flaring yellow teeth. Anybody who wanted to know what was happening had to go out there and ask him. And ever afterwards Morris Henry swore that there hadn't been anything at all in Stanley Albert Thompson's pocket. But then everybody knew Morris Henry was crazy because just a few minutes later when Stanley Albert woke up and walked across to the bar, the change jingled in the pocket and he laid five quarters on the counter. And the money was good enough because Willie bounced it on the counter and it gave the clear ring of new silver.

Stanley Albert had money all right and he spent it; there wasn't anything short about him. He'd buy drinks for anybody who'd come over to his table; the only ones who came were the girls. And he didn't seem to care how much they drank. He'd just sit there, leaning way back in his chair, grinning, his teeth white and big behind his black lips, and matching them drink for drink, and every now and then running his eye up and down their length just to let them know he was appreciating their figures. Most often it was Maggie Mary who would be sitting there, warning all the other girls away with a little slanting of her eyes when they got near. And sometimes he'd sing a song: a song about whisky that would make everyone forget they didn't like him and laugh; or a song about poor boys who were going to be hanged in the morning. He had a good voice, strong and clear, and he pounded time with the flat of his hand on the table. And he'd always be looking at Alberta when he was singing until she'd get up, holding her head high and stiff, and march over to where Willie was and take hold of his arm real sweet and smile at him. And Willie would give Stanley Albert a quick mean look and then pour her a drink of his best whisky.

Stanley Albert had a watch, a big heavy gold one, round almost as a tomato, that would strike the hours. (That was how you could tell he was around sometimes— hearing his watch strike.) It was attached to a broad black ribbon and sometimes he held it up, let it swing before the eyes of whatever girl it happened to be at the time, let it swing slowly back and forth, up and down, so that her head moved with it. He had a ring too, on his right little finger: a white-colored band with a stone big as a chip of second coal and dark green. And when he fought, the first time he came into Willie's, the ring cut the same as a razor in his hand; it was maybe a little more messy, because its edges were jagged.

Those were two things—the watch and the ring—that must have cost more than all the money around here in a year. That was why all the women liked him so; they kept thinking of the nice things he could give them if he got interested. And that was why the men hated him. Things can go as smooth as glass if everybody's got about the same things and the same amount of money knocking around in a jean pocket on Saturday night. But when they don't, things begin happening. It would have been simpler maybe if they could have fought Stanley Albert Thompson, but there wasn't any man keen to fight him. That was how they started fighting each other. A feud that nobody'd paid any mind to for eight or ten years started up again.

54

It began one Sunday morning along toward dawn when everyone was feeling tired and leaving Willie's. Stanley Albert had gone out first and was sitting aside the porch railing. Jim Mastern was standing on the lowest step not moving, just staring across the fields, not being able to see anything in the dark, except maybe the bright-colored patterns the whisky set shooting starwise before his eyes. And Randall Stevens was standing in the doorway, looking down at his own foot, which he kept moving in a little circle around and around on the floor boards. And Stanley Albert was looking hard at him. Randall Stevens didn't lift his head; he just had his razor out and was across the porch in one minute, bringing down his arm in a sweeping motion to get at Jim Mastern's neck. But he was too drunk to aim very straight and he missed; but he did cut the ear away so that it fell on the steps. Jim Mastern was off like a bat in the daylight, running fast, crashing into things, holding one hand to the side of his head. And Randall Stevens folded up the razor and slipped it back in his pocket and walked off slowly, his head bent over, as if he was sleepy. There wasn't any more sense to it than that; but it started the feud again.

Stanley Albert swung his legs over the railing and stretched himself and yawned. Nobody noticed except Alberta, they were so busy listening to the way Jim Mastern was screaming and running across the fields, and watching Randall Stevens march off, solemnly, like a priest.

And the next night Randall Stevens tumbled down the steps of his cabin with his head full of scatter shot. It was a Monday night in November. His mother came out to see and stepped square on him, and his blood spattered on the hoarfrost. Randall Stevens had six brothers, and the next night they rode their lanky burred horses five miles south and tried to set fire to the Mastern house. That was the beginning; the fighting kept up, off and on, all through the winter. The sheriff from Gloverston came down to investigate. He came driving down the road in the new shiny white state police patrol car—the only one in the county—stopped in Willie's Café for a drink and went back taking two gallons of home brew with him. That wasn't exactly right, maybe, seeing that he had taken an oath to uphold the law; but he couldn't have done much, except get killed. And that was certain.

The Stevenses and their friends took to coming to Willie's on Friday nights; the Masterns kept on coming on Saturday. That just made two nights Willie had to keep the place open and the lamps filled with kerosene; the crowd was smaller; shotguns were leaning against the wall.

That's the way it went all winter. Everybody got on one side or the other—everybody except Stanley Albert Thompson. They both wanted him: they had seen what he could do in a fight. But Stanley Albert took to coming a night all by himself: Sunday night, and Willie had to light all the lamps for just him and stand behind the counter and watch him sit at the table adding lightning to the whisky.

Once along toward the end of February when Cy Mastern was killed and the roof of his house started burning with pine knots tossed from the ground, Stanley Albert was standing just on the rim of the light, watching. He helped the Masterns carry water, but Ed Stevens, who was hiding up in top of a pine to watch, swore that the water was like kerosene in his hands. Wherever he'd toss a bucketful, the fire would shoot up, brighter and hotter than before.

By March the frosts stopped, and there weren't any more cold winds. The farmers came out every noon, solemnly, and laid their hands on the bare ground to see if it was time to put in their earliest corn and potatoes. But the ground stayed cold a long time that year so that there wasn't any plowing until near May. All during that time from March till May there wasn't anything doing; that was the worst time for the fighting. In the winter your hand shakes so with the cold that you aren't much good with a gun or knife. But by March the air is warmer and you don't have any work to get you tired, so you spend all the time thinking.

That spring things got bad. There wasn't a crowd any more at Willie's though he kept the place open and the lights on for the three nights of the week-end. Neither the Stevenses nor the Masterns would come; they were too easy targets in a house with wall lamps burning. And on Sunday night the only person who ever came was Stanley Albert Thompson. He'd sit and drink his whisky and lightning and maybe sing a song or two for the girls who came over to see him. By the end of April that was changed too. He finally got himself the girl he wanted; the one he'd been waiting around nearly all winter for. And his courting was like this:

Thomas Henry Lacy and his sons, Luke and Tom, had

gone for a walk, spoiling for a fight. They hadn't seen anything all evening, just some of the cows that had gone wild and went crashing away through the blueberry bushes. Alberta had taken herself along with them, since she was nearly as good as a man in a fight. They had been on the move all night but keeping in the range of a couple of miles and on the one side of the Scanos River. They were for Stevens and there was no telling what sort of affair the Masterns had rigged up on their ground. They rested for a while on the bluff of the river. Tom had some bread in his pocket and they ate it there, wondering if there was anybody in the laurels across the river just waiting for them to show themselves. Then they walked on again, not saying very much, seeing nothing but the moon flat against the sky and its light shiny on the heavy dew.

Alberta didn't particularly care when they left her behind. She turned her head to listen to the plaintive gargling call of a night quail, and when she looked again her father and the boys were gone. She knew where she was: on the second ridge away from home. There was just the big high ridge there to the left. The house was maybe twenty minutes away, but a hard walk, and Alberta was tired. She'd been washing all day, trying to make the clear brook water carry off the dirt and grease from the clothes, her mother standing behind her, yelling at each spot that remained, her light face black almost as her husband's with temper, and her gray fuzzy hair tied into knots like a pickaninny's. The boys had spent the whole day dozing in the shed while they put a new shoe on the mule.

Alberta listened carefully; there was nothing but night

58

noises; her father and the boys would be halfway home by now, scrambling down the rain-washed sides of the ridge. For a moment she considered following them. "Ain't no raving rush, girl," she told herself aloud. The night was cool, but there wasn't any wind. With her bare feet she felt the dry pine needles, then sat down on them, propping her back against a tree. She slipped the razor from the cord around her neck and held it open loosely in the palm of her hand; then she fell asleep.

She woke when the singing started, opening her eyes but not moving. The moon was right overhead, shining down so that the trunks of the pines stuck straight up out of the white shiny ground. There wasn't a man could hide behind a pine, yet she didn't see him. Only the singing going round and round her.

> "Alberta, what's on you mind,
> Alberta, why you treat me so unkind?
> You keep me worried; you keep me blue
> All the time,
> Alberta, why you treat me so unkind?"

She pushed herself up to a sitting position, still looking straight ahead, not following the song around and around. She let the hand that held the razor fall in her lap, so that the moon struck on the blade.

> "Alberta, why you treat me so unkind?"

Nothing grows under pines, not much grass even, not any bushes big enough to hide a man. Only pine trees, like black matches stuck in the moonlight. Black like matches, and thin like matches. There wasn't a man could hide behind a pine under a bright moon. There wasn't a man could pass a bright open space and not be seen.

> *"Alberta, let you hair hang low,*
> *Alberta, let you hair hang low.*
> *I'll give you more gold*
> *Than you apron can hold."*

"That ain't a very nice song," she said.

> *"I'll give you more gold*
> *Than you apron can hold."*

She lifted her right hand and turned the razor's edge slowly in the light. "I got silver of my own right here," she said. "That enough for me."

The song went round in a circle, round and round, weaving in and out of the pines, passing invisible across the open moon filled spaces.

> *"Alberta, let you hair hang low,*
> *I'll give you more gold*
> *Than you apron can hold*
> *If you just let you hair hang low."*

There wasn't a man alive could do that. Go round and round.

> *"Alberta, why you treat me so unkind?"*

Round and round, in and out the thin black trees. Alberta stood up, following the sound, turning on her heel.

> *"You keep me worried, you keep me blue*
> *All the time."*

"I plain confused," she said. "I don't reckon I understand."

>*"I'll give you more gold*
>*Than you apron can hold."*

"I ain't got no apron," she said.

>*"Alberta, let you hair hang low,*
>*Just let you hair hang low."*

The song stopped and Stanley Albert Thompson came right out of a patch of bright moon ground, where there were only brown pine needles.

Alberta forgot she was tired; the moon-spotted ground rolled past her feet like the moon in the sky—effortless. She recognized the country they passed through: Blue Goose Lake, Scanos River, and the steeper rough ground of the north part of the country, toward the Tennessee border. It was a far piece to walk and she wondered at the lightness of her feet. By moonset they had got there—the cabin that the boys had seen one day while they were hunting cows. She hesitated a little then, not afraid, not reluctant, but just not sure how to go on. Stanley Albert Thompson had been holding her hand all evening; he still held it. Right at the beginning when he had first taken her along with him, she'd shook her head, no, she could walk; no man needed to lead her. But he'd grinned at her, and shook his head, imitating her gesture, so that the moon sparkled on his black curly hair, and his black broad forehead, and he took her hand and led her so that the miles seemed nothing and the hours like smooth water.

He showed her the cabin, from the outside first: mustard color, trimmed with white, like the cabins the railroad company builds. One room with high peaked roof.

"A real fine house," she said. "A real fine house. You work for the railroad?"

"No."

He took her inside. "You light with candles," she said.

"I ain't ever been able to stand the smell of lamps," he said.

"But it's a real nice house. I might could learn to like it."

"No might could about it." He smoothed the cloth on the table with his fingers. "You going to like it."

She bent her head and looked at him through her eyelashes. "Now I don't rightly know. Seems as how I don't know you."

"Sure you do," he said. "I'm standing right here."

"Seems as how I don't know nothing. You might could have a dozen girls all over this here state."

"I reckon there's a dozen," he said.

She glared at him, hands on hips. "You old fool jackass," she said. "I reckon you can just keep everything."

He jammed his hands into the back pockets of his denim pants and bent backward staring at the ceiling.

"Ain't you gonna try to stop me?"

"Nuh-uh."

She leaned against the doorjamb and twisted her neck to look at him. "Ain't you sorry I going?"

"Sure." He was still staring upward at the ceiling with its four crossed beams. "Sure, I real sorry."

"I don't see as how I could stay though."

"Sure you could." He did not look at her.

"I don't see as how. You ain't give me none of the things you said."

"You a driving woman," he said, and grinned, his mouth wide and white in the dark of his face.

Then he sat down at the table. There were five candles there, stuck in bottles, but only one was lighted, the one in the center. Wax had run all down the side of the candle and down the bottle in little round blobs, nubby like gravel. He picked one off, dirty white between his black fingers. He rolled it slowly between his flat palms, back and forth. Then he flipped it toward Alberta. It flashed silvery through the circle of lamplight and thudded against her skirt. She bent forward to pick it up: a coin, new silver. As she bent there, another one struck her shoulder, and another. Stanley Albert Thompson sat at the table, grinning and tossing the coins to her, until she had filled both pockets of her dress.

He pushed the candle away from him. "You all right, I reckon, now."

She held one coin in her hands, turning it over and over.

"That ain't what you promised. I remember how you came and sang:

> '*I give you more gold*
> *Than you apron can hold.*' "

"Sure," he said and lifted a single eyebrow, very high. "I can do that all right, iffen you want it. I reckon I can do that."

63

She stood for a moment studying him. And Stanley Albert Thompson, from where he still sat at the table, curled up one corner of his mouth.

And very slowly Alberta began to smile. "I might could like it here," she said. "If you was real nice."

He got up then and rubbed her cheek very gently with his first finger. "I might could do that," he said. "I don't reckon it would be too heavy a thing to do."

The candle was on the table to one side. It caught the brightness of Alberta's eyes as she stood smiling at Stanley Albert Thompson. The steady yellow light threw her shadow over his body, a dark shadow that reached to his chin. His own shadow was on the wall behind. She glanced at it over his shoulder and giggled. "You better do something about your shadow there, Mr. Thompson. That there is a ugly shadow, sure."

He turned his head and glanced at it briefly. "Reckon so," he said.

It was an ugly shadow, sure. Alberta looked at Stanley Albert Thompson and shook her head. "I can't hardly believe it," she said. "You a right pretty man."

He grinned at her and shook himself so that the shadow on the wall spun around in a wild turn.

"I don't reckon you can do anything about it?"

"No," he said briefly. "I can't go changing my shadow." He hunched his back so that the figure on the wall seemed to jump up and down in anger.

She stepped over to him, putting her hands behind her, leaning backward to see his face. "If he don't do any more than dance on a wall, I ain't complaining."

64

Stanley Albert stood looking down at her, looking down the length of his face at her, and rocking slowly back and forth on his heels. "No," he said. "He ain't gonna do more than wiggle around the wall sometimes. But you can bet I am."

The coins weighed down the pockets of her dress, and his hands were warm against her skin. "I reckon I'm satisfied," she said.

That was the way it began. That was the courting. The woman was young and attractive and strong. The man could give her whatever she wanted. There were other courtings like that in this country. Every season there were courtings like that.

People would see them around sometimes; or sometimes they'd only hear them when they were still far off. Sometimes it would be Stanley Albert Thompson singing:

> *"Alberta, let you hair hang low,*
> *Alberta, let you hair hang low.*
> *I'll give you more gold*
> *Than you apron can hold*
> *If you just let you hair hang low."*

He had a strong voice. It could carry far in a quiet day or night. And if any of the people heard it, they'd turn and look at each other and nod their heads toward it, not saying anything, but just being sure that everyone was listening. And whenever Willie heard it, he'd close his eyes for a minute, seeing Alberta; and then he'd rub his hands all over his little black kinky head and whistle: "Euuuu," which meant that he was very, very sorry she had left him.

And sometimes all you could hear of them would be the chiming of Stanley Albert's watch every quarter-hour. One night that August, when the moon was heavy and hot and low, Maggie Mary was out walking with Jack Belden. She heard the clear high chime and remembered the nights at Willie's and the dangling gold watch. And she turned to Jack Belden, who had just got her comfortable in one arm, and jammed her fingers in his eyes and ran off after the sound. She didn't find them; and it wouldn't have much mattered if she had. Stanley Albert was much too gone on Alberta to notice any other woman in more than a passing appraising way.

And sometimes people would come on them walking alone, arms around each other's waist; or sitting in a shady spot during the day's heat, his head on her lap and both of them dozing and smiling a little. And everybody who saw them would turn around and get out of there fast; but neither of them turned a head or looked up: there might not have been anyone there.

And then every night they'd go down to Willie's. The first night they came—it was on a Thursday—the place was closed up tight. There wasn't ever anybody came on Thursday. Stanley Albert went around back to where Willie lived and pounded on the door, and when Willie didn't answer he went around to the front again where Alberta was waiting on the steps and kicked in the front panel of the wood door. Willie came scuttling out, his eyes round and bewildered like a suckling's and saw them sitting at one of the tables drinking his home brew, only first putting lightning into it. After that they came every night,

66

just them. It was all most people could do to afford a drink on Saturday or the week-end, but some of them would walk over to Willie's just to look at Stanley Albert and Alberta sitting there. They'd stand at the windows and look in, sweating in the hot summer nights and looking. Maybe a few of them would still be there waiting when Stanley and Alberta got ready to go, along toward morning.

That's what they did every single night of the year or so they were together. If they fell asleep, Willie would just have to stand waiting. They'd go out with their arms around each other's waist, staggering some, but not falling. And an hour or so later, people who were going out before dawn to get a little work done in the cool would see them clear over on the other side of the county, at Goose Lake, maybe, a good three hours' walk for a man cold sober. Willie had his own version of how they got around. They just picked up their feet, he said, and went sliding off down the winds. Once, he said, when they were sitting over on the bench against the wall, Stanley Albert flat on it with his head on her lap, when the whisky made the man in him come up sudden, so he couldn't wait, they went straight out the window, up the air, like a whistle sound. Willie had the broken glass to show the next morning, if you wanted to believe him.

Willie hated them, the two of them, maybe because they broke his glass, maybe because they made him stay up late every single night of the week, so that he had to hold his eyes open with his fingers, and watch them pour lightning into his very best whisky, maybe because he had

wanted Alberta mighty bad himself. He'd been giving
her presents—bottles of his best stuff—but he just couldn't
match Stanley Albert. Those are three reasons; maybe he
had others. And Maggie Mary hated them; and she had
only one reason.

Once Pete Stokes shot at Stanley Albert Thompson. He
hadn't wanted to: he was scared like everybody else. But
Maggie Mary Evans talked him into it. She was a fine-look-
ing girl: she could do things like that. He hid behind the
privy and got a perfect bead on Stanley Albert as he came
out the door. The bullet just knocked off a piece of Willie's
doorframe. When Pete saw what happened he dropped
the gun and began to run, jumping the rail fence and
crashing face-first through the thick heavy berry bushes.
Stanley Albert pursed his lips together and rubbed his
hands on his chin, slow, like he was deciding what to do.
Then he jumped down from the porch and went after
Pete. He ran through the hackberries too; only with him
it did not seem difficult: none of the crackling and crashing and waving arms. Stanley Albert just put his head
down and moved his legs, and the sprays of the bushes,
some of them thick as a rooster's spur, seemed to pull back
and make way. Nobody saw the fight: the brave ones were
too drunk to travel fast; and the sober ones didn't want to
mix with a man like Stanley Albert, drunk and mad. Alberta, she just ran her hand across her mouth and then
wiped it along the side of her green satin dress, yawning
like she was tired. She stood listening for a while, her
head cocked a little, though there wasn't anything to hear,
then walked off, pulling down the dress across her hips.

And the next night she and Stanley Albert were back at Willie's, and Pete never did turn up again. Willie used to swear that he ended up in the Scanos River and that if the water wasn't so yellow muddy, that if you could see to the bottom, you would see Pete lying there, along with all the others Stanley Albert had killed.

At the last it was Willie who got the idea. For a week, carefully, he put aside the coins Stanley Albert gave him. There were a lot of them, all new silver, because Stanley Albert always paid in silver. Then one morning very early, just after Stanley Albert and Alberta left, Willie melted the coins down, and using the molds he kept for his old outsized pistol, he cast four bullets.

He made a special little shelf for the pistol under the counter so that it would be near at hand. And he waited all evening, sometimes touching the heavy black handle with the tips of his fingers; and he waited, hoping that Stanley Albert would drink enough to pass out. But of course nothing like that happened. So Willie poured himself three or four fingers of his best stuff and swallowed it fast as his throat would stand, then he blinked his little eyes fast for a second or so to clear his vision, and he reached for the gun. He got two shots over the bar, two good ones: the whole front of Stanley Albert's plaid shirt folded together and sank in, after the silver bullets went through. He got up, holding the table edge, unsteady, bending over, looking much smaller, his black skin gray-filmed and dull. His eyes were larger: they reached almost across his face—and they weren't dark any more; they were silver, two polished pieces of silver. Willie was afraid to fire again; the pistol shook where he held it in his two hands.

Then Stanley Albert walked out, not unsteady any more, but bent over the hole in his chest, walked out slowly with his eyes shining like flat metal, Alberta a few steps behind. They passed right in front of Willie, who still hadn't moved; his face was stiff with fear. Quietly, smoothly, in a single motion, almost without interrupting her step, Alberta picked up a bottle (the same one from which he had poured his drink moments before) and swung it against Willie's head. He slipped down in a quiet little heap, his legs folded under him, his black kinky head on top. But his idea had worked: over by Stanley Albert's chair there was a black pool of blood.

All that was maybe eight or ten years ago. People don't see them any more—Stanley and Alberta. They don't think much about them, except when something goes wrong— like weevils getting in the cotton, or Willie's burning down and Willie inside it—then they begin to think that those two had a hand in it. Brad Tedrow swore that he had seen Stanley Albert that night, just for a second, standing on the edge of the circle of light, with a burning faggot in his hand. And the next morning Brad went back to look, knowing that your eyes play tricks at night in firelight; he went back to look for footprints or some sign. All he found was a burnt-out stick of pine wood that anybody could have dropped.

And kids sometimes think they hear the jingle of silver in Stanley Albert's pocket, or the sound of his watch. And when women talk—when there's been a miscarriage or a stillbirth—they remember and whisper together.

And they all wonder if that's not the sort of work they do, the two of them. Maybe so; maybe not. The people themselves are not too sure. They don't see them around any more.

Miss Yellow Eyes

PETE brought Chris home one evening after supper. I remember it was early spring, because the Talisman rosebush by the kitchen steps had begun to blossom out. For that time of year it was cool: there was a good stiff wind off the river that shook the old bush and creaked it, knocked the biggest flowers to bits, and blew their petals into a little heap against the side of the wood steps. The Johnsons, who lived in the house next door, had put their bedspread out to air and forgot to take it in. So it was hanging out there on the porch railing, a pink spread with a fan-tailed yellow peacock in the middle. I could hear it flapping—loud when the wind was up, and very soft when it fell. And from out on the river there were the soft low tones of the ships' whistles. And I could hear a mockingbird too, perched up on top the house, singing away, forgetting that it was nighttime. And in all this, Pete's steps in the side alley, coming to the kitchen door.

"Hi, kid!" Pete held open the door with one arm stretched behind him. Chris came in.

I thought at first: that's a white man. And I wondered

72

what a white man would do coming here. I got a second look and saw the difference, saw I'd made a mistake. His skin wasn't dark at all, but only sun-tanned. (Lots of white men were darker.) His eyes were a pale blue, the color of the china Ma got with the Octagon soap coupons. He had brown hair—no, it was closer to red, and only slightly wavy. He looked like a white man, almost. But I saw the difference. Maybe it was just his way of carrying himself —that was like a Negro.

But he was the handsomest man I'd ever seen, excepting none. I could feel the bottom of my stomach roll up into a hard ball.

"This here's Celia," Pete said.

Chris grinned and his blue eyes crinkled up into almost closed slits. He sat down at the table opposite me, flipping shut the book I'd been reading. "Evening's no time to be busy, kid."

Pete picked up the coffeepot from where it always stood on the back of the stove and shook it gently. "There's some here all right," he said to Chris as he reached up to the shelf for a couple of cups. "You want anything in yours? I reckon there'd be a can of milk in the icebox."

"No," Chris said. "I like it black."

Pete lit the fire under the speckled enamel coffeepot. "Where's Ma?"

"They having a dinner tonight . . . she said she'll be real late." Ma worked as a cook in one of the big houses on St. Charles Avenue. When there was a dinner, it meant she'd have to stay around and clean up afterwards and wouldn't get home till eleven or twelve maybe.

73

"She'll get tomorrow off, though," I told Chris.

"Good enough." He grinned and his teeth were very square and bright.

They sat down at the table with me and stretched out their legs. Holding the coffee cup to his mouth, Chris reached out one finger and rubbed the petals of the big yellow rose in the drinking glass in the center of the table. "That's real pretty."

"Lena's been putting them there," Pete said.

"That's sure the one I want to meet," Chris said, and grinned over at Pete, and I knew that he'd been talking about Lena.

She was the sort of girl you talk about, she was that beautiful—with light-brown hair that was shoulder-length and perfectly straight and ivory skin and eyes that were light brown with flecks of yellow in them. She was all gold-colored. Sometimes when she stood in the sun you could almost think the light was shining right through her.

She was near seventeen then, three years older than I was. The boys in high school all followed her around until the other girls hated her. Every chance they got they would play some mean trick on her, kicking dust in her lunch, or roughing her up playing basketball, or tearing pages out of her books. Lena hardly ever lost her temper; she didn't really seem to care. "I reckon I know who the boys are looking at," she told me. She was right. There was always a bunch of them trying to sit next to her in class or walk next to her down the hall. And when school was

74

through, there was always a bunch of them waiting around the door, wanting to take her home, or for rides if they had cars. And when she finally came sauntering out, with her books tucked up under one arm, she wouldn't pay them much attention; she'd just give them a kind of little smile (to keep them from going to the other girls) and walk home by herself, with maybe a few of them trailing along behind. I used to wait and watch her leave and then I'd go home a different way. I didn't want to interfere.

But, for all that, she didn't go out very much. And never with the same boy for very long. Once Hoyt Carmichael came around and stood in the kitchen door, asking for her, just begging to see her. She wouldn't even come out to talk to him. Ma asked her later if there was something wrong and Lena just nodded and shrugged her shoulders all at once. Ma hugged her then and you could see the relief in her face; she worried so about Lena, about her being so very pretty.

Pete said: "You sure got to meet her, Chris, man."

And I said to Chris: "She's over by the Johnsons'." I got up and opened the door and yelled out into the alley: "Lena!"

She came in a few minutes. We could hear her steps on the alley bricks, slow. She never did hurry. Finally she opened the screen and stood there, looking from one to the other.

I said: "This is my sister, Magdalena."

"And this here is Chris Watkin," Pete said.

Chris had got up and bowed real solemnly. "I'm pleased to meet you."

Lena brushed the hair back from her forehead. She had long fingers, and hands so thin that the veins stood out blue on the backs. "Nobody calls me Magdalena," she said, "except Celia, now and then. Just Lena."

Chris's eyes crinkled up out of sight the way they had before. "I might could just call you Miss Yellow Eyes. Old Miss Yellow Eyes."

Lena just wrinkled her nose at him. In that light her eyes did look yellow, but usually if a man said something like that she'd walk out. Not this time. She just poured herself a cup of coffee, and when Chris pulled out a chair for her, she sat down, next to him.

I looked at them and I thought: they look like a white couple. And they did. Unless you had sharp trained eyes, like the people down here do, you would have thought they were white and you would have thought they made a handsome couple.

Chris looked over at me and lifted an eyebrow. Just one, the left one; it reached up high and arched in his forehead. "What you looking so solemn for, Celia?"

"Nothing."

And Lena asked: "You work with Pete at the railroad?"

"Sure," he said, and smiled at her. Only, more than his mouth was smiling. "We go swinging on and off those old tenders like hell afire. Jumping on and off those cars."

"I reckon that's hard work."

He laughed this time out loud. "I ain't exactly little." He bent forward and hunched his shoulders up a little so she could see the way the muscles swelled against the cloth of his shirt.

"You got fine shoulders, Mr. Watkin," she said. "I reckon they're even better than Pete there."

Pete grunted and finished his coffee. But she was right. Pete's shoulders were almost square out from his neck. Chris's weren't. They looked almost sloped and hunched the way flat bands of muscles reached up into his neck.

Chris shrugged and stood up. "Do you reckon you would like to walk around the corner for a couple of beers?"

"Okay," Pete said.

Lena lifted one eyebrow, just the way he had done. "Mr. Watkin, you do look like you celebrating something."

"I sure am," he said.

"What?" I asked.

"I plain tell you later, kid."

They must have been gone near two hours because Ma came home before they did. I'd fallen asleep. I'd just bent my head over for a minute to rest my eyes, and my fore-head touched the soft pages of the book—*Treasure Island*. I'd got it from the library at school; it was dog-eared and smelled faintly of peanuts.

Ma was saying: "Lord, honey, why ain't you gone to bed?"

I lifted my head and rubbed my face until I could see Ma's figure in the doorway. "I'm waiting for them," I said.

Ma took off her coat and hung it up on the hook be-hind the door. "Who them?"

"Lena," I said, "and Pete. And Chris." I knew what she was going to say, so I answered first. "He's a friend of Pete, and Lena likes him."

Ma was frowning very slightly. "I plain wonder iffen he belong to that club."

"I don't know."

It was called the Better Days Club and the clubroom was the second floor of a little restaurant on Tulane Avenue. I'd never gone inside, though I had passed the place: a small wood building that had once been a house but now had a sign saying LEFTY'S RESTAURANT AND CAFÉ in green letters on a square piece of board that hung out over the sidewalk and creaked in the wind. And I'd seen something else too when I passed: another sign, a small one tucked into the right center corner of the screen door, a sign that said "*White* Entrance to *Rear*." If the police ever saw that they'd have found an excuse to raid the place and break up everything in it.

Ma kept asking Pete what they did there. Most time he didn't bother to answer. Once when she'd just insisted, he'd said, "We're fixing to have better times come." And sometimes he'd bring home little papers, not much more than book-size, with names like *New Day* and *Daily Sentinel* and *Watcher*.

Ma would burn the papers if she got hold of them. But she couldn't really stop Pete from going to the meetings. She didn't try too hard because he was so good to her and gave her part of his pay check every week. With that money and what she made we always had enough. We

78

didn't have to worry about eating, way some of our neighbors did.

Pete was a strange fellow—moody and restless and not happy. Sometimes—when he was sitting quiet, thinking or resting—there'd be a funny sort of look on his face (he was the darkest of us all): not hurt, not fear, not determination, but a mixture of all three.

Ma was still standing looking at me with a kind of puzzled expression on her face when we heard them, the three of them, coming home. They'd had a few beers and, what with the cold air outside, they all felt fine. They were singing too; I recognized the tune; it was the one from the jukebox around the corner in that bar.

Ma said: "They got no cause to be making a racket like that. Somebody might could call the police." Ma was terribly afraid of the police. She'd never had anything to do with them, but she was still afraid. Every time a police car passed in the street outside, she'd duck behind the curtain and peep out. And she'd walk clear around a block so she wouldn't come near one of the blue uniforms.

The three came in the kitchen door, Pete first and then Lena and Chris.

Pete had his arms full of beer cans; he let them all fall out on the table. "Man, I like to drop them sure."

"We brought some for you, Ma," Lena said.

"And Celia too," Chris added.

"It's plenty late," Ma said, looking hard at Chris.

"You don't have to work tomorrow," I said.

So we stayed up late. I don't know how late. Because

the beer made me feel fine and sick all at once. First everything was swinging around inside my head and then the room too. Finally I figured how to handle it. I caught hold and let myself ride around on the big whooshing circles. There were times when I'd forget there was anybody else in the room, I'd swing so far away.

"Why, just you look at Celia there," Ma said, and everybody turned and watched me.

"You sure high, kid," Chris said.

"No, I'm not." I was careful to space the words, because I could tell by the way Ma had run hers together that she was feeling the beer too.

Pete had his guitar in his lap, flicking his fingers across the strings. "You an easy drunk." He was smiling, the way he seldom did. "Leastways you ain't gonna cost some man a lotta money getting you high."

"That absolutely and completely right." Ma bent forward, with her hands one on each knee, and the elbows sticking out, like a skinny football-player. "You plain got to watch that when boys come to take you out."

"They ain't gonna want to take me out."

"Why not, kid?" Chris had folded his arms on the table-top and was leaning his chin on them. His face was flushed so that his eyes only looked bluer.

"Not after they see Lena." I lifted my eyes up from his and let them drop over where I knew Lena was sitting. I just had time to notice the way the electric light made her skin gold and her eyes gold and her hair too, so that she seemed all one blurry color. And then the whole world tipped over and I went skidding off—but feeling extra fine

80

because Chris was sitting just a little bit away next to Lena and she was looking at him like she'd never looked at anybody else before.

Next thing I knew, somebody was saying: "Celia, look." There was a photograph in front of me. A photograph of a young man, in a suit and tie, leaning back against a post, with his legs crossed, grinning at the camera.

I looked up. Ma was holding the photograph in front of me. It was in a wide silver-colored frame, with openwork, roses or flowers of some sort.

Pete began laughing. "Just you look at her," he said; "she don't even know her own daddy."

"I never seen that picture before," I said, loud as I could.

I'd never seen my daddy either. He was a steward on a United Fruit Lines ship, a real handsome man. He'd gone ashore at Antigua one day and forgot to come back.

"He looks mighty much like Chris," Ma said as she cleared a space on the shelf over between the windows. She put the picture there. And I knew then that she'd got it out from the bottom of a drawer somewhere, because this was a special occasion for her too.

"Chris," I said, remembering, "you never did tell us what you celebrating."

He had twisted sideways in his chair and had his arms wrapped around the back. "I going in the army."

Out of the corner of my eye I saw Pete staring at him, his mouth twisting and his face darkening.

Ma clucked her tongue against her teeth. "That a shame."

81

Chris grinned, his head cocked aside a little. "I got to leave tomorrow."

Pete swung back and forth on the two legs of his tilted chair. "Ain't good enough for nothing around here, but we good enough to put in the army and send off."

"Man"—Chris winked at him—"there ain't nothing you can do. And I plain reckon you gonna go next."

"No." Pete spoke the word so that it was almost a whistle.

"I'm a man, me," Chris said. "Can't run out on what I got to do." He tipped his head back and whistled a snatch of a little tune.

"I wouldn't like to go in the army," Lena said.

Chris went on whistling. Now we could recognize the song:

> *Yellow, yellow, yellow, yellow, yellow gal,*
> *Yellow, yellow, yellow, yellow, yellow gal,*
> *She's pretty and fine*
> *Is the yellow gal. . . .*

Lena tossed her head. "I wouldn't like to none."

Chris stopped whistling and laughed. "You plain sound like Pete here."

Pete's face all crinkled up with anger. I thought: he looks more like a Negro when he loses his temper; it makes his skin darker somehow.

"Nothing to laugh about," he said; "can't do nothing around here without people yelling nigger at you."

"Don't stay around here, man. You plain crazy to stay around here." Chris tilted back his chair and stared at the ceiling. "You plain crazy to stay a nigger. I done told you that."

Pete scowled at him and didn't answer.

Lena asked quickly: "Where you got to go?"

"Oregon." Chris was still staring at the ceiling and still smiling. "That where you cross over."

"You sure?"

Chris looked at her and smiled confidently. "Sure I'm sure."

Pete mumbled something under his breath that we didn't hear.

"I got a friend done it," Chris said. "Two years ago. He working out of Portland there, for the railroad. And he turn white."

Lena was resting her chin on her folded hands. "They don't look at you so close. Or anything?"

"No," Chris said. "I heard all about it. You can cross over if you want to."

"You going?" I asked.

"When I get done with the stretch in the army." He lowered his chair back to its four legs and stared out the little window, still smiling. "There's lots of jobs there for a railroad man."

Pete slammed the flat of his hand down against the table. Ma's eyes flew open like a door that's been kicked wide back. "I don't want to pretend I'm white," he said. "I ain't and I don't want to be. I reckon I want to be same as white and stay right here."

Ma murmured something under her breath and we all turned to look at her. Her eyes had dropped half-closed again and she had her hands folded across her stomach. Her mouth opened very slowly and this time she spoke loud enough for us all to hear. "Talking like that—you gonna do nothing but break you neck that way."

I got so sleepy then and so tired, all of a sudden, that I slipped sideways out of my chair. It was funny. I didn't notice I was slipping or moving until I was on the floor. Ma got hold of my arm and took me off to bed with her. And I didn't think to object. The last thing I saw was Lena staring at Chris with her long light-colored eyes. Chris with his handsome face and his reddish hair and his movements so quick they almost seemed jerky.

I thought it would be all right with them.

I was sick the whole next day from the beer; so sick I couldn't go to school. Ma shook her head and Pete laughed and Lena just smiled a little.

And Chris went off to the army, all right. It wasn't long before Lena had a picture from him. He'd written across the back: "Here I am a soldier." She stuck the picture in the frame of the mirror over her dresser.

That was the week Lena quit school. She came looking for me during lunch time. "I'm going home," she said.

"You can't do that."

She shook her head. "I had enough."

So she walked out of school and didn't ever go back. (She was old enough to do that.) She bought a paper on her way home and sat down and went through the classi-fied ads very carefully, looking for a job. It was three days before she found one she wanted: with some people who

84

were going across the lake to Covington for the summer. Their regular city maid wouldn't go.

They took her on right away because they wanted to leave. She came back with a ten-dollar bill in her purse. "We got to leave in the morning," she said.

Ma didn't like it, her quitting school and leaving home, but she couldn't really stop her.

And Lena did want to go. She was practically jumping with excitement after she came back from the interview. "They got the most beautiful house," she said to Ma. "A lot prettier than where you work." And she told me: "They say the place over the lake is even prettier—even prettier."

I knew what she meant. I sometimes went to meet Ma at the house where she worked. I liked to. It was nice to be in the middle of fine things, even if they weren't yours.

"It'll be real nice working there," Lena said.

That next morning, when she had got her things together and closed the lid of the suitcase, she told me to go down to the grocery at the corner, where there was a phone, and call a taxi. They were going to pay for it, she said.

I reckon I was excited; so excited that I called the wrong cab. I just looked at the back cover of the phone book where there was a picture of a long orange-color cab and a number in big orange letters. I gave them the address, then went back to the house and sat down on the porch with Lena.

The orange cab turned at the corner and came down our street. The driver was hanging out the window looking for house numbers; there weren't any except for the

Stevenses' across the way. Bill Stevens had painted his
number with big whitewash letters on his front door. The
cab hit a rut in the street and the driver's head smacked
the window edge. He jerked his head back inside and
jammed the gears into second. Then he saw us: Lena and
me and the suitcase on the edge of the porch.

He let the car move along slow in second with that
heavy pulling sound and he watched us. As he got closer
you could see that he was chewing on the corner of his
lip. Still watching us, he went on slowly—right past the
house. He said something once, but we were too far away
to hear. Then he was down at the other corner, turning,
and gone.

Lena stood and looked at me. She had on her best dress:
a light-blue one with round pockets in front. Both her
hands were stuffed into the pockets. There was a handkerchief in the left one; you could see her fingers twisting it.

White cabs didn't pick up colored people: I knew that.
But I'd forgot and called the first number, a white number,
a wrong number. Lena didn't say anything, just kept looking at me, with her hand holding the handkerchief inside
her pocket. I turned and ran all the way down to the
corner and called the right number, and a colored cab that
was painted black with gold stripes across the hood came
and Lena was gone for the next four months, the four
months of the summer.

It could have been the same cab brought her back that
had come for her: black with gold stripes. She had on the
same dress too, the blue one with round pockets; the same

suitcase too, but this time in it was a letter of recommenda-
tion and a roll of bills she'd saved, all hidden in the fancy
organdy aprons they'd given her.

She said: "He wanted me to stay on through the winter,
but she got scared for their boy." And she held her chin
stiff and straight when she said that.

I understood why that woman wanted my sister Lena
out of the house. There wasn't any boy or man either that
wouldn't look at her twice. White or colored it didn't seem
to make a difference, they all looked at her in the same
way.

That was the only job Lena ever took. Because she
hadn't been home more than a few days when Chris came
back for her.

I remember how it was—early September and real
foggy. It would close down every evening around seven
and wouldn't lift until ten or ten thirty in the morning. All
night long you could hear the foghorns and the whistles
of the boats out on the river; and in the morning there'd be
even more confusion when everybody tried to rush away
from anchor. That Saturday morning Lena had taken a
walk up to the levee to watch. Pete was just getting up. I
could hear him in his room. Ma had left for work early.
And me, I was scrubbing out the kitchen, the way I did
every Saturday morning. That was when Chris came back.

He came around to the kitchen. I heard his steps in the
alley—quickly coming, almost running. He came bursting
in the door and almost slipped on the soapy floor. "Hi,
kid," he said, took off his cap, and rubbed his hand over
his reddish hair. "You working?"

"Looks like," I said.

He'd grown a mustache, a thin line. He stood for a moment chewing on his lip and the little hairs he had brushed so carefully into a line. Finally he said: "Where's everybody?"

"Lena went up on the levee to have a look at the river boats."

He grinned at me, flipped his cap back on, gave a kind of salute, and jumped down the two steps into the yard.

I sat back on my heels, picturing him and Lena in my mind and thinking what a fine couple they made. And the little picture of my father grinned down at me from the shelf by the window.

Pete called: "Seems like I heard Chris in there."

"He went off to look for Lena."

Pete came to the door; he was only half dressed and he was still holding up his pants with his one hand. He liked to sleep late Saturdays. "He might could have stayed to say hello."

"He wanted to see Lena, I reckon."

Pete grinned briefly and the grin faded into a yawn. "You ought to have let him look for her."

"Nuh-uh." I picked up the bar of soap and the scrubbing brush again. "I wanted them to get together, I reckon."

"Okay, kid," Pete said shortly, and turned back to his room. "You helped them out."

Chris and Lena came back after a while. They didn't say anything, but I noticed that Lena was kind of smiling like she was cuddling something to herself. And her eyes were so bright they looked light yellow, almost transparent.

Chris hung his army cap on the back of a chair and then sprawled down at the table. "You fixing to offer me anything to eat?"

"You can't be hungry this early in the morning," Lena said.

"Men are always hungry," I said. They both turned.

"You tell 'em, kid," Chris said. "You tell 'em for me."

"Let's us go to the beach," Lena said suddenly.

"Sure, honey," Chris said softly.

She wrinkled her nose at him and pretended she hadn't heard. "It's the last night before they close down everything for the winter."

"Okay—we gonna leave right now?"

"Crazy thing," Lena smiled. "Not in the morning. Let's us go right after supper."

"I got to stay here till then?"

"Not less you want to."

"Reckon I do," Chris said.

"You want to come, Celia?" Lena asked.

"Me?" I glanced over at Chris quickly. "Nuh-uh."

"Sure you do," Lena said. "You just come along."

And Chris lifted one eyebrow at me. "Come along," he said. "Iffen you don't mind going out with people old as me."

"Oh, no," I said. "Oh, no."

I never did figure out quite why Lena wanted me along that time. Maybe she didn't want to be alone with Chris because she didn't quite trust him yet. Or maybe she just wanted to be nice to me. I don't know. But I did go. I liked the beach. I liked to stare off across the lake and imagine I could see the shore on the other side, which of course I couldn't.

So I went with them, that evening after supper. It took us nearly an hour to get there—three changes of busses because it was exactly across town: the north end of the city. All the way, all along in the bus, Chris kept talking, telling stories.

"Man," he said, "that army sure is something—big—I never seen anything so big. Just in our little old camp there ain't a space of ground big enough to hold all the men, if they called them all out together. . . ."

We reached the end of one bus line. He put one hand on Lena's arm and the other on mine and helped us out the door. His hand was broad and hard on the palm and almost cool to the touch.

In the other bus we headed straight for the long seat across the back, so we could sit all three together. He sat in the middle and, leaning forward a little, rested both hands on his knees. Looking at him out the corner of my eye, I could see the flat broad strips of muscle in his neck, reaching up to under his chin. And once I caught Lena's eye, and I knew that on the other side she was watching too.

"All together like that," he said. "It gives you the funniest feeling—when you all marching together, so that you can't see away on either side, just men all together—it gives you a funny sort of feeling."

He turned to Lena and grinned; his bright square teeth flashed in the evening dusk. "I reckon you think that silly."

"No," she said quickly, and then corrected herself: "of course I never been in the army."

"Look there," I said. We were passing the white beach. Even as far away as the road where we were, we could smell the popcorn and the sweat and the faint salt tingle from the wind off the lake.

"It almost cool tonight," Lena said.

"You ain't gonna be cold?"

"You don't got to worry about me."

"I reckon I do," he said.

Lena shook her head, and her eyes had a soft holding look in them. And I wished I could take Chris aside and tell him that he'd said just the right thing.

Out on the concrete walks of the white beach, people were jammed so close that there was hardly any space between. You could hear all the voices and the talking, murmuring at this distance. Then we were past the beach (the driver was going fast, grumbling under his breath that he was behind schedule), and the Ferris wheel was the only thing you could see, a circle of lights like a big star behind us. And on each side, open ground, low weeds, and no trees.

"There it is," Chris said, and pointed up through the window. I turned and looked and, sure enough, there it was; he was right: the lights, smaller maybe and dimmer, of Lincoln Beach, the colored beach.

"Lord," Lena said, "I haven't been out here in I don't know when. It's been that long."

We got off the bus; he dropped my arm but kept hold of Lena's. "You got to make this one night last all winter."

She didn't answer.

We had a fine time. I forgot that I was just tagging along and enjoyed myself much as any.

When we passed over by the shooting gallery Chris winked at Lena and me. "Which one of them dolls do you want?"

Lena wrinkled her nose. "I reckon you plain better see about getting 'em first."

He just shrugged. "You think I can do it, Celia?"

"Sure," I said. "Sure, sure you can."

"That's the girl for you," the man behind the counter said. "Thinks you can do anything."

"That my girl there all right." Chris reached in his pocket to pay the man. I could feel my ears getting red.

He picked up the rifle and slowly knocked down the whole row of green and brown painted ducks. He kept right on until Lena and I each had a doll in a bright pink feather skirt and he had a purple wreath of flowers hung around his neck. By this time the man was scowling at him and a few people were standing around watching.

"That's enough, soldier," the man said. "This here is just for amateurs."

Chris shrugged. We all turned and walked away.

"You did that mighty well," Lena said, turning her baby doll around and around in her hands, staring at it.

"I see lots of fellows better."

"Where'd you learn to shoot like that?" I tugged on his sleeve.

"I didn't learn—"

"Fibber!" Lena tossed her head.

"You got to let me finish. Up in Calcasieu parish, my daddy, he put a shotgun in my hand and give me a pocket of shells. . . . I just keep shooting till I hit something or other."

It was hard to think of Chris having a father. "Where's he now?"

"My daddy? He been dead."

"You got a family?"

"No," Chris said. "Just me."

We walked out along the strip of sand, and the wind began pulling the feathers out of the dolls' skirts. I got out my handkerchief and tied it around my doll, but Lena just lifted hers up high in the air to see what the wind would do. Soon she just had a naked baby doll that was pink celluloid smeared with glue.

Lena and Chris found an old log and sat down. I went wading. I didn't want to go back to where they were, because I knew that Chris wanted Lena alone. So I kept walking up and down in the water that came just a little over my ankles.

It was almost too cold for swimmers. I saw just one, about thirty yards out, swimming up and down slowly. I couldn't really see him, just the regular white splashes from his arms. I looked out across the lake, the way I liked to do. It was all dark now; there was no telling where the lower part of the sky stopped and the water began. It was all the one color, all of it, out beyond the swimmer and the breakwater on the left where the waves hit a shallow spot and turned white and foamy. Except for that, it was all the same dark until you lifted your eyes high up in the sky and saw the stars.

I don't know how long I stood there, with my head bent back far as it would go, looking at the stars, trying to remember the names for them that I had learned in school: names like Bear and Archer. I couldn't tell which was which. All I could see were stars, bright like they always were at the end of the summer and close; and every now and then one of them would fall.

I stood watching them, feeling the water move gently around my legs and curling my toes in the soft lake sand that was rippled by the waves. And trying to think up ways to stay away from those two who were sitting back up the beach, on a piece of driftwood, talking together.

Once the wind shifted a little suddenly or Chris spoke too loud, because I heard one word: "Oregon."

All of a sudden I knew that Lena was going to marry him. Just for that she was going to marry him; because she wanted so much to be white.

And I wanted to tell Chris again, the way I had wanted to in the bus, that he'd said just the right thing.

After a while Lena stood up and called to me, saying it was late; so we went home. By the time we got there, Ma had come. On the table was a bag of food she had brought. And so we all sat around and ate the remains of the party: little cakes, thin and crispy and spicy and in fancy shapes; and little patties full of oysters that Ma ran in the oven to heat up; and little crackers spread with fishy-tasting stuff, like sugar grains only bigger, that Ma called caviar; and all sorts of little sandwiches.

It was one nice thing about the place Ma worked. They never did check the food. And it was fun for us, tasting the strange things.

All of a sudden Lena turned to me and said: "I reckon I want to see where Oregon is." She gave Chris a long look out of the corner of her eyes.

My mouth was full and for a moment I couldn't answer.

"You plain got to have a map in your schoolbooks."

I finally managed to swallow. "Sure I got one—if you want to see it."

I got my history book and unfolded the map of the whole country and put my finger down on the spot that said Oregon in pink letters. "There," I said; "that's Portland there."

Lena came and leaned over my shoulder; Pete didn't move; he sat with his chin in his hand and his elbows propped on the table.

"I want to stay here and be the same as white," he said, but we weren't listening to him.

Chris got out of the icebox the bottles of beer he had brought.

"Don't you want to see?" Lena asked him.

He grinned and took out his key chain, which had an opener on it, and began popping the caps off the bottles. "I looked at a map once. I know where it's at."

Ma was peering over my other shoulder. "It looks like it mighty far away."

"It ain't close," Chris said.

"You plain want to go there—" Ma was frowning at the map, straining to see without her glasses.

"Yes," Chris said, still popping the tops off bottles.

"And be white," Lena added very softly.

"Sure," Chris said. "No trouble at all to cross over."

"And you going there," Ma said again. She couldn't quite believe that anybody she was looking at right now could ever go that far away.

"Yea," Chris said, and put the last opened bottle with the others in a row on the table. "When I get out the army, we sure as hell going there."

"Who's we?" I asked.

"Lena and me."

Ma looked up at him so quickly that a hairpin tumbled out of her head and clicked down on the table.

"When we get married," he said.

Lena was looking at him, chewing her lower lip. "We going to do that?"

"Yea," he said. "Leastways if that what you want to do."

And Lena dropped her eyes down to the map again, though I'd swear this time she didn't know what she was seeing. Or maybe everywhere she'd look she was seeing Chris. Maybe that was it. She was smiling very slightly to herself, with just the corners of her lips, and they were trembling.

They got married that week in St. Michel's Church. It was in the morning—nine thirty, I remember—so the church was cold: biting empty cold. Even the two candles burning on the altar didn't look like they'd be warm.

Though it only took a couple of minutes, my teeth were chattering so that I could hardly talk. Ma cried and Pete scowled and grinned by turns and Lena and Chris didn't seem to notice anything much.

The cold and the damp had made a bright strip of flush across Lena's cheeks. Old Mrs. Roberts, who lived next door, bent forward—she was sitting in the pew behind us —and tapped Ma on the shoulder. "I never seen her look prettier."

Lena had bought herself a new suit, with the money she'd earned over the summer: a cream-colored suit, with small black braiding on the cuffs and collar. She'd got a hat too, of the same color velvet. Cream was a good color for her; it was lighter than her skin somehow, so that it made her face stand out.

("She ought to always have clothes like that," Mayme Roberts said later, back at our house. She was old Mrs. Roberts's daughter, and seven kids had broken her up so that she wasn't even jealous of pretty girls any more. "Maybe Chris'll make enough money to let her have pretty clothes like that.")

Lena and Chris went away because he had to get back to camp. And for the first time since I could remember, I had a room all to myself. So I made Lena's bed all nice and careful and put the fancy spread that Ma had crocheted on it—the one we hardly ever used. And put the little pink celluloid doll in the middle.

Sometime after the wedding, I don't remember exactly when, Pete had an accident. He'd been out on a long run, all the way up to Abiline. It was a long hard job and by the time he got back to town he was dead tired, and so he got a little careless. In the switch yards he got his hand caught in a loose coupling.

He was in the hospital for two weeks or so, in the colored surgical ward on the second floor of a huge cement building that said Charity Hospital in carved letters over the big front door. Ma went to see him on Tuesdays and Saturdays and I just went on Saturdays. Walking over from the bus, we'd pass Lefty's Restaurant and Café. Ma would turn her head away so that she wouldn't see it.

One time, the first Saturday I went with Ma, we brought Pete a letter, his induction notice. He read it and started laughing and crying all at once—until the ward nurse got worried and called an intern and together they gave him a shot. Right up till he passed out, he kept laughing.

And I began to wonder if it had been an accident. . . .

After two weeks he came home. We hadn't expected him; we hadn't thought he was well enough to leave. Late one afternoon we heard steps in the side alley; Ma looked at me, quick and funny, and rushed over to open the door: it was Pete. He had come home alone on the streetcar and walked the three blocks from the car stop. By the time he got to the house he was ready to pass out: he had to sit down and rest his head on the table right there in the kitchen. But he'd held his arm careful so that it didn't start to bleed again. He'd always been afraid of blood.

Accidents like that happened a lot on the road. Maybe that was why the pay was so good. The fellows who sat around the grocery all day or the bar all had pensions because they'd lost an arm or a hand or a leg. It happened a lot; we knew that, but it didn't seem to make any difference.

Ma cried very softly to herself when she saw him so dizzy and weak he couldn't stand up. And I went out in the back yard, where he couldn't see, and was sick to my stomach.

He stayed in the house until he got some strength back and then he was out all day long. He left every morning just like he was working and he came back for dinner at night. Ma asked him once where he went, but he wouldn't say; and there was never any trouble about it. A check came from the railroad every month, regular; and he still gave Ma part of it.

Pete talked about his accident, though. It was all he'd talk about. "I seen my hand," he'd tell anybody who'd listen. "After they got it free, with the blood running down it, I seen it. And it wasn't cut off. My fingers was moving. I seen 'em. Was no call for them to go cut the hand off. There wasn't any call for them to do that, not even with all it hurting." (And it had hurt so bad that he'd passed out. They'd told us he just tumbled down all of a sudden —so that the cinders along the tracks cut in his cheek.)

He'd say: "Iffen it wasn't a man my color they wouldn't done it. They wouldn't go cut off a white man's hand."

He'd say: "It was only just one finger that was caught, they didn't have cause to take off the whole hand."

And when I heard him I couldn't help wondering. Wondering if maybe Pete hadn't tried to get one finger caught. The army wouldn't take a man with one finger missing. But just one finger gone wouldn't hamper a man much. The way Pete was acting wasn't like a man that had an accident he wasn't expecting. But like a man who'd got double-crossed somehow.

And looking at Ma, I could see that she was thinking the same thing.

Lena came home after a couple of months—Chris had been sent overseas.

She used to spend most of her days lying on the bed in our room, reading a magazine maybe, or writing to Chris, or just staring at the ceiling. When the winter sun came in through the window and fell on her, her skin turned gold and burning.

Since she slept so much during the days, often in the night she'd wake up and be lonesome. Then she'd call me. "Celia," she'd call real soft so that the sound wouldn't carry through the paperboard walls. "Celia, you awake?" And I'd tell her yes and wake up quick as I could.

Then she'd snap on the little lamp that Chris had given her for a wedding present. And she'd climb out of bed, wrapping one of the blankets around her because it was cold. And she'd sit on the cane-bottomed old chair and rock it slowly back and forth while she told me just what it would be like when Chris came back for her.

Sometimes Pete would hear us talking and would call: "Shut up in there." And Lena would only toss her head and say that he was an old grouch and not to pay any attention to him.

Pete had been in a terrible temper for weeks, the cold made his arm hurt so. He scarcely spoke any more. And he didn't bother going out after supper; instead he stayed in his room, sitting in a chair with his feet propped up on the windowsill, looking out where there wasn't anything to see. Once I'd peeped in through the half-opened door. He was standing in the middle of the room, at the foot of the bed, and he was looking at his stub arm, which was still bright-red-colored. His lips were drawn back tight against his teeth, and his eyes were almost closed, they were so squinted.

Things went on this way right through the first part of the winter. Chris was in Japan. He sent Lena a silk kimono —green, with a red dragon embroidered across the back. He didn't write much, and then it was just a line saying that he was fine. Along toward the middle of January, I think it was, one of the letters mentioned fighting. It wasn't so bad, he said; and it wasn't noisy at all. That's what he noticed most, it seemed: the quietness. From the other letters we could tell that he was at the front all the rest of the winter.

It was March by this time. And in New Orleans March is just rain, icy splashing rain. One afternoon I ran the dozen or so blocks home from school and all I wanted to do was sit down by the stove. I found Ma and Pete in the kitchen. Ma was standing by the table, looking down at the two yellow pieces of paper like she expected them to move.

The telegram was in the middle of the table—the folded

101

paper and the folded yellow envelope. There wasn't anything else, not even the big salt-shaker which usually stood there.

Ma said: "Chris got himself hurt."

Pete was sitting across the room with his chair propped against the wall, tilting himself back and forth. "Ain't good enough for nothing around here," he said, and rubbed his stump arm with his good hand. "Ain't good enough for white people, but sure good enough to get killed."

"He ain't killed," Lena said from the next room. The walls were so thin she could hear every word. "He ain't got killed."

"Sure, Lena, honey," Ma said, and her voice was soft and comforting. "He going to be all right, him. Sure."

"Quit that," Ma told Pete in a fierce whisper. "You just quit that." She glanced over her shoulder toward Lena's room. "She got enough trouble without that you add to it."

Pete glared but didn't answer.

"You want me to get you something, Lena?" I started into our room. But her voice stopped me.

"No call for you to come in," she said.

Maybe she was crying, I don't know. Her voice didn't sound like it. Maybe she was though, crying for Chris. Nobody saw her.

Chris didn't send word to us. It was almost like he forgot. There was one letter from a friend of his in Japan, saying that he had seen him in a hospital there and that the nurses were a swell set of people and so were the doctors.

Lena left the letter open on the table for us all to see.

That night she picked it up and put it in the drawer of her dresser with the yellow paper of the telegram.

And there wasn't anything else to do but wait.

No, there were two things, two things that Lena could do. The day after the telegram came, she asked me to come with her.

"Where?"

"St. Michel's." She was drying the dishes, putting them away in the cupboard, so I couldn't see her face, but I could tell from her voice how important this was.

"Sure," I said. "Sure, I'll come. Right away."

St. Michel's was a small church. I'd counted the pews once: there were just exactly twenty; and the side aisles were so narrow two people could hardly pass. The confessional was a single little recess on the right side in the back, behind the baptismal font. There was a light burning —Father Graziano would be back there.

"You wait for me," Lena said. And I sat down in the last pew while she walked over toward the light. I kept my head turned so that she wouldn't think I was watching her as she went up to the confessional and knocked very softly on the wood frame. Father Graziano stuck his gray old head out between the dark curtains. I didn't have to listen; I knew what Lena was asking him. She was asking him to pray for Chris. It only took her a minute; then she walked quickly up to the front, by the altar rail. I could hear her heels against the bare boards, each one a little explosion. There were three or four candles burning already. She lit another one—I saw the circle of light get bigger as she put hers on the black iron rack.

103

"Let's go," she said; "let's go."

Father Graziano had come out of the confessional and was standing watching us. He was a small man, but heavy, with a big square head and a thick neck. He must have been a powerful man when he was young. Chris had a neck like that, muscled like that.

For a minute I thought he was going to come over and talk to us. He took one step, then stopped and rubbed his hand through his curly gray hair.

Lena didn't say anything until we reached the corner where we turned to go home. Without thinking, I turned.

"Not that way." She caught hold of my arm. "This way here." She went in the opposite direction.

I walked along with her, trying to see her face. But it was too dark and she had pulled the scarf high over her head.

"We got to go to Maam's," she said and her voice was muffled in the collar of her coat.

"To what?" not believing I'd heard her right.

"To Maam's."

Maam was a grisgris woman, so old nobody could remember when she'd been young or middle-aged even. Old as the river and wrinkled like it too, when the wind blows across.

She had a house on the *batture*, behind a clump of old thick hackberries. There was the story I'd heard: she had wanted a new house after a high water on the river had carried her old one away. (All this was fifty years ago, maybe.) So she'd walked down the levee to the nearest house, which was nearly a mile away: people didn't want to live close to her. She'd stood outside, looking out at the river and calling out: "I want a house. A fine new house. A nice new house. For me." She didn't say anything else, just turned and walked away. But the people inside had heard her and spread the word. Before they even began to fix the damage the flood had done to their own houses, the men worked on her house. In less than a week it was finished. They picked up their tools and left, and the next day they sent a kid down to spy and, sure enough, there was smoke coming out of the chimney. Maam had moved in: she must have been watching from somewhere close. Nobody knew where she had spent the week that she didn't have a house. And everybody was really too scared to find out.

She was still living in that house. It was built on good big solid pilings so that flood waters didn't touch it. I'd seen it once; Pete had taken me up on the levee there and pointed it out: a two-room house that the air and the river damp had turned black, on top a flat tin roof that shone in the sun. At the beginning of the dirt path that led down to the house I saw a little pile of food people had left for her: some white pieces of slab bacon, some tin cans. Pete wouldn't let me get close. "No sense fooling with things you don't understand," he said.

Maam didn't leave her house often. But when she did, when she came walking down the streets or along the levee, people got out of her way. Either they slipped down into the *batture* bushes and waited until she passed by on the top of the levee, or, in town, they got off the banquette and into the street when she came by—an old woman with

105

black skin that was nearly gray and eyes hidden in the folds of wrinkles, an old woman wearing a black dress, and a red shawl over her head and shoulders, a bright red shawl with silver and black signs sewed onto it. And always she'd be staring at the girls; what she liked best was to be able to touch them, on the arm or the hand, or catch hold of a little piece of their clothes. That didn't happen often, everybody was so careful of her.

And still Lena had said: "We going to Maam's."

"Lord," I said, "why?"

"For Chris."

There wasn't anything I could answer to that.

It was still early, seven thirty or eight, but nights don't seem to have time. The moon wasn't up yet; the sky was clear, with hard flecks of stars. Out on the river one ship was moving out—slipping between the riding lights of the other anchored ships that were waiting their turn at the docks below the point. You could hear the steady sound of the engines.

On top the levee the river wind was strong and cold and heavy-wet. I shivered even with a coat and scarf. There was a heavy frost like mold on the riverside slant of the levee. I stopped and pulled a clover and touched it to my lips and felt the sting of ice.

There was a light in Maam's house. We saw that as we came down the narrow little path through the hackberry bushes, the way that Pete wouldn't let me go when I was little. She must have heard us coming—walking is noisy on a quiet night—because without our knocking Maam opened the door.

I never did see her face. She had the red scarf tied high

around her head so that it stuck out far on the sides. She mightn't have had a face, for all I could tell. The house was warm, very warm; I could feel the heat rush out all around her. She was wearing a black dress without sleeves, of some light material with a sheen like satin. She had tied a green cord tight around her middle. Under it her stomach stuck out like a pregnant woman's.

"I came to fetch something," Lena said. Her voice was tight and hard.

Inside the house a round spot was shining on the far wall. I stared at it hard: a tray, a round tin tray, nailed to the wall. I couldn't see more than that because there wasn't much light; just a single kerosene lamp standing in the middle of the room, on the floor. Being low like that, it made the shadows go upward on the walls so that even familiar things looked strange.

"I came to fetch something," Lena said. "For somebody that's sick."

Maam didn't move.

"To make him well," Lena added.

Maam turned around, made a circle back through her cabin, ending up behind her half-open door, where we couldn't see. I suppose we could have stepped inside and watched her—but we didn't. And in a couple of seconds she was back at the doorway. She was holding both arms straight down against her sides, the hands clenched. And she kept looking from Lena to me and back again.

Lena took her left hand out of her coat pocket and I could see that she was holding a bill and a couple of coins. She moved them slowly back and forth; Maam's eyes followed but she did not move.

"You got to give it to me," Lena said. Her voice was high-pitched and rasping. I hadn't known it could be as rough as that.

Maam held out her hand: a thin black arm, all the muscles and tendons showing along the bone. She held out her arm, palm down, fist clenched. Then slowly, so that the old muscles under the thin skin moved in twisting lines, she turned the arm and opened the fingers. And in the palm there was a small bundle of cloth, white cloth. As we stared at it the three edges of the cloth, which had been pressed down in her hand popped up slowly until they stuck straight up.

Lena reached out her right hand and took the three pointed edges of the cloth while her other hand dropped the money in its place. I could see how careful she was being not to touch the old woman.

Then we turned and almost ran back up the path to the top of the levee. I turned once near the top and looked back. Maam was still standing in the door, in her thin black sleeveless dress. She seemed to be singing something; I couldn't make out the words, just the sound. As she stood there, the lamplight all yellow behind her, I could feel her eyes reach out after us.

Lena had done all she could. She'd gone to the church and she'd prayed and lit a candle and asked the priest for special prayers. And she'd gone to the voodoo woman. She'd done all she could. Now there wasn't anything to do but wait.

You could see how hard waiting was for her. Her face

was always thin, a little long, with fine features. And now you could almost see the strain lines run down her cheeks. The skin under her eyes turned blue; she wasn't sleeping. I knew that. She always lay very quiet in her bed, never tossing or turning. And that was just how I knew she was awake. Nobody lies stiff and still like that if they're really asleep; and their breathing isn't so shallow and quick.

I'd lie awake and listen to her pretending that she was asleep. And I'd want to get up and go over there and comfort her somehow. Only, some people you can't comfort. You can only go along with their pretending and pretend yourself.

That's what I did. I made out I didn't notice anything. Not the circles under her eyes; not the way she had of blinking rapidly (her eyes were so dry they burned); not the little zigzag vein that stood out blue on her left forehead.

One night we had left the shade up. There was a full moon, so bright that I woke up. Lena was really asleep then. I looked over at her: the light hadn't reached more than the side of her bed; it only reached her hand that was dangling over the edge of the bed, the fingers limp and curled a little. A hand so thin that the moonlight was like an X-ray, showing the bones.

And I wanted to cry for her if she couldn't cry for herself. But I only got up and pulled down the shade, and made the room all dark so I couldn't see any more.

Chris died. The word came one Thursday late afternoon. Ma was out sweeping off the front steps and she took the telegram from the boy and brought it to Lena. Her hand was trembling when she held it out. Lena's thin hand didn't move even a little bit.

Lena opened the envelope with her fingernail, read it, cleared the kitchen table, and put it out there. (We didn't need to read it.)

She didn't make a sound. She didn't even catch her breath. Her face didn't change, her thin, tired face, with the deep circles under the eyes and the strain lines down the cheeks. Only there was a little pulse began to beat in the vein on her forehead—and her eyes changed, the light eyes with flecks of gold in them. They turned one color: dark, dull brown.

She put the telegram in the middle of the table. Her fingers let loose of it very slowly. Their tips brushed back and forth on the edges of the paper a couple of times before she dropped her arm to her side and very slowly turned and walked into the bedroom, her heels sounding on the floor, slow and steady. The bed creaked as she sat down on it.

Ma had been backing away from the telegram, the corner of her mouth twitching. She bumped into a chair and she looked down—surprised at its being there, even. Then, like a wall that's all of a sudden collapsing, she sat down and bent her head in her lap. She began to cry, not making a sound, her shoulders moving up and down.

Pete was balancing himself on his heels, teetering back and forth, grinning at the telegram like it was a person. I never saw his face look like that before; I was almost afraid of him. And he was Pete, my brother.

He reached down and flicked the paper edge with his fingers. "Good enough to die," he said. "We good enough to die."

There was a prickling all over me, even in my hair. I reckon I was shivering.

I tried to think of Chris dead. Chris shot. Chris in the hospital. Lying on a bed, and dead. Not moving. Chris, who was always moving. Chris, who was so handsome.

I stood and looked at the yellow telegram and tried to think what it would be like. Now, for Chris. I thought of things I had seen dead: dogs and mice and cats. They were born dead, or they died because they were old. Or they died because they were killed. I had seen them with their heads pulled aside and their insides spilled out red on the ground. It wouldn't be so different for a man.

But Chris . . .

"Even if you black," Pete was saying, "you good enough to get sent off to die."

And Ma said: "You shut you mouth!" She'd lifted her head up from her lap, and the creases on her cheeks were quivering and her brown eyes stared—cotton eyes, the kids used to call them.

"You shut you mouth!" Ma shouted. She'd never talked that way before. Not to Pete. Her voice was hoarser even, because she had been crying without tears.

And Pete yelled right back, the way he'd never done before: "Sweet Jesus, I ain't gonna shut up for nobody when I'm talking the truth."

I made a wide circle around him and went in the bedroom. Lena was sitting there, on the bed, with the pillows

111

propped behind her. Her face was quiet and dull. There wasn't anything moving on it, not a line. There was no way of telling if she even heard the voices over in the kitchen.

I stood at the foot of the bed and put both hands on the cold iron railing. "Lena," I said, "you all right?"

She heard me. She shifted her eyes slowly over to me until they were looking directly at me. But she didn't answer. Her eyes, brown now and dark, stared straight into mine without shifting or moving or blinking or lightening. I stepped aside. The eyes didn't move with me. They stayed where they were, caught up in the air.

From the kitchen I could hear Pete and Ma shouting back and forth at each other until Ma finally gave way in deep dry sobbings that slowed and finally stopped. For a second or so everything was perfectly still. Then Ma said what had been in the back of our minds for months, only I didn't ever expect to hear her say it, not to her only boy.

"You no son of mine." She paused for a minute and I could hear the deep catching breath she took. "You no man even." Her voice was level and steady. Only, after every couple of words she'd have to stop for breath. "You a coward. A god-damn coward. And you made youself a cripple for all you life."

All of a sudden Pete began to laugh—high and thin and ragged. "Maybe—maybe. But me, I'm breathing. And he ain't. . . . Chris was fine and he ain't breathing."

Lena didn't give any sign that she'd heard. I went around to the side of the bed and took her hand: it was cold and heavy.

Pete was giggling; you could hardly understand what he was saying. "He want to cross over, him."

Ma wasn't interrupting him now. He went right ahead, choking on the words. "Chris boy, you fine and you brave and you ain't run out on what you got to do. And you ain't breathing neither. But you a man. . . ."

Lena's hand moved ever so slightly.

"Lena," I said, "you all right?"

"Chris boy . . . you want to cross over . . . and you sure enough cross over . . . why, man, you sure cross over . . . but good, you cross over."

"Lena," I said, "don't you pay any mind to him. He's sort of crazy."

In the kitchen Pete was saying: "Chris, you a man, sure . . . sure . . . you sure cross over . . . but ain't you gonna come back for Lena? Ain't you coming back to get her?"

I looked down and saw that my hand was shaking. My whole body was. It had started at my legs and come upward. I couldn't see clearly either. Edges of things blurred together. Only one thing I saw clear: Chris lying still and dead.

"It didn't get you nowhere, Chris boy," Pete was giggling. "Being white and fine, where it got you? Where it got you? Dead and rotten."

And Lena said: "Stop him, Chris."

She said: "Stop him, Chris, please."

I heard her voice, soft and low and pleading, the way she wouldn't speak to anyone else, but only her husband.

Chris, dead on the other side of the world, covered with ground.

Pete was laughing. "Dead and gone, boy. Dead and gone."

"Stop him, Chris," Lena said, talking to somebody buried on the other side of the world. "Stop him, Chris."

But I was the only one who heard her. Just me; just me.

You could see her come back from wherever she'd been. Her eyes blinked a couple of times slowly and when they looked at me, they saw me. Really saw me, her little sister. Not Chris, just Celia.

Slowly she pushed herself up from the bed and went into the kitchen, where Pete was still laughing.

Ma was sitting at the table, arms stretched out, head resting on them. She wasn't crying any more; it hardly looked like she was breathing.

"Dead and gone, man." Pete was teetering his chair back and forth, tapping it against the wall, so that everything on the little shelf over his head shook and moved. He had his mouth wide open, so wide that his eyes closed.

Lena hit him, hard as she could with the flat of her hand, hit him right across the face. And then she brought her left hand up, remembering to make a fist this time. It caught him square in the chest.

I heard him gasp; then he was standing up and things were falling from the shelf overhead. Lena stumbled back. And right where her hand struck the floor was the picture of our father, the picture in the silver metal frame, the one Ma had got out the night Chris first came.

She had it in her hand when she scrambled back to her feet. She was crying now, because he was still laughing. From far away I could hear her gasping: "Damn, damn,

damn, damn." And she swung the picture frame in a wide arc at his laughing mouth. He saw it coming and forgot for just a moment and lifted his arm to cover his face. And the frame and glass smashed into his stub arm.

He screamed: not loud, just a kind of high-pitched gasp. And he turned and ran. I was in the way and he knocked me aside as he yanked open the door. He missed his footing on the steps and fell down into the alley. I could hear him out there, still screaming softly to himself with the pain: "Jesus, Jesus, Jesus, Jesus."

Lena stood in the middle of the room, her hands hanging down empty at her sides. Her lip was cut; there was a little trickle of blood down the corner of her mouth. Her tongue came out, tasted, and then licked it away.

The Girl with The Flaxen Hair

THERE were only two houses in our block because we lived on the edge of town. There was our house and there was the old Fitzhugh house and about four hundred feet of weedy place between. The Fitzhugh house had been empty ever since I could remember. Only tramps slept in it sometimes, and once a doper had got in. But not real people.

That's why I was so surprised when I saw crazy Willie begin to open all the windows and sweep out the place. It wasn't any use going over to ask him—he had been born peculiar and couldn't talk right. But I could see for sure that real people were moving in.

That night at supper my mother said: "Willie cleaned out the place today."

My father looked out the kitchen window to where the house was over the weeds. "I heard it's somebody named Ramond."

"Ramond," my mother repeated, tapping her fingers on the table. She was thinking back through all the people she knew, trying to find some called Ramond. It took a while because she knew nearly everybody in four counties. "They from here?"

"No," my father said, still staring at the house. The sun had turned all its windows bright yellow.

My mother reached out and broke a loose thread off his shirt. "Wouldn't it be lovely to have nice people in the old place? I hope they're nice people."

The next morning a truck came, not a regular moving-truck but an open one with latticed wood sides, the sort you'd move stock in. It was full too, and all covered up with canvas.

"Lily!" my mother called. "Lily, you come down here right away."

I slid down the banisters. Usually I got a talking-to if Mother saw me, but this time she was too excited to notice.

"What's the letter on the truck license?" She patted my shoulder and pointed to the old house. "I can't make it out."

It was hard to see a little letter at that distance in the bright sun. Finally I said: "It's a C."

Mother sat down and pushed back her hair. "That's Jefferson County. That must be where they're from." My father was coming downstairs then and she said to him: "It's a Jefferson license—I bet they're from Jefferson City."

"That right?" my father said, yawning.

"What ever do you suppose brought them way out here? Why do you suppose they ever left?" Mother had lived in Jefferson City once, and she remembered it as the most wonderful place on earth.

My father rubbed his cheeks. "Damn that water," he

said. He had a very heavy beard and he couldn't get enough lather with the soap, so nearly every day he'd come down with his face stinging and red. That was why he didn't ever say much in the morning.

"I'm going to go over there this evening to kind of welcome her," Mother said, staring at the closed door of the pantry. "I reckon she'd like it if I brought her some of that quince serve."

"Look at your daughter, Becca," my father said, staring hard at me. I was only supposed to have one cup of coffee in the morning and that half milk, but this morning when everybody was so excited, I'd poured myself another—regular strength. She wouldn't have noticed either, but there wasn't much you could get by my father.

My father put his glasses on in a solemn way. "Coffee will make your skin turn yellow." I thought that was funny. You couldn't see if my skin was yellow under my sunburn.

"Don't fuss at the child, Claude," Mother said from the pantry. "She just wanted to celebrate. And you don't get neighbors every day from Jefferson City."

I didn't get to see them right away, because that was the day I had to go spend with my grandmother. She came driving up and I had to go run out to the car and spend the rest of the day with her over at Pine Bluffs.

That evening coming home we passed the old Fitzhugh place, which was now the Ramond place. They had old Willie out in the yard, cleaning it up, and though it was nearly dark, he was still working. I wondered how they got him to do it. Ordinarily Willie was the laziest colored man around here.

"Did you get to see them?" I asked my mother.

"You wait now," she said; "when your father comes down I'll tell you just exactly what happened."

When my father did come he had a bandage around his right hand. "Claude," my mother said, "I didn't notice that when you came in."

"Well"—my father glared at her like he always did when she'd said the wrong thing—"it was there all right."

Mother looked hurt. She pulled her shoulders closer together and shriveled up. I never saw anybody else who could do that. "Yes, Claude," she said very low.

My father's face got red; he patted her shoulder and kissed her cheek. Then my mother unshriveled and stood upright and smiled.

"It was the Crawford kid," my father said. "I was looking at that big cavity he's got in one of his laterals and he was behaving, then, wham—" he hit the table with his left hand—"he bit me. Just clamps down his jaws on the flat part of my hand."

My mother was staring at the bandage, making little clucking sounds of worry.

"Just like that," my father said, "when I'm trying to fill that tooth. I had to near shake his head off to make him let go."

My mother picked up his bandaged hand and felt it carefully. "Oh, Claude—" she said.

My father laughed. "It's not broken, Becca. And I ought to expect things like that."

My mother looked up at him and smiled quick. "You

need something to eat," she said. She could worry one minute and forget the next.

Later on, when she and my father were drinking their coffee and I was eating my second dessert, she told about her visit to the Ramonds.

"They've got the old place looking real nice," she said. "I wouldn't thought it possible. It's a big place for just them. Just the three of them. They only got one little girl about our Lily's age."

"That right?" my father said. I could tell that he wasn't really listening to her. He was thinking about his aching hand. But my mother went on.

"We talked for such a long time. She sure likes to talk, Mrs. Ramond. With the little girl sitting quiet on her chair and listening and never saying a word. She has beautiful manners, that one."

I looked out the window at the Ramond house. The upstairs bedrooms were lighted. Old Willie was burning trash out back. You could see him moving against the fire.

"They don't put much furniture out in summer, and they keep it covered up with white denim slips so it'll be cooler," my mother said. "But they got lots and lots of ferns —not just wood ferns either, but maidenhair and Lady Anne and other kinds I never did see before. They keep them right in the house. You can smell how cool the mud is."

She said a lot more, but I didn't listen: I was watching old Willie throw gasoline to make the fire burn better.

Then my father was laughing, and so hard that he hit his sore hand against the table. "Damn," he said and then:

"Sorry," to my mother. He leaned back in his chair and chewed his lip. "What a line she gave you!"

Mother looked flustered. "Well I never—"

"What she said was true enough," said my father with a laugh; "she just didn't go far enough. Her father was Senator Winslow, all right. But Senator Winslow had to resign fast to keep from being indicted for bribery. I don't know anything about the rest of her family, but I bet there are people who could tell you plenty in Jefferson City."

My mother just sat and looked at him. She always thought of Jefferson City like she rememered it—its main street full of cars and wagons on Saturday and the Bermuda grass lawns and the brick walls around the capitol. She didn't remember what it would be like with people.

"Oh, Claude," she said, and you could tell she was feeling sad.

"Now I'll tell you the rest of it, so you can get it all straight." My father leaned forward, resting his elbows on the table. "No sense your falling for all their talk; you know what Ramond is? A barber. That's all. He cuts hair and shaves and takes tips."

"Claude, please—Lily'll hear." My mother looked anxiously down at me.

"Let her," my father said. "Let her find out just what they are so she won't be taken in." You could tell from the pitch of his voice that he was determined to talk. My mother settled back in her chair with a little sigh. "He's a barber and he works that extra chair in the hotel shop."

"All right, Claude," my mother said patiently. "All right."

121

"When they don't have much furniture around it's not because it's stylish and the way they're doing it in Jefferson City—it's because they don't have any furniture." He began to laugh. He found the sound of his own voice funny, and he kept on laughing until the table shook under his arms. Finally he stopped, gasping for breath. "Ferns are the cheapest things there are and dirt's for free."

"All right, Claude," my mother said. "But I'll tell you this—they had an air—Mrs. Ramond and her little girl. It's not just good manners; lots of people have that. It's something more." She looked out the window to the Ramond house. Willie's fire was still smoldering red in the back yard and all the upstairs lights had gone out. "They have an air."

The next morning I was climbing up the rose trellis along the side of our house just to see how high I could get. It was easy going; the roses didn't have too many thorns. From the trellis I thought I could reach the cross-beams under the eaves and from then it was only a little swing up to the roof. But this particular time I didn't make it.

The door over at the Ramond house slammed hard and a woman came out, running along the street at a dead run. She held something wrapped in pink in her arms. Before I could do more than get turned around and start climbing down, she had got to our porch and was pounding on the door, though the bell was right there under her elbow. My mother opened the door. "Thank God," the woman said. "I didn't know if you'd be home."

I heard my mother's murmur of surprise as they went inside and quick footsteps the length of the house to the kitchen. Then I ripped open the back of my hand on a splinter. It began to bleed; I felt it run warm down my arm. I was still high up, above the second-story windows. My mother didn't hear me yell, she was so busy inside. I just stayed there on the trellis until the funny bleeding feeling stopped. Then when I wasn't so scared I climbed down.

Mother turned around when I opened the screen door. I put my hand inside the pocket of my overalls. "Don't let the flies in, Lily."

"Yes'm." I closed the door carefully behind me, all the while looking at the woman who had come to live in the only other house on our block. She was big: that was the first thing I thought. Not fat, maybe, but big. I thought of my father somehow when I saw her.

"And so this is your daughter," she said.

"Yes," Mother said. "This is Lily." She looked at me with a kind of half smile. "She's something of a tomboy."

Mrs. Ramond smiled at me. She had very white skin and her eyes were light blue. "How are you, my dear?" I gave the little curtsy Mother had taught me. "I have a little girl about your age," she said and then to my mother: "She takes after you, my dear—that black hair."

"Yes," said my mother. "Except for one thing. I didn't ever go around in coveralls with my face dirty. Lily is rather wild."

My mother had never talked like that before. I couldn't make it out. I began to feel uncomfortable.

123

"Your mother has been being an angel," Mrs. Ramond said, smiling at me. There was gold far back in her mouth. "My Rose got stung by some wasps. And I didn't know what to do, but she fixed everything wonderfully."

"Well"—my mother smiled—"we're very used to all sorts of stings out here."

"Oh, dear," Mrs. Ramond said. "Are there other stinging insects?" She pulled a little bit of lace out of the neck of her dress and pressed it to her mouth. "We never had to worry about things like that in Jefferson City."

"No," said my mother, "not there."

Mrs. Ramond nodded then. "Have you been there?"

"Oh, yes," my mother said quickly. "I grew up there." That wasn't quite true. She had stayed there only until she was eight. She'd told me that story over and over again.

"Not really?" Mrs. Ramond looked up with more excitement than she had shown yet. "Not really?" My mother smiled yes. "We must spend a long time together talking over our memories. I'm homesick for it sometimes and Rose misses it so very much."

"The dear child," my mother said vaguely and she glanced to the far corner of the kitchen, which was behind me and out of sight. "Do the stings hurt any more? Shall I put more ice on them?"

"No, thank you."

She had been sitting on the straight wooden chair by the window, and she had been watching me ever since I came in. There was one of our blue-checked towels wrapped around her leg where the wasps had gotten her and there was another one on her arm. She was sitting

124

there with the bandaged leg stuck out straight and holding one bandaged arm with the other. But what I noticed first was her hair. It was yellow and it was wrapped around her head in plaits like an old woman's would be.

Mrs. Ramond stood up; she was the tallest woman I'd ever seen. "No," she said. "We won't take up any more of your time. Mornings are so busy, I know."

"My husband comes home for dinner."

Mrs. Ramond smiled and picked up Rose. She stood holding her wrapped in a pink blanket and smiling. "I had best put the child to bed. She'll probably have fever."

"Oh, I don't think so," my mother said. "There wasn't enough for that. Lily got stung all over last summer on a picnic and she didn't get much fever."

Mrs. Ramond nodded. "But Rose is very delicate. We came here partly for her health, you know."

"Is that right?" My mother clucked sympathetically. "I know—I'll go back with you, to see if there's anything I can do. It's always such work moving."

"How sweet of you!" Mrs. Ramond said. "Isn't it, Rose? She must know how nervous I've been with that crazy old colored man pottering around out in the yard."

"Hilda—that's our cook—she should be coming," Mother said. "She'll fix dinner and I'll be back soon. You stay here, Lily." She reached out her hand and patted my shoulder; then she was gone.

I stayed in the kitchen until I saw Hilda come walking up the street. She stopped at the back gate and put her can of snuff on the top of the gatepost, because Mother wouldn't let her chew while she was around the house. I went out to meet her. "Mother's gone," I said. "She went over to the Ramond's."

"Sure enough?" Hilda leaned on the gate, taking a last slow chew of her snuff.

"They're from Jefferson City," I said.

Hilda sighed and blew the mouthful of snuff out into the grass. "Your ma say what she wanted for dinner?"

"Nuh, nuh. Hilda," I said, "my hand hurts."

She did not stop walking toward the house. She had to get away from that can or she'd take another mouthful. "Have a look," she said.

I held out my hand. The blood had run up my arm in long streaks; it had hardened in drops on my fingernails. And it had turned black. I saw it and began to cry, though it did not hurt very much any more.

"Christ sake," Hilda said, "lemme wash that."

My father came home early because there hadn't been many patients in his office that morning. He came home before my mother got back. When he saw my hand his face got dark and set all over. "What'd you do that on?" I didn't answer; I didn't want to say that I had been climbing the trellis up the side of the house. "Looks like a nail to me. Was it?" I nodded, beginning to cry at the thought of the nail ripping open the back of my hand. "Hush, now," he said, and picked me up in his arms like Mrs. Ramond had done with Rose. "Tell my wife," he said to Hilda, "that we've gone to Dr. Smither's."

Hilda nodded, impressed by the angry sound in his voice. "It ain't looked that bad to me."

"She's going to take a tetanus," my father said, "just in case."

When we came home, my mother was out in the front yard waiting for us. She'd been doing a little digging in the garden to make the time pass; you could see that she'd uprooted the nasturtiums. They had a fight then, my mother and my father. And it ended the way it always ended, with my mother crying and my father patting her shoulder and telling her not to.

"It was just an accident, Becca," he told her.

She twisted her handkerchief. "I should have been here," she said. "I'll never talk to them again if you don't want me to."

My father laughed. "Don't go making promises you can't keep, honey."

"They are lovely people," my mother said slowly. "It's so nice to know people like that."

"All right, then"—my father looked out the window to the old house—"talk to them. Just don't let Lily get killed in the process."

My mother looked relieved because the anger was all gone from his voice. She laughed. "Don't be ridiculous, Claude. Nothing will happen to Lily. She's always getting cut up, you know. If only she wasn't such a tomboy."

My father laughed and ran his fingers through my hair. "Don't you mind, pigeon," he told me. "You'll be a fine lady soon enough."

My mother didn't hear him; she was looking down at me. "I do hope that you and Rose get to be friends. It would be so good for you." Then she turned to my father.

"Why, Claude, isn't that nice?—their names fit together. Lily and Rose. Isn't that nice?"

"Yes," said my father. "That's just swell."

The very next day Mother took me to see Rose. She was sitting on their porch, her leg still bandaged over the stung spot, though the ache would have been gone a long time.

"How are you, honey?" my mother asked.

"Much better, thank you." She had blue eyes, lighter than any I'd seen. There was no other color in them like yellow or black. They were plain blue like the sky in the water color in the dining-room that Mother had done years ago.

Rose was looking at me solemnly, without smiling. "You remember Lily?" my mother said.

"Oh, yes." She smiled then. "You came in yesterday after your mother had attended to my stings—" she turned back to my mother. "That was very neighborly of you. Thank you."

"That's all right, honey. I was glad to," my mother said. "Your mother home?"

"Of course," Rose said. "She's probably heard your voices, but I'll call her." Then she reached out and with her knuckles tapped four times on the wall behind her. "In this old house," she said, "every little sound travels. You might say that was our signal."

"How cute!" my mother said.

Rose said to me: "Wouldn't you like to sit over here and talk to me?"

I guess in all the time I knew her she must have asked me that question a hundred times. It was her favorite one. "Come talk to me"—of course, she didn't mean that at all. She meant that she wanted to talk, wanted somebody to listen to her. And I did.

I thought she was the most beautiful thing I ever saw. And she was used to being admired. Her mother said, "There was a gentleman once—in Jefferson City, when we used to live there—a Mr. Clayton, who told me that Rose had a face like a Botticelli angel."

An angel—no, that wasn't what her face reminded me of. I had seen too many pictures of angels not to know. For one thing, her hair was too heavy, her yellow hair, which she wrapped in braids around her head like an old woman's. And angels' eyes were darker.

She had a way of telling stories, though. She would lean forward, her elbows on the arms of her chair, both her hands pressed to the braids around her head. She would tell the stories quickly, the words rushing out. And yet you never missed a word, somehow. My mother would always stop and listen to her; and Mrs. Ramond, too, if she were there, would nod her head and smile as if she were hearing all of this for the first time, while she had told the stories to Rose in the first place. They sounded better somehow when Rose told them. There were many stories, but Rose talked so much that sometimes she told the same one twice. I didn't mind.

"Once," she would say, beginning a story about her grandfather, Senator Winslow, and most all the stories were about him, "when he was just married a little while and his first child was only nine days old, some robbers came into the house. Muriel, that was his wife, a tall woman with hair like mine, woke him up saying: 'Save me and the baby.' And so he got his pistol out of the drawer of the little table by the bed. It was a French table, gilt and silvered; he'd brought it back with him on his last trip to Europe. He took the pistol out of the drawer and saw that it was loaded; then he went out in the hall to the stairs. Muriel took the baby from the cradle and hid with it behind the big walnut armoire. When he got to the head of the stair, he saw the robbers in the front hall. 'What are you doing in my house?' he called. The robbers looked up and they were afraid. He shot the leader, and the rest ran out the door. They never could get the stain off the rug in the front hall. And he wouldn't change the rug, because he said it was a warning to other thieves to stay away from his house."

She paused and I broke in: "Did he kill the robber?"

Mrs. Ramond laughed behind me. "He never missed a shot. He had the truest eye in the state."

I nodded and closed my eyes to see better the picture that was in my mind: a tall man, but not very broad or heavy, with hair light like Rose's. He was wearing a blue coat with silver buttons, and high boots that shone like water in the sun.

"Once he went campaigning in the back counties of the state. And the crackers saw his fine clothes (he always wore beautiful clothes; he brought them from France), and they began to laugh. He saw them laughing and he got very angry. His eyes would flash and his face would get dark and his hair would rumple up. If he was at home and he got angry, his wife, Muriel, would send all the servants out of the room quickly. Then she would come up to him gently and ask him to sit down. And when he did, she would sit on the arm of his chair and rub his forehead with her cool white fingers, humming his favorite tune very softly. And the anger would go all out of him. She was the only one who could make the anger all go out of him like that.

"But that time when he went campaigning in the back counties of the state he got angry and there was nobody there who knew how to stop him. 'I see you are laughing, sir' he said to one of the men. 'And may I ask at whom?' And the man, thinking that anyone who wore such fine clothes must be weak, laughed even harder. Until the Senator hit him and he lay out on the ground. Then the Senator took off his blue coat and rolled up the sleeves of his cambric shirt and fought with the whole crowd. When it was over, there were fourteen men lying on the ground; four of them had broken jaws. And he had only a little scratch on his cheek from a man who had drawn a knife and stabbed at him from behind. Then he unrolled his sleeves and put on his blue coat and rode twenty miles to the next place he was to speak."

Always when Rose had finished her story she would sit there, nodding her head with the heavy yellow plaits. Usually I'd get too restless and say something or scrape my chair. Then she'd look up frowning slightly and shaking her head. She was so sorry when a story was finished.

One day she talked longer than usual. The shadow

131

from the house reached nearly across the street; it was time for dinner. I was starting to say that, when I saw that her father had come home. He stood leaning against one of the porch pillars and looking at Rose with a kind of twisted smile. "Oh, yes," he said softly. "He was a most remarkable man. Most remarkable. And so very honest a one."

He was a short man, and fat, and dark. His wife was much bigger. He had a strange accent, too, because he had come from France. "Has she ever told you stories about me, Lily?" I shook my head. "No? That is such a pity! How naughty of you, Rose, not to tell stories about your own father!" He looked down at her and twisted the corner of his mouth even more. I thought it was a funny way to smile. "You must ask her sometimes to tell stories about me, Lily. About how I shaved the King of France."

I wondered if I should believe him; but he was French and he was a barber, so I asked: "What—what did the King say?"

He looked at me solemnly. "The King had a very tough beard. And though I had sharpened my razor especially for him, it was not enough. All he said was: 'Ouch.' "

Rose was looking down at her hands folded in her lap. I thought for a moment she was crying. He looked at her, then turned to me. "Do you know what 'flaxen' means?" I shook my head. "Well, it means yellow, like the color of her hair there." Mrs. Ramond came out on the porch and stood staring at him. "Good evening, my dear," he said. She didn't answer and he shrugged and asked me: "Have you ever heard of *The Girl with the Flaxen Hair*?"

I saw the way Mrs. Ramond was looking at him, and I

wondered what I should do. "No, sir," I said. I wondered if I should have told the truth.

He was smiling again, twisting the corner of his mouth. "It's a piece of music I wrote," he said. "I used to be a musician, too. Come inside and I'll play it for you. You come, too, Rose."

I stood by the piano and listened while he played. I thought I had never heard anything as smooth as the way the sounds came. But it didn't remind me of Rose somehow. When he finished he smiled again and said: "It's a lovely piece, isn't it? I wrote it especially for Rose, my daughter, the girl with the flaxen hair."

I saw Rose; she was sitting by the window and this time there was no doubt of it. She was crying. Just sitting there, not making a sound, the tears falling into the hands in her lap. My stomach knotted up and my legs got shaky. I began to back to the door. "My mother told me not to be late to supper. She told me that." I made the little bow Mother had taught me. "Thank you."

"You are very polite." He stood up and bowed very slowly. "You must come back and I will play some other of my compositions for you. Au revoir."

I jumped down the steps and ran all the way home, but I heard Mrs. Ramond's voice come hissing out the windows, soft and full of hating: "Raoul, how could you—"

I wasn't afraid of him exactly; my father was the only one who could scare me really, when his face got dark and he scowled. No, I wasn't afraid of Rose's father. But I didn't know what to make of him. I'd never heard anybody play piano in the smooth rippling way he did, his fingers so fast on the keys they were just a blur. I only heard him play that once: *The Girl with the Flaxen Hair.* Because he went away.

"He's gone back to France to study music," my mother said one night. It was hot like always in summer, without a bit of breeze. It was dry too. There hadn't been rain in ages. There was only a mist high up by the stars that made them shine brighter. Like pieces of ice in the hot sky.

"The hell he did." My father gave a quick laugh. He never got so angry and used words like that in front of my mother unless they were talking about the Ramonds.

"Claude, please—" my mother said.

He took a couple of quick draws on his pipe and blew rings into the air. Then he turned and looked at the Ramond house. The lights were on upstairs although the bedrooms must have been terribly hot.

"Maybe he went to France," my father said, "but it wasn't to study music. And I'll bet my bottom dollar he won't be coming back."

"He just couldn't desert them."

"Why not?" My father laughed again. "It's happened before. Maybe it wasn't such a bad idea. Not after years of that Amazon over there and her background and her stories of the Senator who was just a crook after all. And the girl that looks like she's half dead with that mess of tow hair."

Like my father said, Mr. Ramond didn't come back. If anybody asked Mrs. Ramond where he was, she'd say he was studying music in France. But unless there was a question she didn't talk about him.

"I wonder what they live on, the poor dears," my mother said.

"Go ask her," my father said, grinning.

"Oh, no." My mother looked horrified. "I couldn't ever. You just don't talk about things like that."

"Well, I wouldn't worry," my father said. "She probably has enough from her father, the Senator. After all, he stole enough to have something left over. And they're living on that."

I heard him, though I wasn't supposed to, but I didn't believe him. I knew the Senator too well. He was tall, but not heavy, and he wore a blue coat with silver buttons, and boots shiny as water in the light.

"By the way," my father said, "Rose came to my office this afternoon. She's got an abscessed tooth; one of her second ones. I'm going to pull it for her tomorrow."

Mother and I went to the office with Rose and Mrs. Ramond and sat waiting in the little outside room. My father glared when he saw that we had come, but Mother just looked him up and down and sat down by Mrs. Ramond and put her hand on her arm.

Rose didn't make a sound. My father said afterward that she was just about a perfect patient. When it was finished, she opened the door herself and came out to where we were waiting. My father put his head around the door and said: "You want to keep the tooth as a souvenir?"

"No, Claude, no," my mother whispered to him, and

then to Rose: "Come on, honey. We'll drive you home."

She'd got out of the chair too soon: the bleeding hadn't stopped. There was a little trickle of blood out the corner of her mouth. She stopped it with her handkerchief just like it was a drop of perspiration.

She kept her mouth pressed tight closed as we walked down the street to where the car was parked. I guess the sun was too hot, because Mrs. Ramond nearly fainted. She staggered a little bit, and my mother got her around her waist, holding her up, and started sort of dragging her to the car. Rose let her lips open and the blood came out and down her chin. My mother looked over her shoulder. "Oh, my God," she said. "You grab her, Lily, and get her in the car."

I got one arm around Rose and pulled her to the car. She wasn't making any attempt to stop the blood now. It was all down the front of her dress and some had got on me, too. Her blood was red—red as mine—even if she was so pale and light-haired.

Until Rose got killed they went on living next to us. I was just crazy about Rose. There wasn't ever anybody like her. They didn't seem ever to know many people in town except us; they didn't seem to want to. I remember, after they had been living there a couple of weeks, Mother asked Mrs. Ramond to come to her club meeting, but she just shook her head and smiled and said no very politely. And my mother smiled back at her, and I had the feeling she was very glad Mrs. Ramond wasn't going.

"They just wouldn't appreciate her," she told me as we

walked back home. "They're nice enough people, but they just wouldn't appreciate her."

I thought of the club: Mrs. Farland, the doctor's wife, who was old and fat and had five girls and wanted to be president and was furious when my mother got elected instead; Mrs. Cullers, who ran the drugstore and grocery; Mrs. Henderson, who was little and pretty almost as my mother and who ran the other drugstore and grocery across town; and my grandmother, who drove in from Pine Bluffs for the meetings. And the others, ten or twelve of them, who came from the farms around.

"Yes," said my mother, and she took hold of my hand, swinging it slowly back and forth. "They wouldn't appreciate her."

So most of the ladies in town made one call on the Ramonds, because it was polite. And that was all. They weren't ever friendly with anybody but us; but we were real good friends—my mother and Mrs. Ramond and Rose and I.

My father couldn't ever stand the sight of them, though he was always polite, and it was only afterward that he said what he thought to my mother and me. And he was the one who found out about Rose at last. He told us one morning two winters later. He was sitting in the breakfast room with his chair tilted back against the wall. He hadn't shaved yet; the beard's darkness made his face look strange. He had made coffee, and the pot was on the table in front of him.

"Why, Claude," my mother said, "how nice! You must have got up real early."

"Since around four thirty."

I'd never been up that early in my life. If it was winter like now, the sun wouldn't be up; and it would be freezing cold with the night fog still all over.

"What ever for?" my mother asked.

"Well"—my father craned his neck to look out the window at the other house. "Looks like they went back to bed."

"They haven't got up yet," my mother said.

"Oh, yes, they have," my father said. "You know, last night—or this morning—when you woke me up because the room was chilly? You went right back to sleep, so you didn't notice. But I went over to Lily's room to turn up her radiator. And then I happened to look out the window and I saw a light in the house over there."

"Maybe Rose was sick," my mother said.

My father didn't answer her. "It wasn't a bright light at all. It was sort of yellow and flickering like a flashlight. I thought it was burglars—"

"Was it?" I said. "Was it?"

He looked at me and rubbed his eyes; you could tell that he was sleepy. "I'm talking to your mother," he said. "Go get some milk." I didn't move because he went on talking. "Well, I got to thinking how helpless they'd be if it was burglars." He shrugged and looked at my mother. "You'd have sense enough to get my gun out of the drawer, but her"—he jerked his head backwards to the house— "she'd probably come running down without a thing and get herself hurt or killed. I got to thinking that and I began to get worried." He laughed and twisted his lips. "You

138

know, I guess I got as much chivalry in me after all as the great Senator."

I tried to imagine him in the blue coat with the silver buttons and the high shining boots. I closed my eyes to try the harder, but all I could see him in was the high-collared white smock he wore in his office.

"I got on my clothes because it was cold. Nasty cold, with a heavy wet mist. But by the time I got halfway over there the back door popped open and the girl came out. She was all dressed with a coat and a scarf around her head. And her mother I saw in the door behind her holding a flash with her fingers across the beam to shade it. Then she closed the door and the girl went off at a run."

He stopped and yawned; neither my mother nor I said anything.

"I went after her. After all, a kid like that wandering around alone in the dark of the morning with all the tramps that get thrown off trains here—so I went along. I thought at first I'd catch up with her and tell her what a fool thing she was doing. But I didn't; I got too curious. I just went along behind, close enough if there was any trouble, but not close enough for her to notice. But now that I remember, I don't think she would have noticed no matter how close I got. She didn't notice anything. Just kept going at a run, her head bent a little. Right straight to the railroad yards.

"That's where we went. It's quite a way and I'd been doing it at a trot and I was winded. She'd been running and she didn't seem tired at all. You know the pile of

coal where they load the trains. Well, she made straight
for that, without hesitating even. And then I saw that she
was carrying one of these flexible baskets. They're made
out of straw, I think. She filled it up with coal; filled it
right to the very top, too, because pieces kept rolling off
when she walked. I wonder how much it weighed, that
basket. It was maybe a half bushel or a little more. You
wouldn't think she'd have strength like that, her being so
little and light."

He looked at my mother. "Well," he said. "That's all—"

My mother sat very quietly, chewing on one fingernail.
"Claude," she said, "they must be terribly poor."

My father let his breath go out in a whistling sigh. "I
reckon the Senator didn't steal enough, after all."

The very next afternoon Rose sat in our front parlor. I
looked down at her shoes, expecting almost to see some of
the cinder dust from the railroad yards on them, but they
were dusted clean. She had brought an old album over to
show us and was turning the pages slowly. "That's my
great-aunt and her husband. He was wounded at Siloe and
when they were bringing him home he died." She turned
the page. "This was my grandmother. Her dress is lovely,
isn't it? Pale yellow—she was married in it."

My mother took the book from her and examined it
closely. "It really is," she said.

"My dress will be just like that—yellow, you know, and
with that little high neck. He'll give me a brooch and that
will be my only ornament."

I wondered who he was. My mother smiled. "Isn't it early for planning, dear?" she said to Rose. "You don't know who your groom is going to be."

"No," Rose said. "Mother and I have talked it all over."

They talked over a lot of things. Sometimes when they left the shade up, we could see them at night, sitting in the parlor, talking. And even when the shade was down, we could see the light from behind it and know that they were in there, talking.

"I don't think I'll want any flowers," Rose said. "I'll just brush out my hair and let it hang, perfectly plain. The church will be full of flowers, though. In all shades of yellow—pale like the asters or bright like jonquils or gold like tiger lilies."

(When we told my father about it later, he just laughed. "It'd look nice, all right, but you couldn't ever get all those flowers to bloom at the same time.")

"It'll be all in Jefferson City. Do you remember Trinity Church?"

My mother nodded. "But it's still so far off, dear."

Rose shook her head. "Not so far. I'll be eighteen then and I'm twelve now. That isn't far."

I thought of the light every evening in the parlor and their talking, just the two of them, and Rose's straight blond hair. And for the first time in ages I thought of her father, the man with the accent, who had played a piece called *The Girl with the Flaxen Hair* and said it was a picture of her. He was gone; he had been gone nearly two years. And they didn't seem to miss him. But they were poor, so poor they stole coal from the railroad yards in the winter.

Rose was killed that spring in the railroad yards. It was the Comet, the express to Birmingham. They had changed its schedule, so that it came racing through town four hours earlier than usual.

Rose got on the tracks; she wasn't looking and didn't notice: she didn't ever seem more than half awake at that time of morning anyway.

The people on the train didn't know anything, or if they did they didn't stop or give a sign. It was Pete Lafferty, going out to start up the boiler on the switch engine around about five o'clock, found her a little to one side of the track. She was still holding on to the wicker basket, which had a couple of pieces of coal in it. She must have just gotten started.

And Pete left her where she was lying and ran back and got Tim Maybeck, the station manager, and Tim took one look and called the sheriff and the doctor and my father because he lived next door. And the sheriff woke up his deputy and all of them together—all six of them—wrapped her up in an army-colored blanket and brought her home. They all helped carry her into the house, carrying her gently and slowly.

Mrs. Ramond didn't make a sound. She just thanked them and locked the door behind them. If she cried, nobody saw her.

For a while all the men stood around on the porch, wondering if there was something else they should do.

Then they walked across to our house and my father opened a bottle of whisky.

There wasn't a wake. Mrs. Ramond packed everything into two valises and left. My mother and I went down to the station with her and watched while they put Rose in the baggage car; she was going to her grandfather's plot in Jefferson City. Mrs. Ramond watched the door of the baggage car close and then, not turning or speaking, she got into the day coach. She never came back; she never wrote.

When we got home, my mother cried for hours. "The poor little thing. The poor little dead thing."

My father sat very quietly holding her. "God forgive me," he said very softly, "but it's best. They just couldn't go on."

"Why'd she go?" my mother asked with her head buried in the cloth of his shoulder. "You don't need coal in spring. Why'd she go?"

He shook his head. "I don't know. She just did, that's all. Maybe she got in the habit. Maybe she thought about putting it aside for next winter. Maybe she didn't think at all." He rubbed his forehead slowly. Outside the window a little breeze ran a shadow across the yellow weeds. "All she did was get killed."

I tried to think what it would be like to get killed. I tried to think what it must be like for Rose right now in the baggage car going to Jefferson City.

My father reached over and patted my shoulder. "Don't you grieve, honey. It's over; you'll forget."

He was wrong there. I didn't ever forget. Always I

could sit down and think and see her so clear, like she was standing by me. Even years later, even after my father died, even all the way through high school. By that time, by the time I finished school, it was sort of hard for me to remember my father: his face was blurry and I'd have to look at a picture to be sure. I forgot him.

I forgot him. But I didn't ever forget them. And it wasn't Mrs. Ramond I remembered. It was Rose and the Senator. Always there'd be the Senator with his boots shiny as water in the sun and his blue coat with the silver buttons. And Rose would be standing next to him, smiling at him, wearing the yellow dress. And he'd give her a round pin that sparkled with diamonds and she'd fix it to the neck of her yellow dress. And all around them would be yellow flowers—asters, jonquils, tiger lilies. She'd have her hair loose: the way I'd never seen it. Not in braids around her head, but brushed back and hanging down.

The Bright Day

"Finish, good lady; the bright day is done,
And we are for the dark."

It was quite a summer. It was hot: the sun, even when it had just come up, was yellow hot and small as a quarter. There hadn't been any rain in nearly two months, and outside of town only the early cotton had come up; and the corn had rust.

It was quite a summer, all right. And then, in July, there was a hailstorm: the same morning we heard the news about Pamela Langley coming.

I remember I had been wondering what I should have for supper. Andrew only got to come home from camp on week-ends and I wanted something specially good. I had gone down to the cellar to see what I could find. Half the junk in the cellar was new to me, because Andrew and I had only been married a little over a year.

So I didn't see the hailstorm at all. First I heard of it Cousin Roger was standing at the head of the cellar steps calling. And there they were on the grass, the hailstones, some of them big as a golf ball, most of them the size of marbles, some of them small and white as drops of wax—in little drifts like the light snow we had in winter.

"Every single pane in the greenhouse is broken," Cousin Roger said. "Who would have thought it was going to hail —in July? It hasn't since I was a boy. A little boy."

"Yes," I said without listening. I was thinking about Andrew and wondering if this would make any difference in his coming home. Outside I could see Aunt Mayme walking around and around the greenhouse. Then she came in and said to me: "There's fifty panes broken, best I could count. Melton will be heartbroken when he comes home."

"I was down in the cellar," I said. "I didn't hear anything."

The front door slammed and Uncle Melton's voice was calling: "Mayme, Mayme, where are you?"

He went into the dining-room first and we heard him speak to Cousin Roger. Finally he came in and sat down, pulling the lapel of his linen suit away from his hot body. "What happened to the greenhouse?"

Aunt Mayme lifted her eyebrows. "I reckoned you knew: the hail smashed it up some."

"Oh God," Uncle Melton said. "There just isn't anything left to go wrong."

They were twins and they looked it. The same yellow-red hair, the same white skin that fifty or fifty-five years had creamed up like fine old paper.

"Pamela's coming," Uncle Melton said. "She isn't dead. She's coming home."

Cousin Roger came hurrying into the room. "I found it,"

he said. "We haven't had hail in summer since 1916—July 23, 1916. I found the record I made then."

"1916," Uncle Melton said slowly. "It must have been about then that Pamela went away."

"No," Aunt Mayme said. "It was later. A little later. Just after the war. Because we all wondered if there wasn't a soldier in it somewhere."

I sat listening, wondering who they were talking about. I didn't ask then and there about Pamela. When Andrew got home, he told me.

"We thought Pamela was dead. There hadn't been news from her in so long." He turned and sat down on the bed—heavily and slowly as if he were tired. I stood over by the dresser, brushing out my hair.

"I never saw her," he said. "She was before my time. She's first cousin to Mayme and Melton and second to me —and you." He grinned briefly. "Follow me?"

"I guess so."

"Pamela had a sister, Josephine Fredericks. Now do you see? Josephine married well—very well. Fredericks had money when they married. And he got more. In tobacco. Mrs. Fredericks was Pamela Langley's sister. And Pamela is her heir if there's no valid will. And next to Pamela we're the only relatives. See?"

"But Pamela's turned up again. So she gets it all."

The stem of the pipe he was smoking cracked. He had bitten it through. I hadn't realized he was so angry about the whole thing. Andrew was quiet usually; it was very hard to tell what he was thinking. "She gets the whole damn lot," and he got up and went downstairs.

147

I suppose it was funny, the way Uncle Melton and Aunt Mayme and even Andrew had worked and paid to give Pamela Langley title to a lot of money. I suppose it was very funny. You see, Pamela had been gone so long they were certain she was dead and that they were the heirs. And they set out to prove their title.

The trouble was that old widowed Josephine Fredericks, Pamela's sister, had made a will. Or at least that's what John Woodville said.

He was a doctor of sorts. Josephine had picked him up and moved him into her big house and told everybody that he was her doctor and her best friend. And when she died they found a will leaving everything to John Woodville.

First Uncle Melton and Aunt Mayme and Andrew set out to prove that she wasn't sane when she wrote the will. (Uncle Melton, for all his silly little ways and his red hair, is a pretty good lawyer.) Then they discovered the will wasn't genuine. They had a handwriting expert examine it and he was sure: he swore out a statement and gave it to Uncle Melton, who locked it up in his office safe downtown to wait out the time for the case to come up. So everything was all fixed.

Then Pamela came back after all those years, and all the scheming had done was give her a clear claim to her sister's money.

Pamela was a wanderer. She was in her mid-thirties, not married, when one day she just decided to leave. Since she didn't have any family, except her sister, Josephine, there wasn't anything to stop her. Later she'd sent postcards from places like Detroit and New York and Liverpool. They thought she'd died in one of those places. If she'd stayed away just a little longer, until after the court had decided, it would have been all right for us. But now everything went to Pamela.

At breakfast Uncle Melton said: "Pamela will be in to-day. After church we will drive down to the station and meet her."

Andrew said: "Charlotte and I will stay home."

"I have a headache," I said.

That was how Pamela Langley came home, after thirty-something years: Mayme and Melton brought her back and I knew they'd be just as nice and hospitable to her as any two humans could be. I didn't see her the first day she came because I was really sick. Andrew, of course, saw her, but he didn't seem to want to talk when he sat with me, and I didn't feel well enough to ask.

Andrew went back to camp early that Monday morning. He kissed me and said: "It'll be all right, honey." He'd hardly got out the front door before Aunt Mayme came in.

"How are you, dear?"

"I'm all right, thank you," I said.

"Are you starting a baby?"

I felt myself go red at her abrupt question. "No," I said awkwardly, "I don't think so."

"Well," she said, "that's good. Better that the family waits for happy times." She stood over against the open windows, over against the gray light of the first dawn. The room was lightening fast.

"You really should get up, dear," she said. "You have to meet Pamela."

Of course I had to. I went down and let Aunt Mayme introduce me to Pamela Langley.

She was old, much older than I had expected, in her late sixties. She was tall, about my size, and heavy, and her corsets weren't too good. And you could tell she'd never been even passably nice-looking.

What I noticed most was the material of her dress. When I first came in I thought: she's wearing a gray dress. But it wasn't; over the gray was a close-woven design, tiny threads of red, blue, and yellow. When I told her how lovely the silk was, she only said yes in a vague kind of way and that she'd forgotten where she'd got it.

She'd forgotten a great many things about her travels; I found out that soon enough, because she was always wanting to tell me stories. There was the time she'd been in Athens as the governess in an official's family.

"What sort of official?" I asked her.

"I don't remember." She frowned, just slightly. "But he was dark, I remember, very dark, with heavy black hair. And both of his children were fair. Isn't that strange? But then their mother was English. I never knew her. She was dead when I came; that's why I came: to take care of the children. . . ."

She talked on and on—cities like Athens, Cairo, Paris, whose streets were all tangled like a boy's fish net—and at the end was home. That was the thing she remembered most clearly.

The morning I met her, the very first morning she was

back, she insisted on taking a walk, with the sun blazing and getting along toward noon.

"Why, Cousin Pamela"—Aunt Mayme pressed one hand to her throat—"it's killing hot out there."

Pamela laughed. "I reckon I can survive. I lived through a lot hotter in Algiers."

Aunt Mayme lifted her eyebrows.

"If you're going," I said, "I'll come along."

Aunt Mayme looked at me out of the corner of her eyes. "You better take a sunshade, dear," she said. "You haven't been to Algiers."

Pamela touched my shoulder, briefly, smiling. "She hasn't missed very much; it was a dirty place."

"Yes," Aunt Mayme said. "I imagine it was. Let me give you my big shade. I'll help you get it out of the closet."

In her room she said with a kind of whistling sigh of annoyance: "Charlotte, you can be most trying."

"I want to go for a walk," I said, reaching for the sun-shade hanging on the closet door. "I want to get out the house for a little exercise."

She was holding the sunshade's handle. "Pamela only knows that her sister left a will in Woodville's favor."

"But that wasn't genuine."

She closed the door and leaned on it for a minute. "You are not to tell her that. You understand?" Her face was perfectly blank, not excited, not nervous. "Now take your hot morning walk."

Pamela stayed with us two weeks. She liked me, maybe because I'd sit quiet and listen to her stories.

Shirley Ann Grau

She had been all over the world: to England first, then
China, Japan, and home. It took her nearly thirty years.
And then she'd come back at last.

That's what she'd talk about most—the coming home.
I asked her once: "Why did you leave, then?"

"Why?" she said. "I don't think I know, really. I wasn't
unhappy here. There was enough money from Papa's es-
tate; Josephine didn't need any." I caught my breath at
the mention of Josephine and wondered if she was going
to ask about the will, but she went on: "There wasn't any
real reason for me to stay either. I reckon I wanted to see
what other places looked like."

I smiled at her, making a little joke at Aunt Mayme's
expense. "Aunt Mayme says there's a soldier in the story."

"A soldier?" She laughed. "Mayme is romantic at heart.
It's a pity she didn't get married. . . . I didn't have any
soldier to make me run away. I just left because I wanted
to. And I knew I could come home when I wanted to."

I understood her. She could come home—just as if she'd
never been away. She could go all around the world and
come back without remembering anything. And she
could come back to Josephine's money. She could come
back and ruin all the plans we'd made.

Then Aunt Mayme found the perfect little house for
Pamela. It was a pleasant place, only four rooms, but that
was more than enough. It had been empty for nearly two
years, ever since old Mrs. Sherwood had died there; but it
was nicely furnished and the only thing to do was give it
a good cleaning.

• • •

152

Aunt Mayme and Uncle Melton didn't want me to know what was going on. They didn't quite trust me yet. They didn't intend for me to know what they were planning to do. Nor did Andrew, I felt.

But they had to get me out of the house. So Andrew insisted that I accept an invitation from the Robinsons; they weren't particularly old or close friends, but still they invited us to spend a couple of weeks with them.

One night, while with them, Andrew let something slip. He said it was a great pity we had to go shares at all in the money.

One thing about Andrew: when he's caught he knows he's caught. So when I made him sit down and explain what he'd said about sharing the money, he told me the truth.

When he got through, I didn't say anything. He came over and kissed me and said: "You know how it is, honey. You understand." And I nodded because I did understand. He smoked one cigarette over by the window, then he came to bed. He patted my shoulder once, and soon I could tell he was asleep.

I don't think I got much sleep that night. I kept thinking over and over what they had done.

It was this way: Pamela knew her sister had left a will in Woodville's favor. But she didn't know that there was proof that it was false. She didn't even seem particularly interested—she and Josephine had scarcely been friends, and thirty years had taken all of the feeling out of the relationship. And Pamela had money enough from her father; so it was unlikely she would question the will.

Uncle Melton had had a talk with John Woodville and had made a bargain. The will would not be contested. Uncle Melton would withdraw his charge—for a price. And the price was two thirds of what Woodville would get.

I can see what it was like, that scene. John Woodville trying to bargain, knowing that he had to take what was offered to him. So it was settled with Woodville getting one third; the rest Aunt Mayme and Uncle Melton and Andrew would share. Everything had worked beautifully —except that Andrew told me.

In the morning Andrew said I still looked tired and maybe we'd better go home. All the way back, all the long drive through the heat and dust. In one place the brush fires had worked clear up to the road. There was nothing unusual about them, only maybe there were a few more this year. But they were part of the summer along with the dryness and the heat. And the sun bright and yellow through the smoky sky.

Andrew had turned on the radio because the quiet rustling sound of fire burning under pine bark puts your nerves on edge. When we had driven through the burning strip, Andrew flipped off the radio. "God, that's a relief."

"Yes," I said without really hearing him. All through the trip I hadn't really listened to him. Once in a while I'd notice him looking at me out of the corner of his eye and once he'd asked me if I felt all right. But I was too busy thinking to notice very much. I kept thinking about Pamela and knowing I ought to do something.

We were nearly home when I said to Andrew: "I'm going to tell her."

"Tell her?" There was a puzzled look in his eyes.

"I've got to tell Pamela."

He stared straight ahead at the road. "That'd be a hell of a thing to do." We turned left down the street that was ours. "With everything settled, Pamela could charge us with conspiracy to defraud or something like that."

"I know." I'd gone over and over the whole thing.

There were little beads of sweat forming around his mouth, and under the tan his face was white.

"I'm sorry, Andrew," I said. "But we just couldn't. . . . And I just can't stand the thought of that Woodville creature getting any of the money. He did forge the will."

In two more blocks we would be home. "He won't get much," Andrew said. "We'll get most of it like we should."

I shook my head and didn't answer.

He looked full at me. "You won't do anything."

"There's a car coming," I said, as calmly as I could, though I was beginning to be frightened a bit: I knew how much the thing meant to him. "You better watch the road . . . and how could you stop me?"

He didn't answer. When we turned up our driveway and stopped, he lifted the bags from the back seat and went in the house first. I thought that I would drive over at once and speak to Pamela. I slipped over into the driver's seat, but Andrew had taken the ignition keys with him. I had to stop and look for my set in my purse.

It's funny how a little thing like not being able to find keys right away can change just about everything. If my purse had been in order I would have slipped the key in the ignition and been off down the street and told Pamela.

And I guess that I wouldn't have had a husband any more. But it doesn't matter, because it took a couple of minutes to find the keys and by that time Andrew had put down the bags and was coming out again and Uncle Melton was with him. They saw me sitting on the left side of the car and they ran the rest of the way. I heard their feet coming across the grass when I flipped on the ignition. Then Andrew's arm reached in and pulled out the keys and the engine stopped. I looked up and saw the smear of my lipstick on the sleeve of his khaki shirt.

"I'm sorry, dear," he said. "I didn't mean to knock into you like that. Is your lip hurt?"

I glanced in the rear-view mirror. The lipstick was smeared down across my chin.

"I look like something out of *Treasure Island,*" I said, with a smile, hoping all the while that the edges of my mouth would not tremble. "Give me the keys now."

Uncle Melton slipped into the seat beside me. His round white face was dripping with perspiration, and his tie was knocked just a bit crooked. "Perhaps we should go in the house, Charlotte."

"Give me the keys," I said to Andrew. "Don't stand there looking so foolish."

I heard a shade being raised and Aunt Mayme was looking out the dining-room window. My heart was beginning to thump so loud I wondered if Uncle Melton, sitting close beside me, could hear it. "Andrew," I said, and my voice shook though I tried to keep it even, "give me the keys."

He opened the door quickly and slipped behind the wheel, pushing me over along the slick plastic seat-covers.

My shoulder nudged against Uncle Melton's starched coat.

"Andrew," I said, "I made up my mind."

He pulled the keys out of his breast pocket and drove the car back through the yard to the garage. "Now," he said, "let's go in the house."

He took hold of my arm, pulling me out after him. For one moment I caught hold of the steering wheel. "No."

With his other hand he lifted my fingers, gently enough. "Don't make me lose my temper, dear."

He kept hold of my arm as we started across the yard and Uncle Melton appeared on my other side. "Please," he said, "no scenes. It's too hot to be violent."

We went inside to the living-room, the three of us, three abreast, down the hall. They both kept hold of my arms, not roughly but very gallantly.

Cousin Roger was in the living-room. He was reading a heavy red book. Uncle Melton dropped my arm. "Roger," he said, "do you remember where we stored last year's orange wine?"

Cousin Roger took off his glasses and rubbed his bald head. "I reckon it was in the north corner of the cellar. We planning to use some?"

Uncle Melton winked at him. "We could be having a celebration tonight, if you could find it."

That got rid of Cousin Roger. After he found that bottle, he'd drink most of it; then he'd take himself upstairs to his room and lay himself out straight on his bed. And if anyone came into the room he'd swear up and down that he was dead and embalmed and he'd be buried on Sunday coming after the best wake the town had ever seen.

Andrew dropped my arm and took out his pipe. "Andrew Conners," I told him, so mad now that my voice shook, "you are the biggest coward I have ever known."

"Don't blame the boy, Charlotte," Uncle Melton said. "And don't make a scene. They give me a headache."

I sat down in the nearest chair. My face must have been bright red by this time, and with the lipstick smear down my chin I must have looked pretty silly, but I was furious and a little afraid too.

"I can see what you're doing," I told them. "One of you standing by the window and the other one by the door. And Aunt Mayme's just outside the other door."

Andrew laughed but did not move.

"I will tell Pamela."

Uncle Melton said softly: "That would be very foolish, child."

"That would be very very foolish, dear," Aunt Mayme said as she came into the room.

They looked much alike, the two of them, saying practically the same thing.

"Pamela does not need the money," Uncle Melton said.

"She has enough from her father," Aunt Mayme said.

"She is very old."

"She will die soon."

"She has enough to be more than comfortable."

"She would not be able to handle a large amount."

They kept talking like that, first one, then the other, so that I got dizzy twisting my head back and forth between them. All the while Andrew stood in front of me, not saying anything, just watching.

"We are only getting what is ours."

158

"Had she stayed away a little longer—"

"Things would have been settled this way."

"They are settled now."

My head began to hurt; it was hard for me to turn back and forth, so I stared straight ahead at Andrew.

"We're doing it for you and Andrew."

"For your children."

"But we don't have children," I said.

"But we will," Andrew said.

Uncle Melton said: "You've never met John Woodville."

Aunt Mayme said: "He's a nice man."

"We wanted you to meet him."

"I don't want to," I said, staring at Andrew.

"Wipe the lipstick from your chin," Aunt Mayme said, and held out a handkerchief.

"I've got a compact in my bag."

Andrew handed me the leather pouch. My head was going in wide, singing circles. Little sleep the night before; the long hot ride; the excitement. I put the lipstick on in a wavering line.

"That looks terrible," I said.

"It looks beautiful on you," Andrew said.

He was kneeling on the floor beside me, holding the ridiculous huge purse with all my junk inside. He moved and it rattled. At the shoulders his khaki shirt was wet through, and his face was shiny with perspiration.

"Do you want the money so very much?"

"Very much."

He had loved me very much; he had married me over the objections of his family: I remembered that.

"But some will go to Woodville."

"He deserves something," Uncle Melton said.

"For the three years of service to poor old sick Josephine," Aunt Mayme said.

"Yes," I said. "Yes."

"There isn't as much as we expected," Andrew said.

"And you dont have to worry about Pamela."

"Not about her. She'll be all right," Andrew said. "You know that."

His arm brushed across my head. He must have made a gesture to Uncle Melton and Aunt Mayme to leave the room. He slipped his arm around me. I was very tired and let my head rest on his chest. I could hear his heart: slow and regular. He knew I would agree. And so I did.

Andrew went back to camp the next day. After he had gone, I began to think what I had done. Without Andrew I was not so sure. Lying there in bed alone, in the half dark (we'd kept the shutter fast closed to hold in some of the night's coolness for a little part of the day), I began to wonder at what I had done. And I decided that I should go speak to Pamela.

I dressed and went to look for breakfast. Aunt Mayme was in the kitchen, reading the papers. She looked up and nodded; "Good morning." And I had the feeling she had been waiting there for me ever since Andrew left. I drank one cup of coffee quickly, almost choking, wondering whether I should simply go out without saying anything. In the end I decided to tell her and dare her to stop me.

I said: "How's Pamela?"

She took off her glasses and looked at me slowly. "She's

fine, I believe—though the weather is so oppressive for her."

"Really." I lifted my eyebrows as she herself would have done. "I thought she'd seen a lot hotter."

Aunt Mayme shrugged and didn't answer.

"I think," I said, "I'll drop in on her this evening when it's cooler."

She began to wipe the glasses slowly on her handkerchief. "You must be tired, dear. You should stay home."

I could feel the back of my neck getting red. I was angry—at her or maybe at myself. "I'm not tired," I said. "I think I'll go and see her right now."

Aunt Mayme put the glasses into their velvet case. "If you like, dear."

I went out. I went out with a lot of noise and a slamming of the front door. I walked down the street toward Pamela's house, but when I got there, I went on past her door. Then I remembered that when Aunt Mayme had looked at me, there had been a smile on her face.

She was right to smile. Because I wouldn't have any more walked in and told Pamela than she herself would, or Uncle Melton, or Andrew. And when I came back, hot and dizzy from the sun, she put one arm around me and said: "My dear," and hugged me. "After all, we are one family." And I knew she was right.

I told Andrew once: "I'm glad there isn't so very much. I'm glad there isn't the house."

And he kissed me on the cheek, lightly, and smiled. "You're just tired, honey."

And I let him think that. But I was glad, because that

small disappointment made the whole thing more honest somehow. Of course, it wasn't more honest and I knew it. But I was part of it along with Aunt Mayme and Uncle Melton and Andrew. I could say it was right, like they did, but I might just as well have told the sun to stop shining in that bright dry summer.

I think we've used the money very practically. We've a farm now, a beautiful place with some of the sweetest stretches of pasture I ever saw. We've a lovely house too, built like an old plantation manor, on the highest ground for miles around. Sometimes when we are coming home very late, and the night mists still hug to the ground, it is a fairy castle that will blow away with morning. But of course it won't. It is beautiful and solid. And we love it, all of us, Mayme and Melton and Andrew and I and even Cousin Roger, whom we took along because there wasn't anything else to do with him. He still gets drunk occasionally and is sure that he is dead. Mayme and Melton have changed very little; if anything, they have grown to look more alike. Andrew is out of the army; he threw away all his uniforms, but he keeps the Purple Heart and the Silver Star in a little glass frame hung on the wall next to his dresser. He's put on a little weight, but it's becoming.

And I don't change at all. Aunt Mayme tells me: "Dear, you look as young as the day you married."

So I tell her: "I take care of myself."

And she always shakes her head again. "And you keep your figure—even after Andrew and little Melton."

Pamela lives in town: the same little old-fashioned comfortable house Aunt Mayme and Uncle Melton found for her. She seems quite comfortable on the income from her father; year before last she bought the house. She's made very few changes in the six years: a new sink in the kitchen, and she's torn down the old warped cistern. She is content to live out the rest of her life. But I've noticed that she's feebler. The heat worries her; she uses a palmetto fan constantly now. And she stays in the house nearly all the time.

This morning I stopped in for a minute or two. We talked for a while and she made me a cup of jasmine tea. The supply she brought back from China seems to be without an end. Then I said that I must be leaving because there was a long drive before home.

She kissed me good-by and her lips were as dry and faint as her tea leaves. "It's nice to go home," she said. "It's the best part of being away." Like all old ladies, she is a little too sweet. "No matter where I was, I always wanted to come back here. It is so wonderfully peaceful to come home."

I drove faster than usual going home. And when the house finally came in sight, I felt relieved. It was as though I had expected it to be that fairy mist castle and blow away. But it was of timber and bricks and cement and it would be standing when I was dead. I parked the car and walked across the gravel court. For just a minute I thought I was going to faint, the sun was so hot.

Fever Flower

Summers, even the dew is hot. The big heavy drops, tad-pole-shaped, hang on leaves and stems and grass, lie on the face of the earth like sweat, until the spongy sun cleans them away. That is why summer mornings are always steamy. The windows of the Cadillacs parked in car ports are frosted with mist. By ten the dew is gone and the steam with it, and the day settles down to burn itself out in dry heat.

In the houses air-conditioning units buzz twenty-four hours a day. And colored laundresses grumble at the size of washes. And colored cooks work with huck towels tied around their necks and large wet spots on their black linen uniforms—until by mid-July they refuse to come in the mornings and fix any sort of breakfast. It is a mass move-ment. None of the white people can do anything about it. But then it is not serious. No one needs breakfast in sum-mer. Most people simply skip the meal; the men, those of them who have strict bosses, grumble through the morn-ings empty-stomached or gulp hasty midmorning coffee;

164

the women lie in bed late—until it is lunch time and the cooks have come. Nurses feed children perfunctory breakfasts: cold cereals and juices at eleven o'clock. Summer mornings no one gets up early.

By eight thirty Katherine Fleming was sitting alone in the efficient white and yellow tiled kitchen at breakfast: orange juice and instant coffee. She had somehow spilled the juice and she was idly mopping up the liquid from the stainless-steel counter top when the phone rang. Her hands were sticky when she picked up the receiver.

"Why, Jerry—" She swallowed the last of the coffee. "I really didn't think you'd be up this early. . . . Sure I'm all right."

She leaned her elbow on the counter, remembered the spilled juice and lifted her arm hastily, as she listened. She shook her head. "Let's not try lunch, honey. I'm supposed to run out and say hello to Mamma."

She listened another moment, frowning a bit with the beginnings of irritation. "Don't tease me, honey. I'm going because she's lonesome for me. I ought to, you know. Even if I'd rather be with you. And, anyway, there's tonight."

She listened a moment more, said good-by, and stood up, irritably ruffling the back of her hair with one hand.

It always annoyed her to lie. But it would never have done to tell Jerry Stevenson to his face that she did not want to see him; she felt she owed him that much, because he had been fun the night before. Last night she had adored him; this morning all that was left was a feeling of well-being. She stretched, arching her back. She felt wonderful, soft and rested and fine. He was part of last night; he would be part of tonight. But this sudden intrusion into the morning left her vaguely annoyed, though she knew she could forget about him.

Katherine Fleming went upstairs and dressed quickly: a summer suit of white linen, a pale-green blouse that would bring out the color of her eyes. She finished her make-up and studied herself in the mirror, nodding just a bit in approval: nice brown hair, very nice gray eyes, a figure Grable needn't have been ashamed of. And further-more, she told herself, she had years in her favor. She was twenty-five: she looked twenty-two. She picked up her handbag and went quickly down the hall to tell her daugh-ter good-by.

Four years ago Katherine had been married; two years ago she had been divorced. A house that was new and very modern, a daughter whose name was Maureen, and a siz-able check that came every month on the third: these were left of her marriage.

She did not regret anything. She did not look back on her marriage with anger or any feeling stronger than a kind of vague relief that it was finished at last. She was not angry with Hugh; she had never been. Not even when she heard of his remarriage to one of her college friends. Not even that last time when they had called it quits.

Hugh had sat quietly in the armchair over by the win-dow and listened while she told him that nothing between them was ever going to work. He sat facing her, his eyes lifted a little and focused on the spot of wall slightly above her head, so that he was at once looking at her and not seeing her. He had gray eyes, large ones, with lashes for a man ridiculously long and curly. In the light from the window the gray eyes turned shiny as silver and as hard. When she had finished, he got up and left without a word. He hadn't even stopped to pack. The next morning he called and told the maid to send his things to the hotel. Katherine remembered that the only thing she had felt was a kind of wonder that it had all been so easy.

She had never seen him again. But she was sure that had they met, she could have talked amicably with him. He, however, made very certain that they did not meet. Even on the one day a week when he came to see his daughter, she was not allowed to be in the house. His lawyers had insisted on that during the settlement. She was to have the child and a regular check; he was to have the one day a week when she would not be in the house.

Katherine Fleming walked quickly down the hall to tell her daughter good-by, her bag swinging idly from her fingers. A stupid arrangement, she thought, but then Hugh had been a strange fellow, full of odd ideas. One time he had got fascinated by sculpture. He had even considered lessons from Vittorio Manale, who was making a name for himself as one of the moderns. Hugh would always have the best of everything. But Hugh was also a practical man. He never could quite convince himself that money spent for lessons would have been well spent, so he never took any. But he never quite gave up the idea. He spent his Saturday afternoons—just about the only free time he had —in the museums, walking around and around the figures that interested him, figures in white marble, in polished

167

brown granite. He stared at them with his eyes half-shut, trying to imagine how they had been done.

He couldn't work in marble, of course: he couldn't have used a chisel. But he always had been a marvelous whittler —he kept a row of different knives in his desk drawer— so he went to work in soap. That was when Katherine first knew him, the summer she finished college. The first piece he did was a dog, with the ears of a spaniel and the body of a terrier. He had given the little bit of carved soap to her mother. (Her mother still kept it on the whatnot shelves along with the other things of china and straw and the little basket of true Italian marble that they had sent her from Naples on their honeymoon.)

Katherine thought the whole thing was more than a little silly. A grown man, in his late thirties, and as handsome as Hugh Fleming, ought not to be whittling like a boy. But there were many things about him that were boyish: his clothes dropped all over the room at night (even four years in the navy had not cured him of that habit); the quick brushing back of his hair when he was angry; the open joy in new money or a new car or a new house or a new and beautiful wife. Or his whittling. But then Katherine had to admit that some of the things he made were lovely. As he caught the knack, his products came to have the look of marble; one in particular, a woman's head. He said it was she; he had her sit as a model for him, while he worked, but it did not look much like her. She was not that beautiful: her features were somewhat irregular, her eyes not large enough to be so striking, her hair not so perfectly waved. His work had the perfection of line and contour of the face on a cameo. Perhaps, though, he really saw her like that. After all, by the time the figure was completed they were engaged. In any case, that bit of her was undoubtedly the finest thing he ever did. After they had separated she dropped the head into a pan of water and watched its slow disintegration, which took several days.

A crazy idea, Katherine thought, having me leave the house. But like him, she admitted. She went into her daughter's room. Maureen was three, but the room in which she slept was not a nursery. It was a young girl's room with pale-blue ruffled organdy curtains and an organdy skirt around the vanity table and a blue-chintz-lined closet; a long mirror on one wall—the extra wide kind in which one surveys an evening dress's lacy folds; small colored balls of perfume atomizers: red and gold, empty and waiting for the scent their owner would choose when she got old enough to care for such things.

Katherine had insisted that the room be furnished in this manner a few months ago. She did not quite realize why, why it had seemed very necessary to her that the changes be made at once. Perhaps it was only her longing to get through the awkward growing years, the child years.

Perhaps an unconscious admission that the only real contact between herself and Maureen would come during the four or five years of the girl's first beauty, years that would be terminated by her marriage. They would not see each other very often: Maureen must go away to college; at home her time would be occupied

by her friends. Yet for mother and daughter it would
be the happiest time, although an uneasy one, for they
would both realize that they did not really like each
other very much.

Katherine leaned over and kissed her daughter. "I'm
leaving now, honey."

Maureen stared at her solemnly. " 'By." She had been
drinking orange juice (briefly Katherine recalled her own
breakfast): her upper lip with the soft invisible hairs now
sported an orange mustache.

"Messy." Katherine picked up a napkin from the tray
beside the bed. "Now wipe your mouth."

Solemnly Maureen scrubbed the napkin across her lips,
then turned her attention to the bowl of cereal in front of
her.

"She's eating, ma'am," Annie said, rolling pale-blue eyes
behind her rimless glasses. "And it isn't easy to get her to
eat in the morning."

Katherine shrugged. She had come in at the wrong
time; she admitted the mistake to herself. "I'm glad her
appetite's better," she said sweetly. "I was worried."

"Yes, ma'am," Annie said. Her voice had no inflection to
give the words a second and ironic meaning.

She's angry, Katherine thought, because I interrupted
the routine. And now she's thinking I don't care a bit what
happens to my daughter. But I do. I do.

Then because she did not quite believe herself, she
leaned over and kissed Maureen on top of the head.
"Good-by, honey. I'll see you tonight, I reckon."

She did not say good-by to Annie. She turned and picked up her gloves and bag from the chair and left quickly.

There was nothing else to do. She had to be out of the house. And she didn't like going downtown: shopping, eating lunch alone, going to a movie. And she didn't like to go with any of the women she knew. What they thought showed so plainly on their stupid faces (and Katherine was not stupid by any means). And what they thought was a combination of admiration and pity: she has got rid of her husband; she looks happy over it; and today by court order she cannot go home; it is her husband's house again. Katherine saw these things plainly in their faces and she did not go out with these women who were her best friends and whom she liked on other days of the week.

It was not that she minded being out. Not at all. Her friends and her club work took up all her time. But she could have gone home, had she wanted. On these days she could not, not and keep the settlement. Hugh would be strict on that point, she knew. Katherine was furious, but she was too sensible to object. So she usually drove the thirty-five miles over to Barksfield and visited her mother. It seemed the best thing to do.

After a few more years she would find that she much preferred a solitary day in town. After a few years she would find a positive pleasure in being alone.

Perhaps that was why she never remarried. Not that she did not have a chance to. She was a very beautiful woman. She dressed superbly; she went out a great deal and had hundreds of friends. She could have remarried a dozen times, but she said, No, thank you, in a polite way that left no room for argument or doubt. She did not take lovers either, except in the first few years after the divorce, for she was confused then and afraid of loneliness. But she freed herself from them when she realized she could be happiest alone. Each day she experienced a great pleasure when she woke to her beautiful appointed house, her beautiful daughter. Her own lovely body delighted her. She liked to lie in the tub and feel the water move over her and pour half a vial of bath oil over her shoulders. She also found that it was a delicious pleasure to walk around her room naked and feel her body move. She had a perfect body; she was a superb animal. But she was not quite human. She did not need anyone.

Hugh Fleming unlocked the front door and came into the hall. He still kept his door key, though he used it only one day in the week. He kept it in the leather case along with his other keys—the car, the office, the other house. It was a silver key with his initials on the head, the sort that had to be specially made. Katherine had given it to him for Christmas the first year of their marriage. He folded up the leather case, put it in his pocket, and went upstairs to see his daughter. He was earlier than usual: she was just finishing her breakfast.

"I have not done a thing to getting her dressed, Mr. Fleming," Annie told him, lifting her eyebrows in polite annoyance. "You came on us a bit early."

Hugh picked up his daughter, who hugged him delightedly, one hand grabbing his ear, the other holding his tie. "How's my girl?" he said. "How's my big girl?"

She giggled in her thin high-pitched voice and reached for his coat pocket where he always kept a present for her. She let herself hang limp across his arm while she reached into his left-hand pocket, then straightened up, triumphantly holding a green and white bead necklace.

"Now, that is pretty for sure," Annie said. "And isn't he a nice daddy to be remembering you?"

Hugh brushed the rumpled brown hair with his fingertips and twisted it into ringlets. He was holding his daughter, he thought. It was hard to realize that sometimes, she looked so much like her mother.

The awkward squarish child body in his arms squirmed and shifted; a little hand dug into the cloth of his coat as Maureen climbed up to sit atop his shoulder. Tenderness, a great protecting tenderness, burst its soft petals. "I'll give her the bath, Annie. You go start the water."

"Sure, she splashes like a baby whale, Mr. Fleming," Annie said warningly. "And you'll be ruining your suit."

"She's my daughter." He hugged Maureen tighter and she squealed a little at the sudden pressure. "To hell with the suit. I want to."

Annie lifted her eyebrows slightly. She would have given Mr. Fleming the same lecture on blaspheming and evil words that she gave her nephews but for one fact: he paid her salary. So she went and filled the tub and spread the towels and handed Mr. Fleming Maureen's slip and panties. "I will leave her dress on the bed." She spoke with dignity, her conscience still smarting under his affront. "It would only be wilting up in the steaming bathroom."

"Okay," said Hugh, not noticing the iciness of her tone. "Come on, honey," he told Maureen, "your old man's going to give you a bath."

Contrary to Annie's dour prediction, Maureen did not splash in the tub. She was a bit awed at the unaccustomed turn of events and sat very still, staring up into her father's face with neither anger nor friendliness but only a kind of surprise. Hugh washed his baby carefully, an aching pleasant tenderness in his heart. It was not a usual feeling for him; he had not experienced it often before and it never lasted long. It would fade and be replaced by the vaguely angry, dissatisfied stirring with which he usually viewed his daughter. It was not that he disliked her. Not at all. He was being a very good father to her; he was supporting her well. And that was the point—although Hugh would never have admitted it. He was a businessman, one of the shrewdest; he knew a good deal when he saw one. He was spending quite a bit of money on his daughter and he could not quite convince himself that it was worth it.

Of course, it was, in the long run. Maureen turned out to be a lovely young woman. She had a truly magnificent wedding, and Hugh, circulating among the guests, his head buzzing a little from the champagne, finally realized how fine an investment his daughter had been. After all, it was none of his fault that the man she married turned out to be no good, even though he was handsome and came from a fine family.

At her wedding Hugh could be happy in his investment, and it was a great satisfaction to him.

But it was not the same sort of pleasure he felt that morning when against the sour disapproving looks of Annie he bathed and dressed his daughter. And that emotion, perhaps because more rare, is more precious.

They went to the park that particular morning. "Just like I promised you last week," he reminded her. She stared at him without understanding, her dark eyes puzzled: she had long ago forgotten his promise. For a moment he was annoyed that she had not looked forward to it, as he had done. Then he laughed and told her: "You're only a baby yet," and hugged her soft little body. And all day he was very careful of her.

Toward the end of the afternoon, just as they were walking back to the parked car, they passed the tropical gardens. Through the glass door Maureen caught sight of the huge silver reflecting globe and pointed to it with an insistent nod.

"You don't want to go in there, honey," Hugh told her. But she was already hanging on the chrome handle, trying to pull open the glass door.

They went inside. Hugh had always found the air too humid to be comfortable; he found himself taking shallow quick breaths, panting almost. But Maureen loved the heat and the dampness. She smiled up at him, her dark eyes impish and full of life. She tugged at his hand and would have run off, had he not tightened his grip. Finally she stood on tiptoe, swaying back and forth, her nose crinkling with the heavy scents.

He walked slowly up and down the paths with her, past broad wax-leaved plants dripping moisture, and heavy pollened red flowers, and vines carefully propagated by hand and bound up with straw. And then the orchids, a whole wall of them with their great spreading petals reaching into the heat. "See," Hugh told Maureen. "Pretty. Just the color of your dress." The blooms were forced to grow to gigantic size in half the time; they were beautiful and exotic and they did not last.

"Now let's go," Hugh said, for he was beginning to be very tired himself. He picked up Maureen and carried her to the car. She protested, crying, and then suddenly fell asleep. He watched her with faint stirrings of the tenderness whose great upsurge he had experienced that morning.

And it was the last time he would have such a joy in his daughter, Maureen. That afternoon his wife, his second wife, whose name was Sylvia, decided not to go for a drive as she usually did. Even with a cape she thought she looked just too big; and with the anxiety of the novice, she was desperately afraid that her baby would come on her suddenly and indecently in a field or on a road. In the late afternoon she called Hugh and asked him to come home.

By that time Hugh's pleasant affection for his daughter had worn off and had left only the sense of viewing a not particularly successful venture. They had just come back and were still in the front hall when the phone rang. Hugh shifted Maureen to his left arm and answered it himself, saying yes quickly.

Maureen was still dozing. He carried her upstairs to the room her mother had designed with expensive good taste. Then he left quickly, calling out a brief good-by to Annie, and thinking only of Sylvia, wondering if anything could go wrong. (Sylvia bore him three more children: three boys after the first girl. All of them grew up prosperous and healthy. She was a very fine wife for him. And after his death—she found him one evening, sitting on the porch, erect but not breathing—she discovered that she did not want to live either.)

Annie left Maureen to sleep undisturbed in her clothes. The house was very quiet and empty: Hugh had gone and Katherine had not returned. (She would be just now beginning the drive back, her face white and strained from the effort of being polite, her make-up a little streaked by the heat.) Outside on the dry lawns sprinklers were beginning to throw out fan-shaped streams of water.

Annie went down the hall to her own room, leaving the door ajar in case Maureen should call. She opened the blinds and sat down by the window, the late afternoon heat against her face, and, taking a stiff bound Bible from the table, began to read. She was a very religious woman and read in the Bible every day for a half-hour. She did not like the Old Testament; she could never quite convince herself that its heroes (with their bloody swords and many wives) were men of God. And although she always began the New Testament at the Gospel of St. Matthew—she felt that she should begin at the beginning —she found that she preferred the epistles. (She could make no sense of the Apocalypse at all.) Today it was Paul to the Galatians. "Walk in the spirit and you shall not fulfil the lusts of the flesh. . . . The fruit of the Spirit is joy." She heard the front door open, then slam shut, as Katherine came home.

Annie stood up. Joy. The lusts of the flesh. The chaff which shall be cast in the fire. Hell fire. Which was like summer sun, but stronger seven times. In her mind she saw clearly: Katherine and Hugh revolving slowly in a great sputtering, leaping fire while she stood on the edge, watching, dressed in some sort of luminous stuff which all the righteous wore in the hereafter, holding Maureen by the hand.

(Annie died while Maureen was on her honeymoon, just a week after there'd been a card from Hawaii signed: "Love from your little girl, Maureen.")

No one suspected then that Maureen's husband would turn into the sort of fellow he did. No one guessed that she would have two more ex-husbands when, as a middle-aged, strikingly handsome woman, she took a very beautiful, very expensive apartment for one on the west coast. . . .

Annie found Katherine sprawled on the couch in the living-room. "Is something wrong, ma'am?" she asked politely.

"I've had some day," Katherine said. "Lord, but my head aches."

"Maureen is sleeping." Annie stood with her hands in the pockets of her white apron, holding herself stiffly erect. "She is very tired."

"That's fine," Katherine said. "I knew her father would take good care of her." She rubbed her temples gently. "Annie, go get me an aspirin. What a day I've had!"

"Yes, ma'am," Annie said.

Katherine stretched herself on the couch, one arm across her eyes. "You damn old Puritan," she said. "See if the air-conditioner's working. It's hot as hell."

Later that evening Maureen woke, fretful, and began to cry. Lying on her bed in the orchid pinafore she had worn to the park, she began to cry—softly at first, then louder so that Annie could hear.

"You eat something wrong, lamb?" Annie asked. "Did that father of yours feed you something wrong?"

Maureen spread out her arms and legs and stretched, as if she would grow suddenly, grow to fill the bed, which was too big for her.

"We'll take off your dress, lamb. And you'll rest better."

But Maureen shook her head and dug her fingers into the bed. The orchid dress was wet through in spots with perspiration.

"Annie won't move you, then, lamb. But we'll cool off this old room for you." She walked over to the door and glanced at the thermostat dial: it was as low as it could go. "You're running a fever, lamb."

Annie stood looking down at her. "My pretty little one. My pretty, pretty one."

Annie rubbed her hands together slowly. "Sure," she said, "and you look like a young lady already, there."

Maureen did not answer. She lay on the bed, staring up at the ceiling, her eyes wide.

"Don't look like that, lamb." Annie moved over and sat on the edge of the bed. Half under her breath she began a lullaby, a soft, plaintive little air, with a wide tonal range—too wide, for her voice faltered on the high notes. But the Gaelic words came out soft and clear:

> *"My little lady, sleep*
> *And I will wish for you: A love to have,*
> *A true heart,*
> *A true mind,*
> *And strong arms to carry you away."*

Her fingers brushed away the hair from Maureen's forehead: it was damp and sticking to the skin in little wisps. The child pulled away. The sun had left her cheeks flushed—bright color, high across the cheekbones. Fever sparkled her eyes and enlarged them. Tiredness gave lines to her face and shadows and the illusion of age.

"Sure," Annie repeated, "and you look like a young lady, a lovely young lady already, there."

Maureen lay on her side, the clear lines of her profile showing against the pink spread. She did not turn again: she had stopped crying. And lay there, beautiful and burning.

The Way of a Man

For five years the boy lived with his old father in the house on Bayou St. Philippe.

It was a good house, snug and tight against the brief cold winds of the tumbled gray January sky and the hard quick squalls of August. The house was built on good solid ground, a high bank of shells, that stuck up out of the marsh like the back of an alligator: a great alligator extending nearly two miles from the state highway, winding and twisting out into the Gulf marsh where the tides were salty and sea fish came up into the bayou mouths. The house stood at the end of the winding shell ridge, farthest away from the highway, the end where Bayou St. Philippe made a circle in from the east and let its slow yellow-green waters into the Gulf.

It was a comfortable clapboard house with one room and a lean-to kitchen. Inside was a double bed; a cylinder-shaped oil stove for winter; and a chest that the man had brought from New Orleans once when he was young and had gone into the city for a spree: a low chest and of some light wood—cedar or maple, it was hard to tell after so many years. And tacked carefully to the wall over the chest was a colored lithograph of the Virgin, tall and serene in a bright blue gown; from the same nail dangled a black-bead rosary, its cross missing.

None of the walls were painted—inside or out—but time had given the boards a uniform black stain. Outside, also blacked by time and weather, were racks for drying nets, the small kind that a single man could handle, for he always fished alone; and racks for drying the muskrat pelts when he trapped during the season.

The boy, whose name was William, had been born in this house and until he was five years old had played among the racks and breathed the smell of nets and of drying pelts and watched wind shadows roll over the marsh grass.

He had been born in the house—one hot September afternoon. The sky was a still high arch of bright blue: the sun slid down it like a silver dime. In the south a mass of thunderclouds sat low on the horizon; the waters of the Gulf moved with the peculiar nervous tremor of a storm on them somewhere.

He was not long being born. His mother cried quietly and briefly in the hot afternoon, saw that her child was a man, and fell asleep. No one seemed particularly concerned. When the work was done, his grandmother rolled down the sleeves of her long-sleeved cotton print dress, nodded to her daughter, and began the walk back across the marsh. As she went she saw the old man who was her daughter's husband coming back from a day's fishing.

When the boy was two, his mother left. She was a young

woman, not more than twenty then, with a long lithe body and quick darting eyes. She had married the old man because of two mistakes. She thought he was too old to give her a child and she thought that he was rich. Within a year she had a child growing in her body. And she never saw his money.

A government pension check came regularly each month on the third. They held it for him at the post office over in Port Allen; he walked in to fetch it. He had done this for so many years that the two men who sorted the mail looked specially for his envelope—light brown with the blue check showing through the strip of cellophane—and put it up on a little shelf beside the general-delivery window to wait for him.

"Say, Uncle," one of them asked him once, "how come the government's sending you money?"

The old man took the check in his knotted black fingers. "Account I was in the war."

"Which war?" the man said. "There's been a lot of them."

The old man blinked his eyes slowly.

"It couldn't a been the Civil War," the white man said. He had hold of one end of the envelope. "You ain't that old."

His partner came and leaned on the counter beside him. "I bet it was the Spanish War, wasn't it, Uncle?"

"You in the fighting, Uncle?" the other one asked.

"I done press the pants and shine the shoes for them that's done the fighting," the old man said with dignity and pulled his envelope from the white man's hand.

Holding his check carefully in two fingers, he always went directly across the street to the bank to cash it. When he had the bills in his hand, he would buy food for the month and fishing gear or some new traps, and on his way home he'd pick up a jug of corn likker.

That was it. His young wife never saw his money. She was convinced he had hidden it somewhere; she spent days searching and found nothing. But she was certain he was rich.

It wasn't any life for a young woman, a pretty woman. One day she was gone. When the old man came home, there was only his son in the house, a fuzzy-headed black boy with bright brown eyes and a constant smile. The old man called for his wife once and walked once around the house, looking over the marsh on all sides. Then he went in and began supper himself. The boy followed him inside, climbed on the edge of the table, and waited for food.

The next morning the old man sat in the sun and mended his nets. The boy crouched on the edge of the bayou and tried to catch the little water lizards with his hands.

William was young and agile as a black monkey and noisy. And his father was very old and slow. And so one day the man took down the boy's cap from the nail where it had been hanging and put it on the nervous kinky head, and folded the boy's clothes in a brown paper bag. Then he took his son by the hand and walked into town to give him back to his mother. He stopped only once—in the grocery to ask where she was living—and then went directly to the house. There he knocked on the door and she herself came to answer it—a young woman wearing a pink print dress stretched tight across full hips and heavy breasts. The old man pointed down to the boy and dropped his hand and turned around without a word and walked away. The woman looked down at her son—at his thin long black limbs and his thin quick monkey face—and then up at the broad heavy stooped back of the man as he walked away. And she asked her son: "Don't he feed you none, the old man?"

The boy nodded and grinned. The upper row of his front teeth was missing.

"He can afford to, him," the woman said. "He can sure afford to, him." Then she turned and walked back into the house, leaving the door open behind her. Her son followed her, stopping to pick up the brown paper parcel of clothes that his father had dropped on the steps.

That was how he came to his mother, after his father had shown that he would have no more to do with him. And he lived with her until he was fourteen and the police caught him stealing tires. Then he was sent up to the north part of the state to the reform school.

Three years later he was back knocking on his mother's door. And she opened it and stood leaning against the doorjamb studying him. "You a man grown," she said. "I used to could look down at you and you was a boy. But now I got to look up because you a man."

"Reckon so," he said.

He was a man grown. Not tall but broad: his father's build. There were such muscles across his back that he

185

almost seemed to be stooping. He had the same quick nervous face of his childhood, the same nervous up-twitching of the left corner of the mouth.

Because he was a man, he did not live in his mother's house. She fixed him a bed in the kitchen (her house had only two rooms), a pillow and a blanket rolled up to be out of the way; and she kept it there in case the officer who was in charge of his parole should come around looking. He did come occasionally—a slight dark Negro, whose dark-blue police uniform did not fit him, whose name was Matthew Pettis. The first time he came she met him at the door and asked him in and offered him some coffee and said that her son was working on the oyster boats because he was so strong—for all that he was just seventeen, he was a man grown. She showed him the bed. And Pettis nodded and rubbed his black kinky hair, and his little shiny black eyes danced all over the room.

The next time Pettis came, William happened to be there and he and his mother sat side by side on the bed in the front room and answered yes sir and no sir to the questions and looked with quiet brown eyes into Pettis's restless quick ones.

When the policeman had gone, William stood up and stretched and pulled on his cap and sauntered slowly out of the house. His mother did not notice he was gone until she called to ask him if he wanted anything to eat. She opened the front door and called for him out into the street. Then she went back and began to eat herself. She did not think of him again. She did not know where he had gone or where he was living. She did not wonder about it. A man could make his own way.

He was living in Bucktown, a double line of colored houses strung out along a dirt road and only a couple of miles from the oyster docks. He had a girl there, short, plump, and high-brown colored. Her name was Cynthia Lee. She was always laughing, always showing her short square teeth and her dull red gums. She worked at the shrimp plant that was a little farther down the shore. He'd worked there too, once, when he'd first come back. He'd quit because the work was too light, for a man. And he went to the oyster boats, where the pay was better and the work was enough to try the muscles of a strong back.

He'd been saying hello to her for over a week before he got the nerve to ask her to have a beer with him on Saturday night. She said, "I reckon so," with her quick bright grin and a little jerk of her head.

They went to the Smile Inn, which was the closest bar for Negroes, and they had three beers each, and then, because it was Saturday and the place got very crowded and men kept bumping into her round little body and saying: "Excuse me," with a grin, he pointed to the door.

"It too crowded," he said. "I don't study getting all mashed up by people none."

She just laughed and pushed her way to the door.

He walked her home. It was night and there weren't any lights along the dirt road. They stumbled in ruts and held on to each other, laughing. The moon came up finally over the straggling thin pines and they could see the road in front of them.

"I ain't used to coming home this late," she said.

"Ain't you?"

"No," she said. "Ma'll give me hell."

"Seems like you could handle her with no trouble." He rubbed his chin with the back of his hand. "Seems like you'd better be worrying about your pa."

She grinned; in the uncertain moon glow her little square teeth flashed white in the darkness of her face. "He done picked up and gone a long time ago."

"That right?" William said.

"Ma don't miss him none." She laughed again and stumbled in a deep rut. He caught her around the waist.

"Cynthia Lee," he said, "seems like you can't even walk none. You sure must be drunk."

"Me?" Her laugh went up and down the dark. "I can't ever hold no likker."

He tightened his arm. "I reckon I know one kind you could." He kissed her. Her square white teeth clamped on his lower lip. He hissed with the pain and slapped her away from him. She stumbled backwards and sat down. Her body made a soft sound against the ground. He rubbed his lip for a few moments and then bent over her. He had thought she was crying; but she was only laughing softly.

It was settled after that. He lived with her in her mother's house in Bucktown. And since her mother was a big fat jolly woman who worked as a cook in one of the white houses on the beach, and who thought William was a fine handsome man, things went well.

One evening after work he went out to see his father. He had not been there since he was a little boy and he wondered if he remembered the way. He began to walk down the highway, the highway that led into the city. It was a dry time. The wheels of the cars on the asphalt strip stirred up dust and he coughed and covered his nose and mouth with one hand. He rubbed the other hand across his face and felt the grit of the dust on it. He pulled a handkerchief out of his pocket and wiped his face carefully, for he knew that his skin was black and that the light dust would streak it. And he did not want to appear before his father with a face streaked up like the clowns he had seen in a circus once. (At the reform school once for good behavior they had given him a pass to the circus and had let him go alone. He had been so fascinated and dazed by all that he had seen that he had returned to the school, forgetting his plan to break parole and run away. When it was too late, he remembered with a sick feeling in his stomach. He was calling himself all the names he could think of, whispering them clearly to himself, when the chaplain, a fat little man with a bald pink head, came and shook his hand and told him that he was proud of him, that he had behaved like a man.)

When William saw the white shell road leading off the highway, he knew that he would remember the way, even if it had been years since his father had taken him by the hand and, walking so fast that he had to run and stumble after, had brought him over to his mother.

The shell road ran south and ended with a small wharf where some white fishermen kept their boats dragged up above the tides on slips of rough wood. Just before the road's end a footpath went off straight eastward through the waist-high grasses that moved in any wind. At the end was Bayou St. Philippe and his father's house. Long before he got close, he could see the house on the ridge of high ground, a square little weathered building with a slanting lean-to for a kitchen and a slanting little pile of firewood. Though it was warm spring weather, his father had built a little fire outside on the grass-free stretch of ground. He was sitting alongside it now on a straight-back cane chair he had brought from inside.

William remembered the chair; he was sure it was the same one that had been there when he was a boy. He remembered trying to climb the ladder back and stumbling to the floor with the chair over him like a tent. And his father had pulled him free with one hand and with the other had given him a slap across the head that made his eyes blur and his ears sing. William stopped and stared at the old man and wondered how he had been able to hit so hard.

He wore tennis shoes; the old man had not heard him come up. He had not lifted his head from the redfish he was cleaning. Very slowly, eyes squinting with the effort, he was removing the fish scales.

"Hi," said William.

The old man looked at him slowly over the smoke and

haze of the fire. Slowly he put the fish back in the wicker basket at his side.

"You remember me?" William asked, and stepped closer, his hands jammed down in his pockets, wondering if he had got all the road dust off his face, for he did not want his father to laugh at him.

The old man looked at him slowly, up and down, without answering. His face in the firelight in the dusk was very old and very lined. Even the blackness of his skin was beginning to gray—like a film of dust was gathering over it.

"You remember me?" William repeated.

The old man nodded slowly, very slowly. "You a man grown now. A man grown."

"I past seventeen," William said, and squared his shoulders.

He stepped up to the fire and took the fish out of the basket and held out his hand for the scaling knife, and when the old man gave it to him he finished the cleaning in a few quick movements. "I been working on the oyster boats," he said.

"I worked the boats," his father said, and folded his hands together and rested his chin on them.

"You did?" William studied his father. He was a big man, big as his son, or he had been once. He was stooped now so that he always seemed to be huddling into himself.

The old man took the cleaned fish and went inside. William picked up the chair and followed him.

"You want I should put it on to cook?" William asked.

The old man shook his head.

"You ain't changed nothing," William said. The room was just as he remembered it. He opened the wood shutter on the side that looked out on the bayou and, beyond that, a quarter mile away, the Gulf. "It's rough out there," he said. "It's gonna be a rough night."

It began to rain while they were eating. "First come in over a month." His father did not stop chewing, his jaws moved slowly up and down.

"Lay the dust a little," William said.

In one corner the roof leaked; water ran down the wall. But neither of them noticed. The old man went and lay on his bed and almost immediately fell asleep. William stretched on the floor, pillowed his head on a pile of nets, listened to the rain, and thought about his girl until he fell asleep too.

The water that had leaked in through the roof ran down the smooth boards of the floor and touched his cheek. He lifted his head, rubbing at his face, and saw that it was morning.

The door was open. William rolled over and peered out of it. His father was standing there right on the edge of the bayou, looking down toward its mouth and the Gulf.

When William stood up he saw the skiff too: overturned, half awash, caught just inside the bayou. He jammed hands in his pockets and looked around. The squalls of the past night had not changed the appearance of the marsh; but then the grasses never changed from summer to winter. Even after a hurricane had whipped through them they rose fresh and untouched.

"I plain don't see nobody," he told his father.

The old man swung his head slowly back and forth as if he were looking for somebody.

"Look," William said, "iffen you don't want that boat, I sure enough do."

The old man kept his skiff pulled up alongside the house. William shoved it down into the water. Then quickly he got the oars, which were leaning against the wall; and when he turned he found that his father was sitting in the boat waiting.

"That all right with me," William said. "You just plain remember that my boat."

"Who done seen it?" his father said. "I plain ask you."

"That don't matter." William picked up the oars and fitted them into the locks. "I the one to get it in, and it mine."

"I plain ask you: who done seen it first?"

"Jesus," William said. "I plain telling you: that mine."

His father did not answer. He did not seem to hear.

"I plain telling you," William said. "I done spoke out first."

He began to row down to the overturned skiff. The water was rough and occasionally he felt a wet slap in his face—cool for all the warmth of the day. As he rowed he stared up at the sky, which was low and hazy, and thought about the things he could do with a boat of his own. After a coat of paint nobody would recognize it.

"Look," his father said. "They got a net out."

He lifted his oars and rested them and turned his head.

Strands of net were caught across the skiff and a few feet out were five colored cork floats.

"That net ain't gonna be worth nothing," his father said.

"Jesus," William told him, "I ain't wanting that net. I plain wanting the boat."

His father stared at him. His old face was lined with determination. "Who seen it first?"

"I ain't arguing," William said. "I telling you. That mine."

They came alongside the skiff. Their own prow nosed into the reeds. The old man reached out and touched the other hull, tapping it softly with his fingers. Using one of the oars for a pole, William pushed against it.

"Jesus," he said. "She's fast. She caught up fast."

"She ain't gonna come loose that way," his father said.

"I know that, man." William felt his ears get hot with anger. "I plain know that."

"There ain't no way but get out and push her off."

William stood up and walked down to the prow of the skiff. With the oar he tested the depth of the water. "Jesus," he said when he lifted the oar, "that near waist deep."

He took the pack of cigarettes out of his shirt pocket and put it carefully in a dry place under the seat. Then he swung himself over the side. "I only doing this," he told his father, "account of it my boat. I gonna get it and it mine."

His father did not answer.

"I don't want no trouble with you," William said.

His father did not appear to hear.

William looked at him and knew that he would have trouble and did not care.

The water came to his waist, and it was cold. He felt his clothes hamper his movements and he wished he could have taken them off. But there might be jellyfish about, and even though he knew that their red stinging marks were harmless he was afraid of them.

And because he was afraid and did not want to be, he splashed noisily and quickly around to the other skiff. The bayou floor was a tangled mass of seaweed; he stumbled and his face touched the water. He spluttered and wiped the green weed taste away with the back of his hand. He saw that the stern of the boat was caught on a mound of sand; he climbed up beside it, pushing down the reeds. The water scarcely came to his ankles here.

He stopped and looked at his father, who was sitting without moving and watching him.

"I the one who pushed this loose," William said, "you remember."

The old man blinked his eyes slowly.

William said: "You ain't strong enough to push this off."

The eyes kept blinking at him.

"I got this, so it mine. Man's got a right to what he can get."

His father still did not answer. William felt his ears sing with anger. He bent and hooked his fingers under the stern handles, lifting and pushing. The muscles across his shoulders and back tensed against his shirt. He heard the wet cloth tear as the boat floated free.

They towed the skiff back up the bayou. "There's net all over her," the old man said.

"She pulls heavy," William said.

On the shore William sat down and began to take off his shoes. He shook them and stood them carefully aside to dry out. His father could pull up the skiff, he thought.

He noticed something strange. For a minute he wasn't sure what it was. Then he realized: the quiet. Before, up to a minute before, there had been the sounds of his father moving about the skiff. Then suddenly everything stopped. He lifted his head abruptly and saw his father standing there, his back to him, and looking down at the skiff. And William sat where he was, wiping his face slowly with one hand, and stared at the skiff they had found.

It was right side up now. And he saw that there were more nets tangled around it than he had thought. And through their black crisscross he saw a yellow dress and white skin.

He got to his feet slowly and walked over and stood beside his father and looked down at the snarl of black net —and the girl tangled in it, caught in it, lying there, face down on the shells, one arm pulled up, twisted and broken over her head.

"Sweet Jesus," William said. His heart was beating so fast he could hardly talk. "Sweet Jesus Christ."

"She caught up under the seats," his father said.

"She been to a party," William said very slowly. She was wearing an evening dress, bright yellow, with a full skirt that the water had shredded and wrapped around her legs.

William looked down at her and rubbed his chin and fought down the sickness in his throat. "Maybe she done took too much to drink and went out fishing for a joke."

"That might could be," his father said.

She had red hair, short red hair, bright in the sun. The yellow dress had fallen to her waist, and her back and shoulders shone white and slender. He had never seen such white skin.

There was a quivering in his stomach, but he said calmly, the way a man should: "I done reckon she went out cause she got a little too much, and the storm caught her up and killed her."

"That might could be," his father said.

There was one thing a man had to do. William pulled his heavy knife from his pocket and went to work cutting through the nets, slowly. The tips of his fingers rubbed against the yellow taffeta underskirt. He stared at the white curve of her back and saw that the skin was not so perfect. It had been torn in some places, but the water had washed all the blood away.

He cut through the last of the nets and folded up the knife and put it away and sat back on his heels and tried to get courage to turn her over. He had seen the face of the drowned before.

His father's black old hand took her shoulder and turned her. She was not quite stiff yet; he let her fall on her back. William jerked his head aside and closed his eyes so that he should not see. He got to his feet, stumbling, and walked away.

He heard his father say: "Ain't you a man grown?" But

he kept walking until he got to the house and sat down on the steps.

"A man's got a call not to look at some things," he said aloud. His breath was coming short and quick. When he'd been little and breathed like that, he'd been crying. But he was not crying now.

A man didn't have to look at some things just to prove he was a man. "A man's got no call like that," he said aloud.

He could imagine what her body would look like. The picture had flashed in his mind when he saw his father turn her over, even though he shut his eyes so that he would not see. The picture came into his mind and stayed there—her body shining white and perfect, shining wet and dead.

He felt dizzy suddenly. His head kept going in wide swinging circles, circles that left streaks of color behind them. He reached down both hands and held tightly to the steps. But that did not help any. He lifted both hands and took hold of his head. He held the outside of his head steady, but the inside behind his eyes kept turning.

He was almost afraid . . . he did not know what was happening to him. Then his head was all right. He opened his eyes. And lifted his head and even looked over at the shore where his father had stood. He saw that the girl's boat was still there, but his father's boat was gone. He stood up and saw his father out at the bayou's mouth. He saw the yellow of the dress too, and then his father changed the course of the boat and began to row southward, paralleling the shoreline. William sat down again and listened. And although he knew better, he felt that if he listened hard enough he could hear the splash when his father found a spot that was far enough away and pushed the girl's body over.

"A man's got no call to do some things," he said aloud. "Iffen he don't want to." He straightened up, folded his arms and felt the muscles of his back stiffen. A man had muscles like that.

He sat and stared at the ground that was bare of grass and that last night's rain had crisscrossed with thin little lines. He sat and thought about the things a man could do. And gradually he lifted his eyes until he was staring across the uncertain ground, the marsh, and the straight grasses that moved in the slightest wind.

Finally he heard his father come back. When he turned around, the old man had his skiff up on the bank and was standing looking at the other one. He held his chin in one wrinkled black hand as he studied the boat.

William got up slowly and walked over to him. "It done take you a long while."

"I done went quite a ways." The hand kept rubbing the chin, the thin black chin with the irregular tufts of white whiskers.

William felt in his shirt pocket for the cigarettes, remembered where they were, and walked over to the boat to look for them.

He had put the pack under the bow seat. He remembered very distinctly. He remembered the smooth slick feel of the cellophane on his fingers when he put it there.

"I plain see what happened," he said to the bottom of

the skiff. "I plain see what happened." He straightened up and turned to his father. And held out his hand.

The old man did not move.

William hunched his shoulders slightly. "I ain't no kid," he said, "to get things taken from me. I a man grown that can take what his."

Slowly the old man took the pack of cigarettes out of his trouser pocket and handed it to his son. Slowly William lit one.

The old man put a foot up on the gunwale of the second skiff. "I got me a mighty pretty skiff here."

William looked at him from under his brows. "I wouldn't have a dead skiff for no amount of money."

The old man reached down and scratched his ankle. "Yes, sir, a real pretty skiff."

"Listen," William said. Always when he was angry his ears began to hurt and burn. "Iffen I wanted that boat there . . ."

"Yes, sir," the old man said, and rubbed his foot up and down the gunwale. "A sweet boat. This here is plain my lucky day."

"I a man can take what he wants," William said. "And I plain wouldn't have nothing to do with that there boat."

The old man reached down and pulled off a strip of grass that had caught inside the boat. "Got myself a new boat."

"You damn keep it," William said. Holding the cigarette between his lips, he began to walk away. "I ain't arguing with you."

From behind him the old man spoke. "And you supposed to be a man grown."

"A man don't have to do every single thing. Some things he don't do."

He went to his mother's house. He was very angry. And he was hungry. The door of the icebox stuck. He jerked at it so savagely that it crashed open against the wall. He heard his mother come and stand in the doorway behind him.

"I looking for something to eat," he said, and glanced at her over his shoulder. She had just got up; she still wore a red flower-printed housecoat.

"There ain't nothing there. Stan come in and I fix him a real supper last night." Stan was her husband, a railroad waiter with a lean, hungry black face, who always drew long runs and was very seldom in town.

William slammed shut the door. "I reckon I better go find something."

"You been fishing?" his mother asked. She was staring at his trousers, which were still wet at the seams.

"I been to see the old man." He began to walk toward the door.

She caught his arm, stopping him. "He ain't give you no breakfast?"

"I ain't one to ask," he said.

She hooked both thumbs in the belt of her housecoat and spread her palms downward against her hips. "With all that money he got—"

Stan called sleepily: "That William you talking to, honey?"

"Nobody else," she said. "Don't you go getting jealous." She turned back to her son, but all she saw was the screen door closing behind him.

She called after him: "Why ain't you got him to give you something?"

"I ain't wanted nothing from him," he said.

William did not see his father again for nearly four months. At night sometimes the old black face, its cheeks and jaw studded with tufts of white hair, floated through his dreams. During the day he did not think of him. He had his job on the oyster boats (it was a good season and a heavy one) and he had his girl, whose name was Cynthia Lee.

One Friday evening in November he stood drinking his beer in Jack's Café with some of the other fellows from his boat. Cynthia Lee came up to him and pulled at his arm. Her mouth was open, but this time not smiling. She told him that Matthew Pettis and another policeman were asking for him at his mother's.

He put the glass down on the bar and turned it around and around slowly. He could guess what had happened. Something had gone wrong in the deal he had with Clarence Anderson and Mickey Lane. He thought briefly of the newspaper-wrapped package hidden in his room and the brown dry weeds inside. He wondered if the police had found that. They did not know where he lived; he was supposed to stay with his mother. But there were always people who would tell them.

Maybe he could get to the package before they did. . . . He wondered how much the police knew; maybe they had the package already. They would find it soon if he didn't get back to it. But maybe they were waiting for him there. . . . Maybe . . .

Cynthia jiggled his arm. "What you aiming to do? What you studying to do?"

"I getting out," he said.

She called after him as he left—"William!"—but he did not bother to answer. He did not have time.

He turned away from the houses and the lights in the windows and, running, twisted and turned down back alleys until he found himself in the open country. He stopped for a moment and caught his breath and listened. There were nothing but pines, thin straggling pines growing in the sandy ground; there wasn't even a wind to rustle their needles. But he saw Matthew Pettis's quick black face behind every tree and every hackberry bush. A quivering began deep down in his stomach. "A man got no call to be afraid," he said.

He left the pine ridge and made his way through the swampy grounds. He was tired from a day's work on the oyster boat, but he made himself move at a trot. The close damp night odor was beginning to come up from all around him.

He did not know exactly where he was going until he saw the square boards of his father's house right in front of him over the reeds. Then he stopped and thought for a minute. "There's things a man can ask for," he said. And he knew he would ask the old man for money, for enough money to get him to the city, to New Orleans.

He walked closer. The sun was down, but the light was still good enough for him to see the second boat, the girl's boat, pulled up high against the north side of the house. The old man had painted it dark green, but William still recognized it, and from four months past the memory of the girl flashed into his mind. He shook his head to be rid of it. Death frightened him.

As he had done before, he ate with the old man—fish and canned beans. And because it was near to the time the pension check came (on the third of every month), William began to wonder if the old man would have any money at all.

William sat very still, thinking, rubbing his underlip with his tongue and wondering how he should ask. Finally he said: "I done got myself in trouble."

The old man dunked the two plates up and down in a bucket of water and wiped them on the sleeve of his shirt. "That right?"

"You might could sound more interested," William said. "You might could."

"Ain't no interest to me," his father said. His thick nubby black fingers reached for the package of cigarettes on the shelf beside the door, the shelf that was nothing but a board resting on two wood blocks fastened to the wall with tenpenny nails.

"I gonna need some money."

The old man lit his cigarette slowly and did not answer.

"I gonna need just enough money to get me to New Orleans."

The old man tipped his chair back against the wall and smoked slowly.

"I shoulda been paid tomorrow. So I ain't got any money."

"I ain't got none either."

"Sure you got it," William said. "Everybody know you got it."

"Everybody but me," the old man said.

"I got to get to New Orleans," William said, and rubbed his fingers up and down the edge of the table, bending them and pressing on them hard as he could.

"You can walk."

"It eighty-odd miles," William said.

The ashes from the old man's cigarette dropped to the floor.

"A man's got a right to ask some things," William said.

The old man did not answer.

"Iffen I stay around here the police catch me sure."

"That right?" his father said, and closed wrinkled lids over his eyes.

William got up and stood in the door, looking across the grasses. All he could see was Pettis's thin face under the blue cap. He closed his eyes and shook his head, but the image followed him. His jaw began to tremble and he held it with his hand.

"And you supposed to be a man," his father said softly;

205

his lips scarcely moved. "You supposed to be a man and you afraid. You plain afraid."

William spun around. The rubber soles of his tennis shoes squeaked on the boards. "I ain't afraid." He felt quick tears spurt down his cheeks. "I got a right to ask."

His father laughed, soundlessly as old people always do, and doubled up on his chair. His father opened his mouth and laughed at him. "And you a man . . ."

The tears filmed his eyes and wet his mouth as he stumbled across the room. His hip struck something that must have been the edge of the table; his head was filled with the echo of his own sobbing as he went stumbling toward his father. "A man got a right to some things."

He felt his arm go up, but it was not his arm moving. He could not see when his fist came down, but he felt something crumble. "A man got a right . . ."

He stood there crying until the tears were all used up.

His father was dead. He had gone down like an old wall that has been dry and toppling for years, waiting for someone to push it over. He had fallen from his chair and lay on his side, one arm stretched out gently.

William shook his head slowly, back and forth. Unbelieving. He had forgot that old bones were brittle from wear. He had forgot that the bigness of a man meant nothing against age, that old men die easily.

William held up his hand and looked at it. There was no blood on it. He looked down at his father. In the dusk he could see no marks on the black old face. The boy rubbed his knuckles slowly with the fingers of his left hand. He had not meant to: the old man had died so easily.

After a while William lifted his head and listened, sniffling back the last of the tears. He walked over to the window, pushed open the shutter a bit, and looked out. The night was going to be foggy. You could see it beginning already in the reeds at the edge of the bayou, white fog lying along the ground like a strip of bandage. It would be thick, come night—even thicker when the smoke came down from the cypress stumps they were burning to the north.

He stood looking out the window, squinting his eyes, thinking. He wondered where he should go. There was his mother's; he would trust her. But the police would be sure to watch there. There was Cynthia Lee and the house in Bucktown. But they would have found out about that by now. He had friends, but he did not want to trust them. Not now.

William looked down at the old man lying on the boards of the floor with the chair fallen over him and he shook his head. He had not meant to kill him. He lifted his arm and held it in the same position. He felt the muscles in his shoulder and along the arm. They had killed the old man. He had not done it. Not with his mind. He had lifted his arm, and his muscles and his strength and his youth had done it. He swung his arm outward, repeating the blow. Then he rubbed his head and turned from his father to the window and the stretch of bayou and Gulf and the fog that was coming up slowly.

He would have to sleep out. There were plenty of places

of high ground near the road. Most nights he would not have minded that. But tonight with the fog, the fog that was mixed with cypress smoke, with sweet fleshy cypress smoke . . .

There was no help for it. He pulled closed the shutter and turned back to the room. Like a man should, he straightened his shoulders and looked down at his father. Already it was so dark that he could not see the face at all, only the vague outline of the body. It might have been anyone lying there. It might have been—but he knew it wasn't. He knew that it was his father lying dead with the side of his skull crushed in. Maybe even the mark of a fist along the side of his head.

There was no help for that either. He had not intended to, but he had done it, and now there was no use standing shivering like a baby. A man did what he did and didn't study about it afterwards.

If he were to sleep out, William knew that he would need a blanket. The fog would be cold and the night was going to be long. He stepped over his father and reached for the blanket on the bed. It was tucked in tightly, and when he jerked at it the light mattress came loose. Something hit the floor with the quick sound of metal and rolled toward him and struck his foot. He jumped, then bent down and felt around on the dark floor with his fingers to see what it was that had come jumping out toward him, as if it had been meant for him. His fingers touched and recognized it and lifted it up: a silver dollar.

Then William remembered what he had come for. And what he had nearly forgotten. He reached into his pocket for a lighter. The first two tries the flint did not spark. He shook it, saying softly: "Damn!" Then he was holding a small yellow flame in his hand. He checked the coin in his fingers: a dollar. And he bent down over the bed to see what else was hidden under the mattress.

The light caught the sheen of the round silver pieces lined up on one of the slats of the bed. He held the light down and counted them slowly, using his finger as a pointer. There were six of them, and the one he held in his hand made seven.

One by one he picked them up and dropped them in his pocket. That was all: seven of them.

There was a kerosene lamp by the window. He lit it and searched carefully around the bed. And found nothing. He began to get angry. He jerked the bed from the wall and looked behind it. He yanked open the drawers of the chest and went through them, tossing the stuff on the bed. He felt behind the window frame and found nothing. His anger increased, anger at the old man lying on the floor, the old man who kept only seven silver dollars.

William went out to the lean-to kitchen. There was only a single rough shelf holding four cans; he knocked them to the floor. There was a pot on the stove; he knocked that over too. He noticed a loose floor board. Using the handle of the pot, he pried it open; there was only ground underneath. He put his hand through the opening and pulled up a handful of dry musty earth. He threw it against the wall with disgust.

"God damn, God damn, God damn," he whispered softly to himself. He looked out, this time on the side away from the bayou. Fog was thicker there over the marsh, making the grasses silvery, translucent almost, floating. It was like the fog sucked away all color.

Fog was always sucking away, William thought. When you walked through it you could feel it sucking at your skin, sucking away at your skin, trying to wither you up. When he slept he could cover himself all up with the blanket, head and all, so that it could not reach him.

There were two other loose floor boards. He pried them up and found only ground under them. He broke the boards across his knee and tossed them into a corner.

He went through his father's pockets carefully: three nickels and two pennies and a smooth brown rabbit's foot on a key chain with a single heavy key. William held the key up to the lamp and turned it slowly in the light. Then he looped the chain around his fingers, snapped it, and let the key roll to the floor. The rabbit's foot he put in his pocket with the nickels.

He picked up the chair that had been knocked over and put it against the wall and sat down. He sat and thought what he should do and where he should go. He began to wish he could stay right where he was; but already he thought he could begin to smell the dead. There was always a smell; the girl had had it too, young as she was and as washed clean with salt water.

He would have to go. He stood up, held the chair by the back, and smashed it to pieces against the wall. The wood splintered and cut his hand. He sucked at the palm until there was no longer any blood taste.

If he could only stay where he was—he would be safe.

He glanced out at the fog that was thickening by the moment. The road from town would be almost blocked up by now; a police car couldn't get through.

He could stay where he was and be safe . . . but he couldn't stay. He looked down at his father. The lamp wasn't bright enough to show his face. It might have been anybody lying there. Anybody who was dead.

William leaned against the wall and rubbed his head slowly with both hands. Then he picked up the quilt and folded it around his shoulders to keep the fog away from him. And he opened the door.

The fog was very heavy now, but low: a white strip that covered the grass and the ground and cut the trees in half. William hunched the quilt high over his head.

A man did what he had to do. . . .

Sometimes he did not intend to, but things came to him and he did them.

He did not mean to kill the old man. He looked back into the room. The lamp was running out of oil; the wick was burning with a sputtering blue flame. The light did not reach down to the floor. There mightn't have been anyone lying there at all.

William stared at the dark floor and tried to remember how the old man had looked. And could not.

The police would remember; Matthew Pettis would remember. William saw the smooth black face under the peaked visor of the blue cap, the short slim body, the nervous fingers, and the quick black eyes, shiny as oil in the sunlight. Pettis would remember, and he would follow him; it would be his job to follow him.

211

William pulled closed the door behind him and hugged the quilt tighter around his body. He would find a place to sleep tonight near the highway. In the morning he would flag down the first bus; there would be enough money for the fare. And even Pettis would have a hard time finding him in a city as big as New Orleans.

He turned around slowly. In another hour the fog would be too heavy to walk in, even. He would have to be near the road before it got that thick, so thick that he could not move. He fingered the quilt: a good heavy one. He would need it, sitting by the road waiting for the sun to come with morning. It was a big quilt too, wide and long; he would wrap himself up in it so that the fog could not reach him, the sucking fog that was heavy with the sweet smoke of cypress.

He leaned back against the wall for a minute, shivered, and was afraid, the way a boy is afraid playing a game in the dark. Then he remembered and stood up straight and walked off as quickly as he could with the quilt hunched around his shoulders: the things a man has done he must abide with.

One Summer

You forget most things, don't you? It's even hard to remember in the hurry and bustle of spring what the slow unwinding of fall was like. And summer vacations all blur one into the other when you try to look back at them. At least, it's that way for me: a year is a long time.

But there's one summer I remember, clear as anything; the day, a Thursday in August.

It had been a terrific summer, the way it always is here. There was dust an inch thick on everything. The streams were mostly all dry. Down in the flaky red dust of the beds —where the flood in spring was so fast you couldn't cross it and where now there was just a foot or two of slimy smelling water—you could find the skeletons of fishes so brittle that they crumbled when your foot touched them. The wells were always dug extra deep just for summers like this: there's always water if you go down deep enough for it. There was plenty of water for drinking and washing and even maybe enough to keep the gardens watered, but nobody did; most of the plants withered and crumbled away. By August, cracks were beginning to show in the

213

ground, too, crisscross lines maybe half an inch wide showing under the brown dead grass.

So that when this big pile of thunderheads came lifting
out of the south everybody watched them, wondering and
hoping.

I was sitting on Eunice Herbert's porch, over in the
coolest part, behind the wooden jalousies. There was a
swing there, and an electric fan on a little black iron table,
and two or three black iron stands of ferns, all different
kinds—her mother was crazy about them. Maybe it wasn't
cooler there, but with the darkness from the closed
jalousies and the smell of wet mud from the fern pots, it
seemed comfortable.

Eunice was the prettiest girl in town, there wasn't any
doubt of that. She had hair so blond that it looked almost
silver white. All summer long she kept it piled up on top
of her head with a flower stuck right on top; she got the
idea from the cover of *Seventeen*, she said. Whenever she
was at a party, there was nearly always a fight between
some boys. It was just sure to happen, that's all; I was in
enough to know. I almost had got thrown out of school
because of one of them: at the spring party in the gym of
the big yellow-brick high school. I don't remember how it
started. I was just dancing with some girl when over at
the table where Eunice was sitting two fellows started to
fight. I remember dropping the girl's arm and walking
over. Not wanting to fight, not really, but somehow I did;
and somehow I got a Coke bottle in my hand and started
swinging. It was the bottle that nearly got me expelled. My

father had to do an awful lot of talking so I could go on and finish the year with the rest of my class.

One thing though—it set things up fine between Eunice and me. In those two months she hadn't had a date with another fellow.

That hot Thursday afternoon in August we were sitting on her porch swing, holding hands under the wide skirt of her dress, which she had spread out so that her mother wouldn't see anything but two people sitting and talking. Her mother was inside, doing something, I never found out what, but every ten minutes or so she'd stick her head out the door and ask: "You children want something?" And Eunice would say: "Oh, Mamma, no," with her voice going up a little on the last word.

We were just sitting there swinging back and forth, staring at the green little leaves of the ferns. I was feeling her soft thin fingers. There was a kind of shivering going up and down my back that wasn't just the electric fan blowing on my wet shirt.

Then her mother stuck her head out the front door to the porch for maybe the fifteenth time that afternoon—she was a little woman with a tiny face that reminded me of a squirrel somehow, with a nervous twitching nose. "Children," she said (and I could feel Eunice's fingers stiffen at the word), "just you look out there—" she pointed to the south; "here's a big pile of rain clouds, coming right this way."

"Yes, ma'am," I said. We'd noticed the clouds come up half an hour past.

And then because she kept staring at us we had to get up and walk over and peer out through the little open squares in the jalousies and look at the sky.

"It looks like rain," I said, because somebody had to say something.

Without turning around I heard Mrs. Herbert take a seat in one of the wicker chairs. I heard the cane creak and then the rockers begin to move softly back and forth on the wood flooring. Alongside me I could feel Eunice stiffen like a cat that's been hit by something. But there wasn't anything she could do: her mother was going to sit and talk to us for the rest of the afternoon. I might just as well go sit in one of the single chairs.

The afternoon was so quiet that from my house—just across the street and one house down—you could hear our cook, Mayline, singing at the top of her voice:

> "*Didn't it rain, little children,*
> *Didn't it rain, little children,*
> *Didn't it rain?*"

So she'd noticed that big mass of clouds too.

"Is that Mayline I hear?" Mrs. Herbert said. The words came out slowly, one for each creak of her rocker.

"Yes, ma'am," I said and sat down in the red-painted straight chair.

Eunice dropped down in the middle of the swing and folded her hands on her lap and didn't say anything.

"Well," her mother said with just an edge of annoyance, "if you children are doing anything you don't want me to see . . ."

216

"Oh, Mamma," Eunice said, staring down at her hands.

"Yes, ma'am," I said, and then changed it to "No, ma'am," and all the while I was thinking of a way to get us out of there.

From the corner of my eye I saw that Eunice's mother was getting that hurt bewildered look all mothers use.

And then—just at that right minute—we heard Morris Henry come running down the street. He was a poppy-eyed little black monkey Negro, no taller than a twelve-year-old, but strong as a man and twice as quick. He had little hands, like a child's or a girl's maybe, with nails that he always chewed down to the quick. Even when there wasn't anything more to bite on, he'd keep chewing away at the fingers with his wide flaring yellow teeth.

He came running down the road—you could hear the sound of his bare feet on the dirt road quite a ways in front of him. He took a short cut through the empty lot at the corner and came bursting through the high dry grass that went up like a puff of smoke all around him.

With the dust in his nose he started sneezing, but he didn't stop. He tore down the middle of our street at top speed, both hands holding to his trousers so they wouldn't fall off. He took our fence with a one-hand jump, made a straight line through the yard to the kitchen door, and was up the steps two at a time. The door slammed after him.

It was quiet then with him inside my house. All you could see was the path he'd broken for himself through the dry stalks of the zinnias in the front yard.

"My goodness," Mrs. Herbert said. "Hadn't you better go see what's wrong?"

"Yes, ma'am," I said.

"I'll come with you," Eunice said quickly.

We yanked open the screen door and we were all the way down the steps and halfway to the front gate before we heard it slam, we were running that fast.

"The front way," I said. And we rushed up the front steps and in the front door.

We had to stop for a minute: the parlor was always kept with the blinds drawn, and coming out of the sun we couldn't see a thing. I could hear Eunice breathing heavily alongside me. She was so close it was the easiest thing in the world to put my arm around her. I kissed her hard, and for as long as I dared with people so close—the voices in the kitchen sounded excited.

"You hurt," she said.

And I just grinned at her; it was the sort of hurt she liked.

And then we went into the kitchen to see what had happened.

Little Morris Henry was sitting in a red-painted kitchen chair and my mother was holding his thin little shoulder, that was all bulged and lumpy with muscle. Over in a corner Mayline stood with her mouth open and a streak of flour on her black face.

Next to my shoulder I could hear Eunice let her breath out with a quick hissing whisper. No one seemed to have noticed that we had come in. Mayline was looking over in our direction and her eyes rested right on us, but there wasn't any recognition in them. They were just empty

brown eyes; only they weren't brown any more, but bright
live metal. They were eyes like flat pieces of silver.

Because we didn't know what to do, we stood very still
and waited.

In a minute my mother looked around. She seemed to
feel that we were there; she couldn't have seen us, we
were behind her. But she looked over. Keeping her hand
on Morris Henry's shoulder she twisted her head around
and looked at us.

"He says there's something wrong with the old gentleman. . . ." Her voice wandered off. She had spoken in
such a whisper and the words had slipped so gradually
that you couldn't quite tell when she stopped. I wondered
if I had really heard anything at all.

She seemed to realize this, because she repeated louder
this time, in a way that you couldn't mistake: "He says
there's something wrong with the old gentleman."

That would be my grandfather. Everybody called him
that. They never did use his name. When they were talking about him it was "the old gentleman" and to his face
they always said "sir."

"The old gentleman's gone fishing on the Scanos River,"
they'd say. And that would mean he'd taken his little
power boat out into the middle of the muddy red yellow
river and stopped the motor and thrown over his line and
was sitting there waiting for the fish to bite; and they always did; he was a fine fisherman.

Or maybe Luce Rogers, who was Mayline's husband—
of a sort and not a legal sort—would stick his head in the
kitchen door and wipe his shiny face with his broad hand

and look at Mayline and shake his head and say sadly: "Baby, I can't set with you this morning. I got to go to work." And Mayline would look at him from under her lids, not quite believing him because he didn't like to work and he sure had a wandering eye. So she would suck in one corner of her mouth and hold it between her teeth and stare at him, nodding her head just a little. And he would open his eyes very wide and shake his head and say: "You ain't got no cause to suspicion me, baby. I was just plain walking past the place when the old gentleman yells at me from the porch."

And Mayline would relax for a little while anyhow, because that would mean that my grandfather had found some work for him to do, like mowing the grass maybe or washing the windows, or doing some other work that the regular girl, whose name was Wilda Olive, couldn't do. It was just about the only time Luce Rogers worked—when my grandfather caught him.

That Thursday afternoon in the kitchen, it was Eunice who moved first. She slipped around me—she was standing almost half behind me in the doorway—and went up to my mother and put her arms around her.

"You better sit down, Mrs. Addams," she said. She had the chair all pulled out from the table and ready. "You look a little pale."

That wasn't true; my mother looked perfectly all right. But that was Eunice's way—she'd used that line in the high-school play a couple of months before and she didn't see any reason not to use it again. Or maybe it was because she didn't really know what to say either.

Anyhow, my mother did sit down. And she leaned one arm against the table and beat a little tattoo on it with her fingers.

The minute she sat down, Morris Henry bounced up and went over and stood by the window, chewing his little knuckles. Eunice stood next to my mother and looked over at me. And I looked down at the ground.

My mother began tapping the heel of her shoe against the floor. That was a sure sign she was thinking. Finally she said to me: "MacDonald—"

"Yes, ma'am," I said.

She was the only one who ever used my full name like that. To most people I was just Mac. But she liked that full name, maybe because it had belonged to her family. Or maybe she just liked the sound of it.

"Go see if there's a car in the neighborhood we can borrow. . . . Go outside and look.

"Eunice," she was giving orders now, "put in a call for Dr. Addams. . . . I've got to put on a regular dress." She only wore a kind of smock-like affair around the house, because of the heat.

I went out in the yard and looked up and down the block. There wasn't a single car in any driveway. It wasn't surprising, because most people either took the car down to the business section with them if they were going to work, or if they left them at home their wives took them to the market or the movies. I had known that I wasn't going to find anything when I went out.

I went back up the stairs into the hall. Eunice had finished calling and had put the phone back on the little black wood table that teetered if you touched it too hard. She was leaning against the wall, at an angle with it, and her legs were crossed. The way she had hunched her shoulders her peasant blouse was slipping way down on one side.

Eunice waved at me to come back. She had just called my father's office. He wasn't there. Nobody had expected that he would be. He was out making his calls. He had a big practice—he was probably the most popular doctor in the county or maybe even in this part of the state—and there was no telling exactly where he was.

Eunice put down the phone for a minute. "Isn't it just dreadful, Mac?" she said in a whisper; "about your grandfather, I mean."

"Yeah," I said. I was looking at the smooth stretch of her shoulder.

She saw my gaze and pulled up the cloth.

"You the prettiest girl in this town," I said, "bar none." I had told her that before, and she always answered the same way.

She gave a little giggle and said: "Men . . ."

My mother came out into the hall. She just looked at us and walked over and took the phone off the hook. There was somebody on the party line. She broke through that in a minute and had the operator. "Can you find Dr. Addams?" she said. "Tell him it's his father."

That was the way you located either of the two doctors in this town, if you needed them fast. You just called up Shirley Williams, who was the operator, and told her. And sooner or later my father would make a call and she'd recognize his voice and give him the message. It worked fast that way; much faster than you'd think. I was sure that in about half an hour my father would know about it wherever he was.

She hung up the phone and looked at us. "This is just no time for you to behave like children. . . . MacDonald, is there a car we can borrow?"

"No, ma'am," I said.

"I'll just have to walk then." She took a sunshade out of the closet and slammed the door. She was halfway down the walk before she turned to look at me.

"I reckon you better come along," she said slowly. "I might need you to take a message."

My grandfather wouldn't ever have a telephone in his house. There was always somebody passing by soon enough to take a message for him, he said.

She pointed me back into the house. "Go get a hat," she said. "It's killing out here."

On the way out I said to Eunice: "I'll see you to-night."

It was an agreement we had. During the last two months, almost every night I'd slip out of my room and throw one small piece of gravel against her window screen. And then when she looked out I'd blink my flashlight real quick, just once. And she would slip down. . . . If her folks ever found out, there'd really be a row. Though they didn't have to worry. Eunice wasn't that sort of a girl. We'd just stand out in the dark, not even talking, so no one would notice us. Until the mosquitoes got too bad; and then I'd kiss her good-night.

"I'll see you tonight," I told her as I grabbed my hat and rushed out after my mother.

The sun was so hot you could feel it tingling your skin right through the clothes. It was so hot you didn't sweat any more. My mother went right on walking very fast, so that we covered the five blocks to my grandfather's house in maybe two minutes. And all the while I had my eyes on the big pile of thunderheads, the ones that had just come up and were hanging there in the sky promising rain. The people we passed, sitting on their shaded porches, who nodded or waved to us, were watching them too and they called out to ask us if we had seen them.

My mother answered them, hardly politely sometimes, we were walking so fast.

As it turned out we needn't have been in such a hurry after all.

My grandfather had died that hot afternoon in August, while everybody for miles around was watching the big pile of thunderheads. And nobody was paying much attention to an old man.

He had tumbled out of his chair in the living-room and died there on the floor with his mouth full of summer dust from the green flowered carpet. Wilda Olive, the colored woman who kept house for him, found him there about an hour later. She'd been puttering around in the back yard, making like she was sweeping off the walk, but really, just like everybody else, keeping an eye on those clouds.

She came in to tell him about the rain that might be coming and found him where he'd done a jackknife dive into the carpet. For a while she just stood looking at him, with his seersucker coat rumpled up in back and his bald head buried under his arm, bald head that was getting just a little dusty on the floor. She took a couple of steps backwards (she didn't even go near or touch him) and she lifted up her apron and put it over her head and began to cry. It was one of those long aprons that wrap all around and it was big enough to cover up her head. She just stood there, bent over in the dark from the heavy linen folds, and wailing. Not high, not the way a white woman would cry, but a kind of flat low tone that you could almost see curling its way up through the layers of heat in the day.

Morris Henry, who happened to be passing by in the street, had heard it and gone in to look. After one look his poppy eyes stuck out even more than usual; and he headed straight for our house, at a run. And my mother and I came rushing over in the full heat of the afternoon sun. . . .

Minute we stepped through the front gate we began to hear Wilda Olive's moaning. My mother nodded toward the pecan tree in the north corner of the yard. "You just sit down there and wait for me," she said.

Of course, I didn't do anything of the sort. I followed her right inside.

She pushed past Wilda Olive and bent over the old man and stretched out her hand but didn't quite touch him and pulled back her hand and straightened up and just stood there. Finally she reached over and pulled the apron from Wilda Olive's head. "Stop that," she said sharply.

Wilda Olive didn't seem to hear her. My mother held up her own hand, with fingers outspread, and looked at it carefully. Then slapped Wilda Olive hard as she could. That hushed her.

"We'll need some ice water," my mother told her. "It's perishing hot out, walking."

Wilda Olive went to the kitchen. And my mother came and stood out on the porch. "MacDonald," she said when she saw me, "I thought I told you to stay out in the yard under the tree."

She wasn't really paying any attention to me; I could tell that from her tone; so I didn't move. She took one of the cane rockers from where it was leaning backwards against the porch wall and turned it around and sat down, very slowly. Very slowly, with one hand she rubbed the left side of her face, the two skins rubbing together smoothly and squeaking just a little from the wet of the perspiration.

Wilda Olive brought the ice water and disappeared. "Let's hope she doesn't start that racket again," my mother said, and listened carefully. But everything was quiet. "We'll just wait for your father," she said.

I sat down on the edge of the porch, my feet stuck through the railing and hanging down. It was so hot it was hard to breathe.

There was a little bead of sweat collecting very slowly on my neck, right over the little hump of bone there. I hunched my shoulders so that the shirt would not touch and break it. I felt it getting bigger and bigger until it had enough force to cross the bone and begin to wiggle slowly down my back. It was all the way down to within an inch of my belt when my father came driving up.

My mother jumped up and went out to meet him. Her feet in their white sandals went by me very fast and I noticed for the first time how small they were and how brown and smooth the turn of her ankle. I'd never thought of my mother as having nice legs before. . . .

My mother stood against the side of the car, leaning in through the window, the sun full and hard on her white print dress. I saw the line of her thighs and her narrow hips. It was funny for me to be thinking of my mother that way now, with my grandfather lying all doubled up on the floor inside and dead. I saw something I'd never seen before: she had as good a figure as Eunice Herbert.

When my father went inside, she sat down, not saying anything to me, rocking herself slowly, her foot beating out the time. There was a fuzz of yellow hair all up her leg; I saw that out of the corner of my eye.

Then my father came out and sat on the arm of her chair. I looked up and saw how she sat there with her eyes tight closed. My father was writing out the death certificate, the way he had to; I recognized the form. I'd seen them lying around his office enough.

And I thought how he was writing his father's name: Cecil Percival Addams. I could see his hand printing out the name, slow and steady. He was writing out his father's name on a death certificate.

Shirley Ann Grau

Just the way it would be for me someday. What he was doing now, I would be doing for him someday. I would sit where he was now; and there would be my wife alongside me, crying a little bit and trying not to show it. I would be a doctor, too, writing just the way he was now. And he would be lying dead inside.

And then we'd all move up one step again. And it would be my son who'd be looking down at me, lying still and dusty. I'd never thought of that before.

The trickle of sweat reached to my belt, broke, and spread, cold on my hot skin. I shivered. The thunderheads were still piled up in the south, shining gray-bright in the sun. They struck me as being very lonesome.

My father signed the paper and laid it out on the railing. "Jeff'll need that," he said quietly. Jeff was the undertaker, a little man, quick and nervous and bald, who wore black suits in the winter and white linen ones in the summer. His wife had run off with a railroad engineer and disappeared. He had a married daughter over to the north in Birmingham and he visited her twice a year.

My mother bent her head over in her lap with a quick sharp movement. My father slipped his arm around her.

"Honey," he said, "don't. Let's go home."

He lifted her up and they walked to the car. I could tell from the way he braced himself that he was almost carrying her. And even a small woman like my mother is a heavy load in one arm. I hadn't thought my father was that strong.

My mother slipped in the front seat and made room for me alongside her.

"No," my father said. "Let him stay here."

My mother shook her head doubtfully.

"Somebody's got to," my father said as he got behind the wheel. "He's almost a man. And there isn't going to be anything for him to do."

My mother didn't look convinced.

"Look," my father said shortly, "he's staying."

"There's a phone next door in the Raymond place," my mother said faintly, "MacDonald, if you want to call."

"Yes, ma'am," I said.

"Stay on the porch, son, if you want to," my father said. "Just see that Jeff gets the certificate. And keep an eye on Wilda Olive."

"Yes, sir," I said.

As they drove off, my mother rubbed her face deep down in my father's shoulder, the way a girl does sometimes on a date coming home.

And just for a second I could really feel Eunice's cheek rubbing against my shoulder and hear the soft sound it made on the cloth. And there was the tickle of her hair on my chin. And the far faint odor that wasn't really perfume —though that was part of it—but was the smell of her hair and her skin.

Then all of a sudden I didn't have that picture any more. I was back on my grandfather's porch, watching my father drive off with my mother. She had her face buried deep down in his shoulder. My father's arm went up and around to pull her closer to him. Then I couldn't see any more, the dust on the road was so thick.

I looked around. In the whole afternoon there wasn't a

thing moving, except me. Except my breathing, up and down. And that seemed sort of out of place.

For a while I sat on the porch. Then I thought that maybe I ought to have a look at Wilda Olive. I didn't want to go through the house, so I walked all the way around it, outside, around to the kitchen door. "Wilda Olive." I thought I called loud but my voice softened in the heat until it was just ordinary speaking tone.

She was in the kitchen, scouring out the sink, quietly, like nothing had happened. She looked up and saw me. "Yes, sir," she said.

She'd never said "sir" to me before. The old man's death had changed that. I had moved up one step. I was in my father's place. It was funny how quick it all happened.

"Yes, sir," she said.

"You all right?" That sounded silly. But I'd said it, so I stuck my hands down deep in my pockets and lifted up my jaw and waited for her to answer.

"Yes, sir." She dropped her eyes. Ordinarily she would have gone back to her work and let me stand there to do what I wanted. But that had changed, too. Now she stood waiting for me. Not going on with her work because of me.

"You were cutting up pretty bad when we came," I told her.

"Yes, sir," she said. There wasn't the slightest bit of expression in her face now.

"Well," I said, "I'll be out front if you want me—on the porch, because it's too hot inside." That wasn't the reason.

I didn't want to stay inside with the old man. But she mustn't know that. I wanted to go around, the way I'd come—through the garden—but I knew she was expecting me to go straight through the house. And so I did, walking fast as I could without seeming to hurry.

I had hardly got back out on the porch before I saw Eunice coming. She had a red ruffled parasol held high against the sun and she was carrying something wrapped in a checked kitchen towel in her other hand. I watched her open the gate and come up to the porch.

"I thought you'd be steaming hot," she said, "so I brought you over a Coke." She unwrapped the towel and there it was, the open bottle, still with ice all over the outside.

"Thanks," I said. I drank the Coke, but I couldn't think of anything else to say. Somehow she didn't belong here. Somehow I just didn't want her here.

She took the bottle from me when I had finished. "I got to get back," she said. "I promised Mamma to help with dinner."

"Thanks," I said again.

At the foot of the steps she turned. "I'm awful sorry."

The sun was shining on her just the way it had on my mother.

"It's okay," I said. "It's okay."

She was gone then. And there was only the Coke taste in my mouth to remind me that she had been there. And that was gone soon, and there was just the dust taste. And there wasn't a trace of her. I just couldn't believe that she had been there . . . it was funny, the way things were beginning not to seem real.

That evening they came, the little old people who had been my grandfather's friends . . . or maybe his enemies. Time sort of evened out all those things.

Jeff, the undertaker, had come and gone and the house was really and truly empty now; I found I could breathe better. (That was another strange thing: I had never feared my grandfather, living and moving; but dead, he made me afraid. . . .)

Matthew Conners was the first. I saw him way off down the road, coming slowly, picking his way carefully between the ruts, testing the deepest ones with his cane, lifting himself carefully over them.

The sun had gone down but the sky was still full of its light, hard and bright. The rain clouds hadn't moved.

Matthew came up the walk and stood at the foot of the steps. "He come back yet?"

"No, sir," I said. "Jeff'll have him along soon."

Matthew Conners nodded. His head bobbed quickly up and down on the sinewy cords of his neck. He'd been a handsome man once, they said; the bad boy of the southern counties. There was a picture of him in an album of my grandfather's; very tall, very thin, with hair carefully pompadoured in front. Even in the picture you could see how bright the stripes of his tie were. He'd never married. He'd gone on living in the two rooms behind his hardware store (which was on the busiest corner in town, next to the post office). Until one day he sold the business to a nephew. He kept the rooms, though, and lived there. He spent most of his days there, sitting on the doorstep, not saying much to people who were passing, just sitting there, as if he were waiting.

Matthew Conners climbed slowly up the porch steps and sat down on the chair where my mother had sat and put the cane down between his knees and crossed his hands on it and waited.

I saw those hands, blue spots and heavy-veined, crossed and folded together, and I thought how maybe at that very minute Jeff was pressing my grandfather's hands together. . . .

They came all evening, the old people. After Matthew Conners came Vance Bonfield and the short, very fat woman who was his wife, Dorothy, her double chins dripping with perspiration.

I said: "Good evening." They nodded but didn't answer.

And then Henry Carmichael, walking because he didn't live far at all. By this time the porch chairs were all filled—there were only three of them. I started to bring out another chair, but the old man just shook his bald shiny head in my direction and went in the house. Slowly and with great care he began bringing out a dining-room chair, his old hands trembling with its weight. He brought two chairs out, stopped and counted them carefully with one finger. Then he took a handkerchief out of his coat pocket, wiped his face carefully, and with a tired sigh sat down with the others.

They didn't seem to talk to each other at all, beyond the first hello, just sat there waiting, with their hands folded.

So I sat down on the steps and waited, too. Only thing is, I was careful not to fold my hands. I put them out flat, one on each knee.

The long summer twilight had just about worn out when Jeff and his four Negro helpers brought my grandfather back, in a shining wood coffin this time, and put him in the living-room. I heard Wilda Olive begin to cry, softer this time; so I didn't bother to stop her. I don't think I could have anyway. The old men didn't seem to notice; they didn't turn their heads or say anything. They just sat staring out at the front lawn.

I moved out into the side yard and sat down under the locust tree. The dry ground had cracked up, pulling apart the tangled grass roots. In one of the cracks there was a lily bulb, shriveled and dry. I tried to think what kind it must have been, but I couldn't ever remember seeing a flower in that spot.

My father came back. He parked his car, came in the gate, and walked straight up to me. He held out his hand. I wasn't sure whether he wanted to shake mine or give me a pull to my feet. I reckon he did both.

"Go ahead home, son," he said, still holding my hand.

I found myself saying very softly and slow and sure, as if I wasn't in a bit of a hurry: "Don't you reckon you going to need me here?"

234

"That's all right," my father said.

"You be all right?"

"Sure," my father said, and turned away, walking toward the house. "You just hurry. Your mother's waiting supper on you."

I couldn't help feeling that my father wanted me to stay, that he wanted company somehow, but couldn't have it. So I left, walking as fast as I could.

When I caught sight of our house, even if it was so hot, I began to run.

My mother was sitting very quietly in the parlor waiting for me. She had a copy of the *Ladies' Home Journal* in her hands, but she wasn't reading it. She was just using it for something to hold on to. She was wearing the same light print dress she had on before, but now the fresh starchness was gone. The lace on the organdy collar wasn't standing out stiff any more and there were perspiration spots on the shoulders.

She didn't look up from the book when I came in. "Just wash your hands down here, MacDonald. Mayline won't mind if you use the kitchen sink this once."

"Yes'm," I said.

"And we'll eat dinner right away—and then get dressed."

"Yes'm," I said.

"We can keep fresher that way—for the evening." She hesitated over the last words. It was one thing about my mother; wakes always scared her a lot; she'd said so once.

"You hungry, MacDonald?" she asked finally, standing

235

up and putting the magazine back on the table under the lamp.

"No'm," I said. "Not much, just sort of."

After supper my mother and I walked back over to the house. She was wearing a black chiffon dress; and the dye gave off a peculiar smell in the heat: not sour like perspiration, nor sweet like some flowers, nor bitter like Indian grass, but a mixture of all three. I had got dressed too, because I had to: a white suit and a tie, a black tie that had been part of my father's navy uniform. Under the coat I could feel the cotton of the shirt get wet and stick to my body.

Mrs. Herbert was out in the front yard cutting zinnias with a big shiny pair of scissors. She was the only woman I ever knew who kept her house filled with zinnias, and the strong woody odor of them was in all the rooms. Standing there in the half dark she looked like one of those flowers, with her thin body and her frizzy ragged-looking red-brown hair. (Eunice said her mother never had her hair just cut, but singed; she thought it was good for it.)

Eunice was sitting on the top step of the porch. When my mother stopped to say a word to Mrs. Herbert, she came down and stood a little way farther down the fence, leaning on the top rail, her fingers crumbling the dry heads of cornflowers.

"You look nice, all dressed up like that," Eunice said to me softly.

"It's plenty hot," I said. "With a tie and all."

"It makes you look different."

"How?"

"I don't know," she said. "Just different."

My mother had turned around now and was standing waiting for me.

"I got to go," I said. "I got to be there. . . ."

Eunice nodded. It was funny how, being a blonde like she was, her eyelashes were almost black. And when she stood looking down the way she did now, they were just a black semicircle on her cheeks. Usually I would have spent the evening on her porch or at a movie with her. And now I couldn't because my grandfather had to have a wake.

"Look," I said. "I won't be all that late tonight. . . . I'll let you know when I get home."

She nodded, still looking down, the eyelashes still making that dark mark on her cheeks.

I turned around and walked off quick as I could after my mother. And all the way over—in the first dark, which was dusty and uncertain to the eye—I was angry. I kept asking myself why I had to be a part of the old man's dying.

My mother took my arm, formally, and I wondered suddenly if I did look different or something.

The windows of the house were all wide open, it was so hot, and there was a light in every room. Very dim light, from a single bulb that was either small or shaded over with brown paper. The rooms were crowded and full of talk, buzzing whispers that didn't seem to say anything, and vague nodding heads. There were people here who'd

237

come from all parts of the county and some from Montgomery, even. All people I knew, but I had a hard time recognizing them, their faces were so different in the half light.

Out in the kitchen there were two new colored women, working under Wilda Olive's direction. They were cooking everything, emptying out the cupboards. There wasn't any reason to watch the larder any more; the stuff had to be used up. Wilda Olive had never had anyone to help her before; she'd never had anyone to boss about—the way she did now. And she was really fixing a supper, for all the people who'd come. Not even the white women stopped or interfered with her. The smell of cooking was all over the house, making the air so heavy I couldn't catch my breath. I had to go outside.

There was only one light globe burning with all its brightness, full away—the one out in the yard. The summer moths were flying around in big swooping circles, and two little kids—a boy and a girl—were standing in the circle of light, swatting them down with pieces of folded newspaper. Each time they hit one, it would disappear with a tiny popping sound and a puff of something like smoke.

The whole yard was full of kids, the youngest ones who were not allowed in the house. They were wandering around, making up games to play or fighting or just sitting, or calling for their mothers in hushed uncertain voices. Mamma Lou Davis, a big fat colored woman, had posted herself at the front gate, to make sure that they didn't wander away.

ONE SUMMER

In the far corner of the garden, next to the row of
leathery old live-forever bushes, a bunch of the kids had
begun to play funeral. They'd found a trowel somewhere
and they dug a little hole. Then very carefully they filled
it and heaped it so that the mud came to a mound on top.
The sticks they'd tied together like a cross wouldn't stand
up in the loose dry ground, so they pulled off the silvery
leaves from bushes and stuck them all over the mound, like
feathers. Then they stood in a circle, solemn all of them,
with their hands folded behind their backs, and sang:

> "We will gather by the river,
> The beautiful, beautiful river,
> We will gather by the river . . ."

There were more verses, dozens of them, but they only
seemed to know those three lines. So they sang them over
and over again.

There was one—a girl with a fat round face—who was
sitting on the ground a foot or two away from the group.
Her fresh starched pinafore dress was getting all dusty
and rumpled, and every time the group paused for breath,
in that second or two of quiet, she'd ask: "Which river?
Which river? Where?" Not paying any attention to her,
they'd go on singing:

> "Gather by the beautiful river."

Their voices together were thin and high-pitched and
ragged.

Eunice and her mother came (her father was the drug-
gist and had to stay at the store until it closed at eleven);

they didn't see me. I could tell from the polite and cautious way Eunice was looking around that she was searching for me as she followed her mother inside.

I just stood there in the far corner of the yard, not thinking much of anything, just sort of letting my mind float out on the heavy waves of jasmine odor. It couldn't have been long—not much more than a half-hour—when I saw Eunice come out on the porch again. She walked right straight over to the railing this time and stood there, with her right hand rubbing up and down her throat. You could see that she wasn't steady on her feet. Almost immediately her mother came rushing out of the door and put her arm around her and whispered in her ear, and then the two of them came down the steps and got in their car and drove away.

Mamma Lou Davis spoke to me from her stand near the gate: "That little girl sure got plenty sick, green sick. . . ."

"Yeah," I said.

"It plain affect some people that way, dying does." One of the kids, a little boy, made a dash for the gate and the street beyond. Mamma Lou's broad black hand caught him neatly on the top of the head and turned him back into the yard.

"She weren't in there long," Mamma Lou said. "But she got plenty sick."

"Yes," I said, "I could tell that."

I looked over on the porch and saw the extra chairs had been filled. Asa Stevenson had come, a short man, almost

a midget. (They said he had killed three wives with his
children. He had ten or eleven kids, all told, and every one
of them was big and strapping; every one of them was
exactly his image.) And Mrs. Martha Watkins Wood, a
big woman with yellow wrinkled skin stretched tight
across her heavy bones, and with the long sad face of a
tired old horse, had come out from Montgomery.

Now in the circle on the porch, all the chairs were filled.
Old Carmichael had known just who was coming, had expected them. With the arrival of Mrs. Wood the circle was
complete. You could almost see it draw up on itself and
close—a solid circle of wooden chairs. And at that precise
moment I noticed that the silence was gone. They began
talking, their voices light and rustling in the hot night air.
Nobody went near them.

Over in the corner of the yard one of the kids was still
singing:

> "We will gather at the river,
> Gather at the beautiful river. . . ."

By ten o'clock it had turned very quiet. The kids had
fallen asleep—most of them—on the porch steps or out on
the grass. A couple of them were using the little grave
they had dug for a pillow. Mamma Lou was still at the
gate, but she was sitting now, on a camp stool somebody
had brought her from the house. I recognized the stool—
it was the one my grandfather used when he went fishing.

Inside, the people seemed to have no more to say. They
sat in the chairs that had been brought from all parts of the

house for them, and looked at each other, and occasionally one of the women managed a smile, a kind of hesitant one, that seemed even littler in the half light.

From her position on the lowest step little Trudy Wilson shivered with a nightmare and began to cry. Her mother's heels made a kind of running clatter on the straw matting of the hall. They were the first to leave, the Wilsons, even though Trudy had waked up from her dream and was smiling again. The people with the children left first, and then the people who had a distance to drive. And then the people who had a business day coming with tomorrow. Until there were only my parents and me and the old people on the porch.

"Do you suppose they'll stay all night?" my mother asked.

"How could I know?" my father said. "They'll leave when they get ready and not before."

That was true enough. Hoyt Stevenson, who'd driven over with his wife and their three daughters and his father, had tried to get the old man to drive back with them. He tried for at least ten minutes, talking to the man in a low voice. And the old man just didn't answer, just kept shaking his head.

That's the way it was with all of them. So their families got together and figured out a way that they could get home to bed and not worry about the old people's getting home. Jim Butts, who owned the sawmill and who could afford a big car and a chauffeur, offered to ride home with somebody and leave his car and the colored driver. That's the way they did it. Finally there was just Butts's big light-yellow-colored Cadillac parked out front with the fuzzy-haired Negro asleep at the wheel, his arms wrapped all around it. And our car, which was parked up the drive, next to the house.

"Ruby, honey," my father said, "why don't you go to bed?"

My mother smiled at him limply. "I reckon I will. . . ."

Wilda Olive came in softly, carrying a round wicker tray with small cups of coffee.

My father took two. "I'll need them to stay awake."

"Thank you," my mother said. "I nearly forgot you were here, Wilda Olive."

"Yes'm," she said softly, gave me my cup of coffee, and went out on the porch to bring the rest to the old men.

I tasted the coffee. It had brandy in it.

"Say," my father said, "she sure made this a stiff dose."

"I'm so tired," my mother said. "It'll make me light-headed as anything."

"You can be in bed by that time," my father told her; "go ahead."

She stood up. "Come on, MacDonald," she said to me.

"I'm staying."

She appealed to my father. "I couldn't ever walk home alone at this time of night."

"MacDonald," my father said.

"Okay." I got up.

My father put his coffee cup down slowly. "What did you say?"

"Yes, sir."

My mother was tugging at my arm.

"Can I come back?"

My father shook his head.

"Don't you want company?"

"Go home," my father said.

My mother pulled my arm. "MacDonald, please—" And outside she gave a sigh of annoyance. "I'd think you'd have some sense. Can't you see your father's all upset without you pestering him?"

"Yes, ma'am," I said.

When we were almost home I asked her: "Why do you suppose he didn't want company?"

"Sometimes you want to be alone, MacDonald."

"I wouldn't," I said.

I saw her staring at me with a funny kind of look. I rubbed my hand quick all over my face to wipe off whatever expression she was worried about.

On our porch I stopped and took off my coat and tie. I dropped them on a chair. Meanwhile she had opened the door.

"Come on in, son."

I shook my head. "I reckon I need a walk." I started down the steps.

"MacDonald," my mother said, "you aren't coming to bed?"

"No'm."

"Your father said—"

"I don't care—" and because I didn't want to hear her answer to that, I bolted around the corner of the house. I didn't quite know where I wanted to go, so I just stood for a minute, just looking around. There was a thin flat hard sliver of moon pasted up in the west. The sky was almost bright blue and there were piles of thunderheads all over it now, shining clear in the light. There wasn't a bit of air. The dust wasn't even blowing. Everything was still and moldy and hot in the moonlight.

It was the sort of night when you breathe as shallow as you can, hoping to keep the heat out of your body that way, because your body is hot enough already. And you feel like you have a fever and maybe you do—on a thermometer—but you know it's just summer, burning.

I began to walk, not going anywhere, just wading through the dark and the heat. There were mockingbirds singing, like it was day. In the houses all the windows were wide open, and even out in the streets you could hear the hum of electric fans.

I passed a couple of colored boys walking, in step down the sidewalk. They rolled big white eyes at me as they went past. They were wearing sneakers; you couldn't hear their steps at all even in the quiet.

I wasn't thinking of anything. I was just moving around feeling how good the little breeze that made was. I walked through the town, through the business section, the closed stores and the grocery and the movie house; and the railroad station, open, but empty; and the rails shining white in the light, but empty too. I kept on walking until I had swung back through town in a circle and started back toward home. And the first thing I knew I was passing my grandfather's house. I saw the big jasmine bush at the corner of the lot—dusty but full of yellow flowers.

I went around to the side yard out of the reach of the

street light and climbed over the fence. It was just a wire
and wood fence and I had to swing over quick before my
weight brought it down.

I was right by the kitchen window, so I looked in. Wilda
Olive was standing there, at the kitchen table. She was
dressed in a black linen dress so starched that it stood out
all around her like stiff paper. And her hair was just
combed and pulled straight on top her head and shining
with lacquer. She wasn't asleep; her eyes were open.

Out in the yard, so close that I could almost put my
hand down and touch it, a mockingbird was singing. I
looked around carefully trying to see him. I saw a spot of
gray close by the back porch that could have been the
bird, but I wasn't sure.

My father was in the dining-room—I slipped over and
looked through that window. He was sitting in one of the
armchairs, all hunched down in it so that his head rested
against the back. He was facing toward the living-room
doors. My grandfather was in the first room, the one with
the curtains drawn and the light shining dull brown
through them.

And the old people were still on the porch. I could hear
their voices, light and rustling.

I walked around the house and stood on the front steps,
listening to them.

"There was plenty of timber for a house," Vance Bonfield was saying. He was a little wrinkled man, with a full
head of clear black hair, which he dyed carefully every
week. "But Cecil Addams wouldn't have any of plain pine.
He had to have that cypress brought out from Louisiana."

"Wasn't him," Matthew Conners said. "His wife wanted it. Wanted a house just like she used to have. That's what it was."

Vance looked at him, blinking his pale-blue eyes slowly.

"Her name's plain gone from my memory," he said. "Do you happen to recall it?"

"Linda," Mrs. Wood said.

"Louise." Mrs. Bonfield's double chin quivered with the word.

"It was Lizette," Matthew Conners said.

"Ask him," Vance said, and lifted his thin old hand to point to me. (I jumped; I hadn't really thought they'd noticed me.)

"Ask him," Henry Carmichael said; "young people always remember better."

"Not so," Matthew Conners said, and banged with his cane on the porch boards. "They just got less to remember."

And then I said as loud as I could, because some of them were deaf: "Her name was Eulalie."

They looked at me and slowly shook their heads.

And I added quickly: "Lalia for short."

They sighed together: "Aahh"; they looked relieved.

"That's a bright young boy," Matthew Conners said. "A bright young fellow."

They looked at me. "He's a fine young fellow."

"Looks like his grandpa," Vance said. "A man's looks goes on in his sons."

Wilda Olive brought out a round of whiskies.

Looking at her, Vance said: "I can remember when she

was the prettiest high-brown girl in this part of the state."

Matthew Conners cackled to himself, remembering. "And wasn't it a hell of a to-do when he brought her home after his wife died."

"I remember," they said.

I stood looking at them, wondering what it was they remembered, all of them together. Something I didn't know, something I couldn't know. Nor my father. Something my grandfather had known, who was dead.

Wilda Olive served them the drinks as if she never heard.

Vance held the glass in his hand, which shook so that the ice tingled. "Yes, sir," he said. "She was the prettiest thing you ever laid eyes on. Skin all yellow and burning."

Wilda Olive went inside. I looked after her and tried to see how she had looked years ago, when she had been pretty, so pretty that she'd caught my grandfather's eye. But all I saw was a colored woman, middle-aged and getting sort of heavy, with grieving lines down her cheeks.

"Prettiest thing," Vance said. "Sort of thing a young man can have, if he wants it."

"Man can't have anything long," Matthew Conners said.

They were looking at me. I began backing away.

"He's got a girl already," Asa Stevenson said, and hunched his dwarfed shoulders. "He got in a fight over her and near got thrown out of school."

"Who?" Mrs. Bonfield's fat chin lifted up and stared at me.

And Vance put in: "The Herbert girl, what's her name?"

I was backing off. They called to me: "Wait."

248

I had to stop.

"What's her name?" Matthew Conners leaned forward and rested his thin wrinkled chin on his cane. "What's her name?"

"I don't know," I said. The words sounded stupid and I knew they heard that too, but the only thing I could do was repeat: "I don't know."

"Not know your girl's name," Carmichael said, shaking his head. "Not know your girl's name . . ." His voice trailed off. "How do you call her to come out to you?"

Matthew Conners cackled softly. "You plain got it twisted, man. He's the one that come out. . . ."

"She's a pretty girl," Mrs. Wood said, her voice high and shrill in her solemn long face.

"You're right to pick a pretty girl," Vance said. "While you can."

I saw the hate in their eyes and I began to be sick. I backed away, down the steps and around the corner of the porch. This time they didn't seem to notice and let me go.

"It isn't long a man has anything," Matthew Conners was saying, and the ice cubes in his glass rattled. "It isn't long."

I climbed back over the fence, and the wire squeaked with my weight. I walked along the other side, slowly, curling my toes in the hard dry grass at each step.

Finally I sat down under the big locust tree near the street; I knew they couldn't see me there.

There was a funny sort of quivering in my stomach. I leaned back against the rough bark of the tree and looked up through the leaves at the sky that was almost bright blue. Out of the corner of my eye I could catch the sheen of the moon on the car waiting in the street. And that same moon made little blobs of light all around me. It was hot; I just sat there with my arms wrapped around my knees, feeling the sweat run down my back. I noticed a movement over on the porch. I looked more carefully. One of the old men, my grandfather's friends, was wiping his face slowly on a white handkerchief.

I sat under the locust tree and stared up at the sky that was so bright the stars looked uncertain and dim. I don't know how long I sat there before I began to notice something different. The rustling of voices was changing. I shifted my eyes from the sky to the porch.

Their talk was drying up quickly. The words got fewer and farther apart. They began watching each other with a quick sidewise slanting of eyes. And mouths came to a stiff closed line. They began to fidget nervously in their chairs.

Then one by one, with an imperceptible murmur, they slipped away. Singly, each singly, they left. I watched them leave, quiet and alone, and I thought: that's how they came.

The road ended here. They had to walk one way. And soon there were five of them, scattered down the length of the road, poking their way along, feeling the way with their sticks, black on a bright road.

I got up and went over and woke Claude, the chauffeur. He pushed his cap back on his head and rubbed his face with one hand.

"Claude," I said, "there they go."

"Huh?" He held his hand pressed to his face so that his stub nose was all pushed to one side.

"There they go," I repeated. "You better catch them."

He opened his eyes and looked down the road. "Christ Almighty," he said, starting the engine, "they plain near got away."

He swung the car around and went after them. I stood leaning on the gatepost watching. He drove up to the last man, drove a little past him and stopped, got out, opened the door quick. The old man never stopped walking, just kept walking until he was right abreast of the car, and then Claude stepped up and took his arm and almost lifted him into the car. Then he closed the door, quietly (I couldn't hear a sound), and went on after the next one. He did that until they were all safely in the car.

I started home then, and all the way I kept thinking of the picture of the old people moving down the road.

And suddenly I remembered the last time I had seen my grandfather—two days ago. We had both gone to the same place fishing. In deep summer there was only one place around here that you could fish in, only one place where the water stood deep and cool. He'd showed it to me himself the summer past—in an old gravel pit, way back behind the worn-out holes and the sandy ridges. It was quite a trick getting into it; it's hard climbing in loose gravel. I got to the top of the ridge and stood looking down at the line of aspens and willows and red honeysuckle bushes that grew around the pool. Then I noticed that my grandfather was already there, sitting on his camp stool, his rod in his hand. And at first I grinned and thought how surprised he would be to see me; and how much better it was to fish with company, even though you never say a word.

I started to climb down to him, and some loose gravel rolled away under my feet. He looked up and saw me. And he got up and grabbed his stool and his bait box and hurried away up the other side of the ridge. And I noticed a funny thing: his line wasn't out. He'd been sitting there, holding his rod, and waiting, but he hadn't cast out his line. He'd just been sitting there, waiting. . . .

And I understood then. . . . Why Matthew Conners had sold his store and didn't seem to notice the people passing by who talked to him. Why Mrs. Martha Watkins Wood wouldn't keep a servant full time in the big old empty house of hers in Montgomery, just day help. Why Vance Bonfield and his wife suddenly took separate rooms after sleeping in the same bed for forty-six years. Why Henry Carmichael shouted at the noisy grandchildren who climbed the wisteria vines to peer into the windows of his room. Why old people wanted to be left alone. . . .

There was the fear in my grandfather's eyes the day at the gravel pool. Even from a distance I had seen it. The fear that had made the old man pick up his bait basket and scurry off as fast as his stiffening legs could go.

The fear of dying . . . the fear that grows until at last it separates you from the people you know: the dusty-eyed old people who want to be left alone, who go off alone and wait. Who fish without a line.

One day I'll be that afraid. . . . All of a sudden I knew

that. Knew that for the first time, I'll be old and afraid.

I'll be old and restless in company and want to be alone. Because loneliness is more bearable than company, when you are waiting; because it's a kind of preparation for that coming final loneliness.

I could feel it starting, just the beginning of fear.

I'll be old and sit on porches and talk in dry rattling whispers and remember the past and the things that I had when I was able to have them. And in the shaded parlors, in the faces of dead friends, see the image of my fear. The fear that will live with me: will follow me through the day and lie down with me at night and join me again in the morning, until there isn't any more morning and I don't get up at all. . . .

I began to run, not knowing where I was going, not caring. And there was the fear running with me, just with me.

It was so hot, I was running through a blank solid wall. I had to breathe and I kept trying, but there wasn't any air, just heat.

From far away there was the pounding of my own feet on the ground. I looked down at them, moving. I could hear the strangling sound of my own breathing, but that was far away too.

Only, the mockingbird was singing louder and louder and there was a spot of gray flying alongside me. Like it was laughing at me, trying to run away from it.

I was getting tired, so tired; I tried but I couldn't keep up the pace. It was hard too to keep my balance; I kept falling forward. I stretched out my arms; they touched something and I held on to it tightly. I stood shaking my head until my eyes cleared.

It was a fence, a picket fence. And just beyond was our house. I had come home. Not thinking about it, I had come home. All the hot noisy outside had come down to this: our green-painted clapboard house with the olive-colored shutters and the big black screen porch all around it. But somehow I couldn't go inside.

I lifted my eyes. And there were the thunderheads. They were right behind the house, right in line with it, but miles up in the sky. Just where they'd been all day. They'd turned red with the sunset and disappeared with the first dark and then reappeared silver-white with the moon. And there they were, hanging cool-looking and distant.

I looked away from them, down and across the street, to the light in the side window of the Herberts' house. That would be Eunice, waiting for me. For just a minute I saw her face and her eyes that crinkled at the corners and the way her hair was piled up on top of her head with a flower stuck in it.

I thought of all these things and I just turned away from the yellow square of light. And took a couple of steps backward until I pressed up against the big thick barberry hedge. One of the crooked thorns scratched my hand; I looked at it, bleeding slightly; it didn't hurt. Somehow nothing much seemed real—not Eunice, nor my house, nor the hedge that had cut me. Nothing but the pile of thunderheads up in the sky and the fear that had caught up with me, was running circles around me.

Circles and circles around me. Like the mockingbird that was singing louder and louder. The brown-gray bird.

Very slowly I sat down, leaning my back against the sharp thorns of the hedge. And listened.

Joshua

SOUTH of New Orleans, down along the stretch that is called the Lower Coast, the land trails off to a narrow strip between river and marsh. Solid ground here is maybe only a couple of hundred feet across, and there is a dirt road that runs along the foot of the green, carefully sodded levee. It once had state highway markers, but people used the white painted signs for shotgun targets, until they were so riddled they crumbled away. The highway commission has never got around to replacing them. Maybe it doesn't even know the signs are gone; highway inspectors hardly ever come down this way. To the east is the expanse of shifting swamp grass, and beyond that is the little, sheltered Bay Cardoux, and farther still, beyond the string of protecting islands, is the Gulf. To the west is the Mississippi, broad and slow and yellow.

At intervals along the road there are towns—scattered collections of rough, unpainted board houses with tin roofs, stores that are like the houses except that they have crooked painted signs, and long, flat, windowless warehouses to store the skins of the muskrats that are taken every year from the marsh. Each building perches on stilts two or three feet high; in the spring the bayous rise. The waters always reach up to the roadbed and sometimes even cover it with a couple of inches of water.

There is no winter to speak of. Sometimes there is a little scum of ice on the pools and backwaters of the bayous and a thin coating over the ruts in the road. But the temperature never stays below freezing more than a day or two, and the little gray film of ice soon disappears under the rain.

For it rains almost constantly from October to March. Not hard; not a storm; there is never any lightning. There is just a steady, cold rain.

The river is high. The trees that grow out on the *batture* —on the land between the river's usual bed and the levee, on the land that all summer and fall has been dry and fertile—are half-covered with water.

The inside walls of the houses drip moisture in tiny beads like sweat, and bread turns moldy in a single day. Roofs begin to leak, and the pans put under the leaks have to be emptied twice a day. From the bayous and the swamps to the east come heavy, choking odors of musk and rotting grasses.

It is mostly all colored people here in the lower reaches. Poor people, who live on what they find in the river and the swamps and the Gulf beyond them.

Joshua Samuel Watkin sat at the kitchen table in one of the dozen-odd houses that make up Bon Secour, Good Hope, the farthest of the towns along the dirt highway, which ends there, and the nearest town to the river's mouth.

Joshua Samuel Watkin leaned both elbows on the table and watched the way his mother used her hands when she talked. She swung them from her wrist, limply, while the fingers twisted and poked, way off by themselves.

His small, quick, black eyes shifted from her hands to her lips, which were moving rapidly. Joshua stared at them for a moment and then went back to the hands. He had the ability to shut out sounds he did not wish to hear. His mother's flaming, noisy temper he could shut out easily now; it had taken the practice of most of his eleven years.

He glanced at the doorway, where his father was standing. He had just come in. The shoulders of his light-gray jacket were stained black by the rain, and the tan of his cap had turned almost brown. Joshua glanced briefly down at his father's hands. They were empty; he would have dropped the string of fish outside on the porch. Pretty soon, Joshua knew, one of his parents was going to remember those fish and send him outside to clean them for supper. It was a job he had never liked. No reason, really. He would have to squat outside, working carefully, so that most of the mess fell over the side into the yard, where the cats could fight for it.

His father yanked one of the wooden chairs from under the table and sat down on it heavily. He was answering now, Joshua noticed, and his face was beginning to get the straight-down-the-cheek lines of anger. He tilted his chair back against the wall and jammed both hands down deep into his pockets.

From the way things were beginning to look, Josh thought, it might be just as well if he got out for a while.

But he'd better stay long enough to see if there was going to be any supper. He still hadn't bothered to listen to them, to either of them; he knew what they were saying. He balanced his spoon across the top of his coffee cup and then tapped it with his finger gently, swinging it. He miscalculated, and the spoon hit the oilcloth with a sharp crack.

His father's chair crashed down and with an extra rattle one of the rungs came loose. "Christ Almighty," his father said. "Ain't I told you a million times not to do nothing like that?"

"He ain't done nothing," his mother said, and, reaching out her limp black hand, balanced the spoon across the cup again.

Joshua smiled to himself, though his face did not move. It was one sure way to get his mother on his side—just let his father say a word against him. It worked the other way, too; let his mother fuss at him and his father would be sure to take his part. It was as if they couldn't ever be together.

His father let his breath out with a high-pitched hiss.

"He ain't done nothing," his mother repeated. "Just drop his spoon a little."

His father kept on staring at her, his head bent a little, the dark eyes in his dark face glaring.

"Leastways he ain't just sitting around the house on his tail end, scared to stick his nose outside."

"Woman," his father said, "iffen you ain't the nagging-est—"

"Scared." His mother stuck out her underlip. "You just plain scared."

"I ain't scared of nothing a man ain't got cause to be scared of."

"I hear you talking," his mother said. "Only I plain don't see you moving nohow."

"Nagging bitch," his father said, almost gently, under his breath.

His mother's underlip stuck out even farther, and she whistled sharply, derisively, through her teeth.

His father bent forward, slapping a hand down, one on each knee. "Sure I scared!" he shouted in her face. She did not even blink. "Everybody scared!"

Joshua turned his eyes toward the window. All he could see was gray sky. Raining, solid, gray sky in all four directions—east over the swamps and west over the river and north to the city and south to the Gulf, where the fishing boats went, and the U-boats were hiding.

His father was saying: "Like Jesse Baxter, you want me to plain get blown to bits."

Joshua did not take his eyes off the square of gray sky, but he was seeing something else. The fishing boats from Bon Secour, three of them, had come on the two U-boats, surfaced in the fog and together, exchanging supplies. And one of the ships had lobbed a couple of shots from its deck gun square into Baxter's boat. There wasn't anything but pieces left, and the two other fishing boats hadn't even time to look for them, they were so busy running. All they'd heard, just for a second or so, was the men around the gun laughing. The two surviving boats had not gone out again. Nobody would take them out.

Joshua had heard the story and he had dreamed about

it often enough. He would wake up sweating even in the cold and shaking with fear. He couldn't quite imagine a U-boat, so its outline and shape changed with each dream. But the action was always the same—the gun pointing at him and the laughing.

With a little shudder, Joshua turned his eyes back to his parents. "That been a week and a half," his mother was saying, "and how you think we gonna eat? How you think we gonna eat iffen you don't find a boat?"

"We been eating." His father had his chin pressed down against the rolled collar of his gray wool sweatshirt. "Ain't we been eating?"

His mother snorted. "Why, sure," she said. "You man enough to go sneaking out in the little old back bayous and catch us a couple of fish."

"Fish ain't bad," his father said. "Ask *him* iffen he going hungry."

Joshua felt their eyes focused on him, and he squirmed.

"Don't go putting words in the boy's mouth," his mother said.

"Just you ask him."

"Ask him iffen there ain't things you got to have money to buy. Ask him iffen he don't got no coat to wear with the cold. Ask him iffen he don't need a new coat." She turned to Joshua. "You tell him what you want. You tell him what you plain got to have." Her voice ended in a kind of ragged shriek.

"I get him a coat," his father said.

"When that gonna be? He plain gonna freeze first."

"Ain't no son of mine gonna freeze," his father said.

"You plain scared," his mother taunted. "You just plain scared."

Joshua got to his feet and slipped around the edge of the table and outside. On the porch he found a square of black canvas and wrapped it around himself, letting it make a cowl above his head. It had been used to cover an engine, and it smelled of grease and was slippery to the touch, but it would keep him dry and very warm.

He noticed the string of fish that his father had brought home. With the toe of one blue canvas sneaker, he kicked the string down into the yard. It hit the soggy ground with a little splash. The cats would be coming around at dark.

He walked down the road, stepping carefully, watching for the biggest puddles, keeping to the levee side, where the ground was highest. The rain was falling noisily on his square of tarpaulin. Wth the steady, quick, clicking sound of drops all around him, falling on his head but not touching him, tapping on his shoulders but not really being there, after a while he wouldn't be sure of his balance any more, or his direction, there would be such an echo in his head. He kept blinking to steady himself, but that didn't seem to do much good. He had heard men say they would rather get drenched to the skin and maybe get the fever than spend hours under a tarpaulin with a slow, steady winter rain falling.

The wind blew in swirling eddies—like puffs of smoke, almost, the drops were so fine. Joshua rubbed the wet from his eyes. Over the noise of the rain he heard the faint sound of the river against the levee, a sound that went on day and night, winter and spring, until you got so used to it you had to make a special effort to hear it. Squinting, he looked up. The tops of water aspens on the other side of the levee shuddered under the rain, showing the frightened white underside of their leaves.

Joshua hunched the tarpaulin higher over his head and walked faster. Over to the right now he could see the landings where Goose Bayou swung in close and deep. And there were the boats, moored and wet under the rain, and empty, just where they'd been for the last week or more, and, at the far end of one of the landings, the empty space where Jesse Baxter's boat belonged.

Joshua stopped and stared at the empty space, at the muddy, rain-specked water and Baxter's mooring posts with the ropes still around them but dragging down into the water. Like it was in his dreams, he thought, when, cold and sweating, he saw the shape of a ship in the fog and heard the sound of a deck gun.

He reached the shelter of the overhang of a building and let the tarpaulin drop from his head. He still kept it wrapped around his shoulders, because he was shivering. In the middle of the board platform in front of the building, a yellow dog with black-marked flanks was scratching behind one ear, slowly, limply, and overhead a double-board sign hung upside down at a sharp angle. On one side of it was painted, in white letters: "Bourgeois Store." Years ago the wind had lifted it and turned it on its hook, and it had jammed that way, with only the blank side showing. Nobody ever seemed to notice. Maybe because nobody ever looked up.

Joshua peeped in through the window. A single electric-light bulb way up against the ceiling in the center of the room was burning, because the day was so dark. It was a little bulb and almost worn out—you could see the red, glowing coils of wire inside it; and it wasn't much brighter inside the store than out.

Joshua rubbed his fingers against the glass and stared harder. There were two tables set together lengthwise across the front of the room, and behind them two more. They were covered with clothes in neat little piles, according to size and color. There were wall shelves, too, filled with a clutter of hardware. There were so many things in the room that you couldn't find any single object quickly, even if the thing you were looking for was as big as a man.

Joshua finally located Claude Bourgeois at the side of the room, over by the stove, almost hidden behind small crab nets that were hanging by long cords from the ceiling. There were two men sitting with him. Joshua could have known he would be there; he hardly ever moved from that spot during the winter, his bones ached so. Now that he was old, he'd stopped fighting the rain and the cold; he just let them have their way outside the store. He didn't move outside at all. His wife, Kastka, who was part Indian, rubbed his arms and legs with liniment and kept the fire going full away in the silver-painted potbellied stove.

Joshua opened the door. Just inside he let his tarpaulin fall in a heap. Claude and the two men with him turned and looked, and Claude said: "Close that there door quick, boy," and they went back to their talking.

Joshua recognized the two other men: Oscar Lavie and

Stanley Phillips. Lavie ran Claude's fishing boat for him now that he was too old to go out, and Phillips was never very far away from Lavie. They always worked together; it had been that way since they were kids.

Joshua walked over to the small glass case that stood against the left wall, the case that was filled with knives. He stood looking down at them, at one in particular, one in the middle of the case. It had a blade at least six inches long, and its handle was of some white stuff, white and iridescent and shining as the inside of an oyster shell that is wet and fresh. Someday, he told himself, when he had money of his own, he would buy that. If just nobody got to it first.

Not that he needed a knife; his father had bought him one a month or less ago, with the money from the last haul the men had made. He remembered how angry his mother had been. "God Almighty," she'd said. "Iffen you ain't plain crazy, you. Buying that there trash when the boy needs a coat."

His father had just winked at him and said: "You don't hear him complaining none."

"Maybe he ain't got no more sense than you," his mother had said, "but he gonna be mighty cold this winter without no coat."

"Woman," his father had said, "ain't you got but one idea in you head?"

Little Henry Bourgeois came and stood alongside of Joshua. He was Claude's son, the son of his old age, the son of the woman who was part Indian. Henry had the round Negro features of his father and the skin color of his mother, a glowing red, deep and far down, so deep that it wasn't so much a skin color as a color under that. It was almost like seeing the blood.

"You heard the news?" Henry asked. His father had a radio in the store, a small one in a square green case. It was the only radio in Bon Secour.

"No," Joshua said.

"They come almost up the river," Henry said. "They sink one of the freighter ships again."

The war and the shooting and the submarines. And just a little way off. Joshua felt his breath catch in the middle of his chest, catch on the lump that was so big and cold that it hurt. And he remembered all his dreams: the fog, and the other ship, and himself in the gray, rain-speckled water, dying, in a million pieces for the fish to chew. His face did not change. He kept on looking at the knife. "That right?" he said.

"Josh," old Claude Bourgeois called to him. "You come over here."

He turned and crossed through the maze of tables and ducked under the hanging skeins of nets.

"Boy," Claude Bourgeois said, "iffen you don't quit leaning on that there glass it gonna crack through, sure as anything."

Joshua looked down at his feet in the blue canvas sneakers, blue stained darker by the water he had been walking through. He wiggled his toes, and they made little bumps on the outside of the canvas.

"You papa home?" Claude Bourgeois asked.

Joshua nodded.

"He wanting to go out fishing?"

"I reckon—it Ma wanting him to go out."

Oscar Lavie shifted in his chair, lifted one bare foot, and hooked it between his cupped hands. "Iffen you want you boat out," he told Claude Bourgeois, "I reckon you plain better take it out yourself."

Claude opened his mouth, and then, thinking better of whatever he was about to say, closed it again.

"I seen that there ship popping up out of the fog," Oscar went on, "and it ain't nobody's fault it ain't blown me up, place of Jesse Baxter."

Stanley Phillips nodded his head slowly. He stuttered badly, and when he talked people hardly ever understood him. So he let others do the talking. But his lack of speech had given him an air of confidence. Sometimes when he stood leaning against the corner of a building, his hands jammed down in his pockets, his slight body arched back and braced for balance, he seemed to own everything he looked at—the streets and the houses and the people. All the women liked him; some of them got a dreamy look in their eyes when he passed. "He don't have to talk, him," they would say. Only last year Stanley Phillips had married—all proper, in the church over at Petit Bayou—a wife, by far the prettiest colored girl anywhere along the river. And when he'd been out fishing, gone for maybe a couple of days or a week, he'd always head straight home, and when he got within fifty yards of his house, he'd stop and give a long, loud whistle and then walk on slowly, counting his steps, and every fifth step giving another whistle, so his wife would have time to get ready for what was coming.

"Iffen you was in the army," Claude Bourgeois said softly, "you wouldn't have no chance to say no."

Neither Stanley nor Oscar had bothered registering for the army. They just disappeared whenever any stranger came around asking questions, which wasn't very often.

"You figure on anything there?" Oscar asked, his eyes resting on the fat, lumpy body of the old man.

"Not me," Claude Bourgeois said hastily. "Not me."

"That real fine of you," Oscar said. "Then I reckon I ain't gonna have to slice up all you fat and feed it to the gators."

"Me?" Claude rolled his eyes around so that they almost disappeared. "I ain't gonna do nothing like that."

"That nice of you," Oscar said.

"Why, man," Claude said, changing the subject quickly, "you plain got to go out eventually."

"That ain't yet," Oscar said, and Stanley nodded. "It ain't worth nothing going out to get blown to pieces."

"How they gonna find you in all that water out there?"

"It ain't worth the chance," Oscar said.

Joshua stared over at the pot of coffee on the stove top, where it always stood to keep warm. Nobody offered him any, so he looked away.

"Why, man"—Claude was holding his hand outspread in front of him—"you can't go on living on bayou fish forever; there other things you got to have money for." He nodded at Joshua. "This here boy need a coat, only his daddy ain't working to give him none."

"Leastways his daddy ain't lying in pieces all over the bottom of the Gulf, with the fishes eating on him," Oscar

268

said. "Leastways, iffen you are so concerned, you plain can give him a coat. Just you give him one on credit now."

"You gonna do that?" Joshua asked.

Claude coughed. "There ain't no cause to do nothing like that," he said. "This here a matter of business, and this ain't good business, any way you looks at it. There all sort of money waiting for his daddy out there, iffen you wasn't too scared to go get it."

Joshua drifted away toward the door. He picked up the tarpaulin, studied it for a minute, then flipped it around himself and went outside. Little Henry Bourgeois followed right behind him. The low gray sky was thickening with the evening. In the branches of a chinaberry tree a hawk and a catbird were fighting. "Where you going?" Henry asked.

Joshua went down the steps and out into the road. The mud was soft and gummy, and stuck to the bottom of his shoes in heavy cakes. Each step was a sucking sound.

"Damn gumbo mud," he said. He could hear Henry's steps behind him.

They walked about a block, with their heads bent way down, so they really couldn't see where they were going. Henry gave a quick little squishing skip and came abreast of Joshua. "Where you going?" he asked again. "You going there?"

Joshua nodded.

They came to the warehouse. The fur-trading company had put it up maybe ten years ago, when they first discovered all the muskrat around here. There'd been need for extra space then. But things had changed; a couple of hurricanes had drowned out the animals, and they were coming back slowly. It hardly paid for a man to set his traps during the season, since he had to take the skins up to Petit Bayou now to sell them.

But the old warehouse still stood, at the north end of the string of houses. It was a rough building with plain, unpainted wood sides that time and rain and fogs had stained to an almost uniform black. On the far side, behind some low bushes—barberry bushes, with thick thorns and pronged leaves—Joshua had discovered a loose board. It had taken him nearly three hours to work it loose.

The two boys wiggled through the bushes, pried down the board, and slipped inside. They shook themselves like wet puppies and kicked off their shoes. The building was unheated, but somehow it always seemed warm, maybe only because it was dry. The floor boards were double thickness and carefully waterproofed with tar. It was a single room, big and almost empty. There were no windows, and when Henry put the board back in place, the only light came from the thin cracks between the boards. The two boys had been here so often that they knew their way around the room; they did not need to see.

They both walked straight out into the center of the room, until their bare feet felt the familiar rough texture of burlap. There had been a big heap of old bags in the warehouse, and the boys had carefully piled them in a circle, leaving a clear place about four feet across in the middle. When they sat there, the bags were higher than their heads and kept off drafts and cold. In the corners of the warehouse they had found a few furs—tattered, mangy things, too poor to be sold—and they used these as seats or beds, for sometimes they slept here, too. Their families did not miss them; after all, a boy should be able to look out for himself.

Joshua and Henry settled themselves, and Joshua lit the kerosene lantern he had brought a couple of days before. His mother had stomped and raged for a whole day after she discovered it was missing. Joshua did not even have to lie about it; before she had thought to ask him, his father came home and her anger turned on him, and they argued long and hard, and ended as they always did, going in their room to make love.

"I done brought something this time," Henry said. He pulled a paper-wrapped package from under his jacket. The greasy stains of food were already smearing the brown paper. "This here is our supper."

They divided the cold fried fish and the bread, and then Joshua put out the lamp—it was hard to get kerosene for it—and they ate in the darkness, with just the sound of rain on the tar-paper roof and the sound of their own chewing and the occasional scurry of a rat or maybe a lizard or a big roach.

"Man," Joshua said slowly. "This is fine, no?"

"Sure," Henry agreed, with his mouth full. "Sure is."

"Look like they gonna be a fog tonight."

"Sure do," Henry said. "It a good night to be right in here. It a fine night to be in here."

Joshua's fingers brushed the surface of one of the moldy-smelling pelts with a faint scratching sound. "You might

271

even could make a coat outa these here, iffen you had enough," he said.

"No," Henry said scornfully.

Joshua did not argue.

They fell asleep then, because it was dark and warm and they weren't hungry any longer. And Joshua dreamed the same dream he dreamed almost every night. There was a thing that he knew was a submarine. Even the way its shape kept changing—from long, like a racing boat only a hundred times bigger, to narrow and tall, like the picture postcards of the buildings in New Orleans. But it was always fog-colored. At times it slipped back into the fog, and when it came out again, it was a different shape. And he was always there, too, in a boat sometimes, a pirogue or a skiff, hunched down, trying not to be seen, or on foot in the marsh, in knee-high water, crouched down behind some few, almost transparent grasses. Hiding where he knew there was no hiding place.

Joshua shook himself, turned over, bent his other arm and pillowed his head on it, and went back to the dream. He did not wake again, but from time to time he whimpered.

That night one of the submarines was destroyed. The patrol boats found it almost a quarter mile inside the pass, heading for the shipping upriver. The heavy, cold, raining night exploded and then exploded again. Joshua woke up and couldn't be sure he wasn't still in his dream, for the waking was like a dream. Alongside him, Henry was whispering: "Sweet Jesus. Sweet Jesus." With fumbling fingers and a quick sharp scratch of matches, Joshua lit the lantern. The light raced to the roof and stayed there, holding back the darkness. Quickly, afraid, he glanced around the room. He was almost surprised to find it empty.

"What that?" Henry asked. His eyes caught the light and reflected it—bright, flat animal eyes.

Joshua did not answer. His throat was quivering too much. He looked around the empty room again and shook his head slowly.

"What that?" Henry repeated.

Joshua turned up the wick high as it would go. The top of the glass chimney began to cloud with smoke, but he did not lower the flame.

Henry jiggled his elbow persistently. "What that go up out there?" he asked.

"Ain't nothing."

Outside, people were yelling, their voices frightened and sleepy. Their words were muffled and garbled by the walls.

"You reckon maybe we ought to go out and see?" Henry asked.

"I reckon not," Joshua said, and there was a flat note of decision in his voice. "I reckon we best stay right here."

A plane flew by, close overhead. The building shook and the lamp flame wavered.

"I reckon the war come plain close," Joshua said.

"It quiet now," Henry said, and even managed to smile.

Joshua moved his lips but no sound came out. His tongue fluttered around in his throat.

The shouting outside was stopping. There were now just

two voices, calling back and forth to each other, slower and slower, like a clock running down. Finally they stopped, too.

Henry said: "It smoking some."

Joshua turned the lampwick down. The circle of light around them contracted. He watched it out of the corner of his eye and quickly turned the wick back up again.

"Ain't you better put that out?" Henry said. "We ain't got all that much kerosene."

"We got enough," Joshua said.

"You scared."

"Me?" Joshua said. "Me? No." Even he did not believe this. He tried hard to stay awake, knowing that just as soon as he fell asleep, just as soon as he stepped over that line, the indistinct shape, gray like the fog, would be waiting to kill him.

Suddenly it was broad daylight. The lamp had burned out; its chimney was solid black. Henry pointed to it. Joshua nodded. "You left the lamp burning till it run out of oil," Henry said.

Joshua walked slowly across the room. "Me?" he said. "No."

"I heard you talking in you sleep."

"I don't talk in my sleep, me." Joshua put his shoulder to the loose board and pushed. He felt the cold, damp air in his face. He blinked and looked out at the gray day.

"You was crying," Henry said. "You was crying and saying 'Don't.' That what you was doing."

Joshua wriggled through the opening without answering.

Henry stuck his head out after him. "You was scared," he shouted.

Joshua kept going steadily. He could feel a trembling behind his knees, and he had to concentrate with all his might to keep his walk straight.

As he went up the splintered wooden steps of his house, he could hear his father singing:

> "*Mo parle Simon, Simon, Simon,*
> *Li parle Ramon, Ramon, Ramon,*
> *Li parle Didine,*
> *Li tombe dans chagrin.*"

Sober, his father wouldn't even admit to understanding the downriver version of French. He'd near killed a man once who'd called him a Cajun. Drunk, he would remember that he knew hundreds of Cajun songs.

Joshua opened the door and went inside. His father and Oscar Lavie were in the kitchen, sitting at opposite ends of the table. Stanley Phillips was not around; he wasn't ever one for leaving his wife before afternoon.

In the middle of the green-checked oilcloth table cover were two gallon jugs of light-colored orange wine. One was already half empty. And on the table, too, next to the big wine bottles, was the small, round bottle of white lightning. Just in case they should need it.

They were so busy with their song they did not notice Joshua. He looked at them, wondering where his mother was. Then he went looking for his food. He found some beans on a plate at the back of the stove, and a piece of bread in the wall cupboard. He ate them, standing up in a corner.

Slowly his father swung his head around to him and said: "Look who come in."

Oscar Lavie said: "We celebrating way they blow up everything last night."

"You ma gone rushing out of here like the devils of hell hanging on her petticoat."

"I ain't done nothing of the kind." His mother popped her head in through the narrow little door that led to the lean-to at the back of the house. "I just went to get some kindling wood, so you crazy fool drunks ain't gonna freeze to death."

Oscar began singing, almost to himself:

> *"Cher, mo l'aime toi.*
> *Oui, mo l'aime toi.*
> *Vec tou mo cœur*
> *Comme cochon l'aime la bou."*

"Ain't I told you to get out?" his father said softly to his mother. "Ain't I told you I sick and tired of looking at you?"

Joshua finished eating silently. Oscar gave a deep sigh. "Us all gonna starve to death," he said. "Us all."

His father poured himself another glass of the wine. Joshua's mother did not move. She stood in the doorway holding the kindling in her arms.

His father's heavy-lidded eyes focused on Joshua and lifted a little. "What you gonna eat tonight?" his father asked.

The boy turned and put the dish back where he had found it, on the stove. "I don't know, me," he said.

His father began to laugh. He laughed so hard that he had to put his head down on the tabletop, and the table shook, and the wine in the bottle swished back and forth. When he spoke, it was from under his arms. "You hear him, Oscar, man," he said. "He don't know what he going to eat. He don't know."

Oscar did not even smile as he stared off into space. The black of his skin seemed almost blue under the morning light.

"He don't know what he going to eat. I don't know either, me."

Joshua stood watching them.

"I ain't going out today, me, to look for nothing," his father said. "I plain sick of catching a couple of fish or shrimp with a hand net."

"Han Oliver, he got a pig," Lavie said, with a dreamy look on his face.

"Man," Joshua's father said, "Han plain swears he gonna kill anybody what tried to touch his pig, and he been sitting guard on it."

"I seen a dog out front there."

"I just ain't that hungry yet."

Lavie sighed deeply. "It ain't gonna hurt us none not to eat for one day."

"No," his father said, and was silent for so long that Joshua began walking toward the door. He had no clear idea what he would do outside; he only felt he had to leave. His father's head jerked up. "Unless *he* go out."

Joshua stopped short. "Me?" he said.

Oscar looked at him. His eyes faltered, focused again, and held. "He a fine little boy," he said. "He can go run my lines."

"No," Joshua said.

"He ain't gonna do that," his mother said. She came into the room now and dumped her armload of kindling alongside the stove.

"That kindling plain all wet," Oscar said vaguely, scowling.

"You ain't never found nothing dry in winter," his mother snapped.

"It gonna smoke," Oscar said plaintively.

"No skin off my nose," his mother said.

"Ain't I told you to get out?" his father said.

"You done told me a lot of things," his mother said. "I tired of hearing you—"

"You ain't sending that little old boy out where you scared to go."

"Ain't scared," Oscar corrected. "Drunk."

"Woman," his father said, "I plain gonna twist you head around till you sees where you been."

He stood up, a little uncertain on his feet, and his chair fell over. His mother turned and ran out. They could see her through the window, scurrying over to the Delattes' house, next door. She was yelling something over her shoulder; they couldn't make out what.

His father looked at Joshua, his eyes traveling up and down every inch of his body. "You going out," he said.

"I ain't," Josh whispered.

"You going out and save you poor old papa some work," his father said. "Or I gonna twist up every bone in you body till you feels just like a shrimp."

Joshua edged his way carefully to the door.

"You know I mean what I done said."

Joshua ducked out the door. Behind him he heard his father laugh.

Henry was down at the landing, leaning against one of the black tar-coated pilings and teasing a big yellow tom-cat with a long piece of rope. Joshua walked past without a word, and righted his father's pirogue and pushed it into the water.

"You going out?" Henry asked, and his voice quivered with interest.

"Reckon so." Josh bent down to tie the lace of one of his sneakers.

"Why you going out?"

"Reckon somebody got to see about getting something to eat."

"Oh," Henry said.

"My papa, he gonna stay drunk today."

"I heard."

"I reckon I could let you come along."

"That okay. We ain't needing no fish at my house."

"You afraid." Joshua looked at him and lifted his eyebrows. "You plain afraid."

"No-o-o," Henry said, and scowled.

"Why ain't you come along with me, then?"

"I ain't said I ain't coming." Henry tossed the piece of

279

rope away. The cat pounced on it in spitting fury. "I ain't said nothing like that."

"Let's get started, then."

"I tell you what," Henry said. "I gonna go borrow my daddy's shotgun. Maybe we see something worth shooting at. I seen a couple of ducks yesterday or so."

Joshua nodded. It would feel better, having a shotgun with them. Wasn't much good, maybe, but it was something. In his nightmares, he'd wished often enough that he had one with him.

While he waited, he got down in the pirogue and took his place in the stern. Carefully he wrapped the grease-stained black tarpaulin around him. "It cold, all right, man," he said aloud. The yellow tomcat turned his head and watched him. For a minute Joshua stared into the bright yellow eyes and at the straggling broken tufts of whiskers.

Joshua made the sign of the cross quickly. "If you a evil spirit, you can't touch me now," he said. The cat continued to look at him, its black pupils widening slightly and then contracting. Joshua began to wonder if maybe this wasn't one of his nightmares, if this wasn't all part of something he was dreaming. Maybe when he woke up he'd just be back in his bed, and maybe his mother would be shaking him and telling him to stop yelling and his father would be laughing at him for a coward. He took one of his fingers, cracked and almost blue with the cold, between his teeth. He bit it so hard the tears came to his eyes. But he'd done that before in dreams and still he hadn't waked up. No matter how scared he was, he had to finish it out, right to the end.

He held the lightly moving pirogue in place with his paddle and waited for Henry, impatiently, humming a little tune under his breath—the one he'd heard his father singing:

Mo Parle Simon, Simon, Simon,
Li parle Ramon, Ramon, Ramon . . .

and told himself that the cold in his stomach was the weather outside.

He noticed something different. He lifted his head, sniffing the air; it had stopped raining. The sky had not cleared or lifted, and the air was still so heavy you could feel it brushing your face. Everything was soaked through; the whole world was floating, drenched, on water. But for a little while there was not the sound of rain.

And he missed that sound. He felt lonesome without it, the way he always did in spring—suspended and floating. For there isn't any real spring here—just a couple of weeks of hesitation and indecision between the rainy winter and the long, dry summer. There are always more fights and knifings then.

Henry came running back, a shotgun in one hand and four or five shells in the other. "I done got it," he said.

"Don't you point that there thing at me," Joshua said, and jerked his head aside.

"Us can go now," Henry said. He laid the gun in the bottom of the boat and then quickly got in the bow and wrapped a narrow blanket around his shoulders and knees. "I feel better with that along, me."

Joshua shrugged. "It don't matter to me."

They paddled out, following the curve of Goose Bayou, grinning to themselves with the fine feel of the pirogue— the tight, delicate, nervous quiver of the wood shell, the feel of walking across the water the way a long-legged fly does.

A couple of hundred yards down Goose Bayou they turned south, into a smaller bayou, which, for all anybody knew, had no name. It circled on the edge of a thick swamp, which nobody had bothered to name, either, though most people at one time or other had gone exploring in the tangle of old cypress and vines and water aspens and sudden bright hibiscus plants. Way back in the center somewhere, so that people hardly ever saw them, some cats lived—plain house cats gone wild and grown to almost the size of a panther, living up in the tangled branches of the trees, breeding there. Some nights you could hear their screaming—pleasure or maybe pain; you couldn't tell.

Nobody had ever had the courage to go all the way through the swamp. It wasn't all that big; people simply went around it. Except for one man, and that was an old story, maybe true, maybe not. Anyhow, it had been on to fifty years past. There'd been a white man with yellow hair, the story said, and he'd jumped ship out there in the river. He'd had a long swim in from the channel to the levee, but by the time he climbed up the muddy *batture*, he wasn't as tired as he should have been. Maybe he was hopped up on dope of some sort. Anyhow, when he came walking out of the river, just a little above Bon Secour, his clothes dripping and sticking to his body, his yellow hair all matted and hanging down over his face, there was a girl walking on the levee top. She stopped, watched him stumbling and slipping on the wet, slimy river mud, waved to the people she was with to wait a little, and went down to help him, making her way carefully through the tangle of aspens and hackberries, so that her dress wouldn't get torn.

It was torn clear off her, almost, when they found her half an hour later—those people she'd been walking with. They'd finally got tired waiting for her and gone down to see. They'd have killed him, white man or not, if they'd found him. For nearly two days the men hunted for him while the women went ahead with the funeral. They trailed him at last to the small stretch of swamp, and then they stopped, because none of them wanted to go in there themselves and they couldn't ever have found him in there, in a stretch about four miles long and maybe a mile wide. They did look in the outer fringes—in the part they knew. They could see the signs of where he'd been; they could see that he was heading right straight for the middle of the swamp. Nobody ever saw him again. Maybe he fought his way out and went on like he intended to, though the way he went crashing around, he didn't seem to know where he was going. Or maybe he kept on living in there; it wouldn't have been hard. He had a knife; he'd killed the girl with it. Or maybe he just died, and the fish and the ants and the little animals cleaned his bones until they were left shining white and the shreds of his hair shining yellow.

Joshua and Henry paddled past the thick swamp and remembered the story, and listened for the screaming of the cats, but since it was daylight, they heard nothing.

"It good to get out, man," Joshua said.

Henry did not answer, but then nobody talked much in the swamps. People got suddenly embarrassed and shy of their words and spoke only in whispers when they said anything at all, because the swamp was like a person listening. The grasses and bushes and trees and water were like a person holding his breath, listening, and ready to laugh at whatever you said.

Joshua and Henry found the trotlines that Oscar Lavie had set out the day before across a little cove that the bayou made in the swampy island. Oscar had tied a red strip of handkerchief to the end of a vine to mark the place. Henry reached up and unknotted the cloth. "Man," he said, "this wet through." He squeezed the rag over the side of the pirogue.

"It been raining," Joshua said. He gave the pirogue a quick shove up among the cypress knees to the one the line was tied to. "Iffen you loose that, we see what all we got." A sudden swinging vine hit his cheek. He jumped slightly, then grinned.

They worked their way back across the little cove, checking each of the seven single lines. The first three were empty, the bait gone. The next two held only the heads of catfish; the bodies were eaten clean away. "That plain must have been a gar," Henry said, and Joshua nodded.

They could tell by the drag of the lines that the last two were full. Joshua coaxed the lines slowly to the surface— two catfish with dripping whiskers, and gigs, sharp and pointed and set.

"Watch 'em," Josh said. "They slice you up good."

"You ain't gonna worry about me," Henry said. "You just bring 'em up where I can get at 'em." He picked up the steel-pointed gaff from the bottom of the boat and jabbed it through the whiskered bottom jaw of one of the fish. While Joshua steadied the boat, Henry held the fish until its convulsive movements had all but stopped.

When they had finished, Joshua coiled up the trotline and dropped it in the center of the boat with the fish. "Granddaddies, them, all right," he said.

Henry nodded, breathless from exertion.

Joshua turned the pirogue back out into the bayou and paddled rapidly. Soon they passed the swampy island and were in the salt marshes, miles of grasses rustling lightly and stretching off flat on both sides, with just a few *chênières*—shell ridges with dwarfed, twisted water oaks —scattered on the trembling, shifting surface.

"Man, it cold!" Joshua said. "Sure wish I had me a big old heavy coat."

"Look there," Henry said. From a *chênière* away to the left, four or five shapes pumped heavily up into the air.

"Too far away to do us no good."

"Leastways they still got some duck around."

"That a bunch of pintails," Joshua said.

"How you tell?"

"I just plain know, man. I just plain can tell, that all."

Henry was staring over where the indistinct shapes had faded into the low sky. "It mighty late for them to be around."

Joshua dug his paddle deeper in the water. The pirogue shuddered and shot ahead.

"You can't tell what they are from way over here," Henry said.

"I plain can."

Henry turned his head and studied him. "What the matter with you?"

"I hope to God that that there moccasin chew out you wagging tongue," Joshua said.

Henry jerked around; the pirogue swayed wildly. "Where a moccasin?"

"There." Joshua pointed to a long, dark form that was disappearing among the reeds and the Spanish-fern bushes. "And, man, you plain better stop jumping or you have us in this here water."

"I ain't liked snakes."

"You plain scared," Joshua said softly.

"Maybe we get in shooting range of some ducks," Henry said.

Joshua snorted.

Henry said: "Wonder why they all afraid to come out. Ain't nothing out here."

After a moment Joshua said: "I aim to have a look at

where all the trouble was. I aim to keep on going till I can plain see the river." He had been afraid last night; and Henry had seen him. Now there was something he had to prove.

For a while Henry was quiet. Then he said: "Man, I'm colding stiff. Let's go back."

"Ain't no use to yet," Josh said.

"I'm freezing up."

"Me, too," Josh said. "But there ain't no use to turn back yet."

They moved steadily south, in a twisting line through the narrow waterways, following the pattern of a curve that would bring them to the river, far down where it met the Gulf.

In about an hour they were there, in a narrow passage of water sheltered by a curve of reeds from the full force of the river, but where they could see into the broad stream and across to the faint, low line of grasses on the other side. Here the river was just a yellow-brown pass flowing between banks of sifting mud and reeds and tough, tangled bushes and twisted, dead trees brought down years ago and left far up out of the usual channel by the flood waters.

The wind was high. The grasses all around bent with a small screaming sound. The water was swift and almost rough. The pirogue shuddered and bounced. They let their bodies move with it, balancing gently. "Watch that old alligator grass there," Henry said as the craft swung over near the tall reeds. "They plain cut you up like a knife."

Joshua turned the pirogue crosswise in the channel. Behind them a pair of ducks rose, hung for a minute, and then began a quick climb up the strips of wind.

"God Almighty!" Henry said. "There more duck!"

Joshua stood up in the pirogue, following the sweep of their flight. They disappeared almost at once in the low sky. He sat down.

"You reckon we ever gonna get close enough for a shot?" Henry said.

Joshua did not answer. Out of the corner of his eye he had seen something—something blue-colored. And that was one color you did not see down here in the marsh, ever. There were browns and greens and yellows, but never blue—not even the sky in winter. Still, when he had stood up in the pirogue, so that he was taller than the surrounding reeds, and had followed the flight of the ducks, his eyes had passed over a bright blue. He stood up again, balancing himself gently in the moving boat, and let his eyes swing back—carefully this time.

He found it. Down a way, on the other side of the stretch of reeds, right by the open stream of river. There must be a little shell mound there, he thought, a little solid ground, because bushes grew there, and there was one bare, twisted, dead chinaberry tree. The river was always throwing up little heaps like that and then in a couple of years lifting them away. His eyes found the spot of blue color again. "Look there," he said.

Henry got to his feet slowly, carefully. The wooden shell rocked and then steadied. Henry squinted along the line of the pointing finger. "Sweet Jesus God!" he whispered. "That a man there!"

They were still for a long time. The pirogue drifted over to one side of the channel and nudged gently against the reeds. They took hold of the tops of the grasses, steadying themselves. The water got too rough; they had to sit down quickly.

Joshua found a small channel opening through the grass. He pushed the pirogue through it until there was only a dozen yards or so of low oyster grass ahead of them. The river there was full of driftwood, turning and washing down with the slow force of a truck.

"We plain can't get around the other side," Joshua said.

"Ain't no need to get closer," Henry said.

"I plain wonder who he is."

They could see so clearly now: bright-blue pants and a leather jacket.

They were bent forward, staring. "He got yellow hair," Henry said. The water made a sucking sound against the hull, and he looked down at it with a quick, nervous movement. "Water sound like it talking, times," he said.

"I plain wonder who he is."

"Ain't been here long, that for sure," Henry said. "Ain't puffed up none."

"That right," Joshua said.

"Remember the way it was with the people after the hurricane? And they only out two days?" Henry's voice trailed off to a whisper.

"I remember," Joshua said.

The man had been washed up high into the tough

grasses. He was lying face down. He would stay here until the spring floods lifted him away—if there was anything left then.

"He got his hands stuck out up over his head," Henry said. They could not see the hands, but the brown, leather-clad arms were lifted straight ahead and pointing into the tangle of hackberries.

"His fingers is hanging down so the fishes nibble on them," Joshua said, and felt his shoulders twitch.

"I done felt fish nibble on my fingers," Henry said.

"Not when you was dead."

They were quiet again. All around them the sound of the miles of moving water was like breathing.

Suddenly Henry remembered. "I bet I know who he is."

"Who?" Joshua did not turn his eyes.

"I bet he off that there submarine that got sunk out in the river."

"Maybe," Joshua said.

"Or maybe he off one of the ships that got sunk."

"It don't make no difference, none."

"It ain't no use to hang around here," Henry said finally. "What we hanging around here for?"

Joshua did not answer. Henry turned and looked at him. Joshua was rubbing his chin slowly. "He got a mighty nice jacket there," he said.

"Ain't no use hanging around admiring a dead man's clothes, none."

"I might could like that jacket, me," Joshua said.

Henry stared back over his shoulder.

"You think I scared," Joshua said.

"No," Henry said. "I ain't thinking that."

"I ain't scared of going over there and getting that coat that I like," Joshua bragged.

Henry shook his head.

"Him there—he ain't gonna need it no more," Joshua said.

"You ain't gonna do that."

"You think I afraid. I reckon I just gonna do that."

"You plain could get killed going on that riverside, with all the driftwood coming down."

"Ain't going on that side," Joshua said. "I gonna climb over from this here side."

"Iffen you ain't drown yourself," Henry said, "you gonna get cut to pieces by swordgrass or get bit by one of them snakes we seen a little while ago."

"I ain't afraid," Joshua said.

He handed Henry the paddle. "You steady it now, man," he said. He got to his feet, and the pirogue did not even tremble with his movement. He took a firm grasp on the top of the toughest grasses and jumped over the side. The boat dipped heavily and the yellow, cold water splashed in.

"God Almighty," Henry said. "You like to upset us for sure."

Joshua fought his way through the twenty feet or so of matted oyster grass and waist-high water until he reached the little shell mound. The water was shallower there; it came only a little above his ankles. He began to move slowly along through the tangle of bushes, working his way across to the riverside. A heavy branch snapped away from his shoulders and clipped him in the face. He jerked his head back and clapped his hand to the cut spot.

"What that?" Henry called. "A snake ain't got you?"

"No," Joshua said. "I ain't afraid of no snakes when I sees something I want, me."

He could feel a quivering deep down inside himself. But he said aloud: "That just the cold, just the cold water, boy. I can just think how warm and fine it gonna be with a nice coat, me."

He took his hand away and looked at it. There was blood all over the palm. The branch must have cut his cheek deeply.

"It beginning to rain again," Henry called.

"I ain't afraid of no little rain," Joshua called back.

The ground under his feet must have been covered with moss, for it was slippery walking. He lost his balance once and almost fell. He felt the water splash cold up to his shoulders.

"That a gator got you?" Henry's voice was thin and ragged.

"I ain't afraid of no gators," Joshua called back. He had reached the man now. He bent down and touched the soft brown leather of the jacket. From the feel, he knew that it was buttoned across the chest. He'd have to turn the body over. He tugged at one shoulder, but the arms were caught somehow.

"You come help me," he told Henry, and, getting no answer, he looked around quickly. "Iffen you got any ideas of getting scared and running off, I just gonna peel you hide off."

He spread his legs and braced himself and pulled harder and harder. The body turned over stiffly, with a swish of water. Joshua did not look at the face. He stared at the two buttons, and then his cold fingers fumbled with them. They would not loosen.

"What you doing?" Henry called.

Joshua took out his knife, the one his father had given him, and cut off the buttons. One fell in the water. The other he caught between two fingers and dropped in his own pocket.

"Ain't you near got it?"

Joshua looked up and over at Henry when he pulled the jacket off.

"Come on," Henry said, and waved the paddle in the air.

Joshua, still without looking down, turned and worked his way back, dragging the jacket from one hand, in the water.

By the time they got home, it was almost dark and the rain was falling heavily. All the color had washed out of the country, leaving it gray and streaked and blurry, like the clouds overhead. The marshes off a little way looked just like the lower part of the sky.

Joshua picked up the fish with one hand, and with the other he tossed the jacket over his right shoulder.

He could feel the leather pressing cold against his neck.

It had a smell, too. He crinkled his nose. A slight smell, one you wouldn't notice unless you were taking particular notice of such things. Faint, but distinct, too—like the way the swamp smelled, because it had so many dead things in it.

There was a cold wind coming up with the night; you could hear its angry murmuring out in the marshes. Wet as he was, and shivering, Joshua stopped for just one moment and turned and looked back the way they had come, down Goose Bayou, across the gray grasses, and he blinked and shook his head, because he couldn't quite see clear. It had gotten that dark.

A NOTE ON THE TYPE

The text of this book is set in Caledonia, a Linotype face designed by W. A. Dwiggins, the distinguished American designer, typographer, illustrator, and puppeteer. Caledonia belongs to the family of printing types called "modern face" by printers—a term used to mark the change in style of type-letters that occurred about 1800. Caledonia is, in some respects, similar to Scotch Modern in design, but is more freely drawn than that letter. It was first cut in 1939, and is one of the most readable and handsome faces available.

The book was composed, printed, and bound by Kingsport Press, Inc., Kingsport, Tennessee. Typography and binding by Charles Skaggs.